'As the CEO of Destiny Rescue Australia, I see and hear of these atrocities every single day. Penny has captured the strength & determination of Meena beautifully as a shining example of all rescued children. A truly riveting read! The only way evil can triumph is if good people do nothing.'

Michelle Winser
CEO, Destiny Rescue Australia

'Out of the Cages reveals the physical, mental, emotional and spiritual suffering of young girls trafficked into global systems of prostitution. Young adult readers will gain insight into the deception, the betrayal of trust, the systemic collusion, and, above all, the extreme suffering of vulnerable girls whose bodies have become fodder to fuel a global industry. I hope this book will compel all who read it to do all they can to bring an end to sexual slavery.'

Melinda Tankard Reist
Writer, speaker, activist

'Amazing. One cannot read this gripping and beautifully crafted novel of Meena and her rehabilitation without being moved by the plight of trafficked children … [it is] ultimately inspiring, showing the strength of the human spirit to hope and believe in friendship during traumatic times.'

Rosanne Hawke
Author of *Shahana: Through My Eyes*

'Compelling and confronting, this is a story that provides an insight into a life seldom seen and gives voices to women who are seldom heard. The journey of a girl from being trafficked to rehabilitation is raw and gritty but also filled with glimpses of hope.'

Melody Tan
At the Table

Out of The Cages

PENNY JAYE

rhiza edge

Out of the Cages

Published by Rhiza Edge
An Imprint of Rhiza Press
PO Box 1519
Capalaba QLD 4157
Australia

www.rhizaedge.com.au
© Penny Jaye, 2018
Cover Design by Carmen Dougherty, Book Whispers
Editing by Emily Lighezzolo, Rhiza Edge
Layout by Rhiza Press

ISBN : 9781925563412

A catalogue record for this
book is available from the
National Library of Australia

For those who have not yet returned,
and those that fight for them.

Prologue

Nepal. Three years ago …

Two girls squat by the bank of a river. Their brown hands plunge sudsy clothes into water, and out again. A blouse, a skirt, a colourless handkerchief. They talk as they work; the taller one, Meena, often looks up, laughing. Her hair sits in a dark oiled braid down her back. The gold-plated stud she wears in one side of her nose shines in the morning light. She is twelve years old.

The girl beside her is not yet eleven. Her smile is softer, her cheeks fuller. Her name is Putali—Putali Maya—which means 'butterfly' and 'love'.

They work by the river until their hands hurt and the wet clothes are stacked, twisted and wrung in metal basins. Then, still talking, the girls carry their basins to a nearby fence. A group of younger children walk along the road towards the school. Their uniforms starched white and blue. Red ribbons laughing in the small girls' hair.

'Pretty, pretty,' Meena mutters under her breath.

There are no ribbons in Meena or Putali's hair.

'I'd go back to school if I could,' Putali murmurs. She lowers her basin.

Meena shakes her head. '*Hoina*. I wouldn't. Can't make money at school, and my *baa's* not like yours.'

Putali doesn't comment. She knows what Meena means. Their fathers are as different as day and night. Before he went away, Putali's father used to save his daily wage to buy his children twisted toffee from the sweets seller. But Meena's drunken father beat her because they didn't have enough to eat. She understood now why Meena chose to store food among Putali's mother's supply, and why Meena often joined them for the night. Her laughter quiet, her shoulders trembling in the darkness. Still, she follows the school girls with her eyes. 'I'll go back to class, once my mother is better,' she says.

They let the school children pass and begin to hang their washing out. One by one, they stretch the clothes over the barbed wire to dry in the sun. Putali's long shirt catches on the wire and tears slightly. She groans. Her clothes are always worn. Always old; always from someone else.

As the last piece of clothing is hung out to dry, the boys ride up. Rajit and Santosh. They are Meena's uncle's boys. They're on motorbikes and have spare money. Syringe packets lean out the top of their jacket pockets.

'*Timi-lai kasto chha?*' Rajit asks Meena with his usual coy grin. 'How are you?'

Meena just giggles in reply and Putali ducks her head to hide a smile. It's obvious Meena likes the boys. She always has, but it's gotten worse since the boys started meeting them at the river several months ago. At first, they just brought sweets, but it soon progressed to larger gifts. Like a pretty hair clip, or a bunch of bananas for Putali's sick mother. Lately the boys have been offering them rides on their motorbikes. Putali never goes, but Meena does—she laughs and laughs until her face glows and her cheeks don't look so hollow.

'Did your *baa* tell you about the job?' Rajit asks Meena as he rolls a cigarette.

Meena shakes her head.

Rajit nods slightly, as if he understands. 'Our fathers have been talking,' he says. 'They've found out about a job. It'll pay well.'

Meena smiles quickly, hiding a flash of disappointment. 'Congratulations. When do you start?'

Rajit raises his eyebrows. 'Me?' He and Santosh share a chuckle. 'It's not a job for me. It's for you, both of you. You won't have to chip rocks or wash some rich *rani's* filthy laundry ever again!'

'A job for me?' Putali asks, lifting her face to stare openly at the boys.

Santosh shrugs like it's no big deal. 'Yeah, Meena's *baa* said your mum is sick. She could do with the extra money, couldn't she? And your dad's, where——?'

'Arab.' Putali's answer is barely a whisper. 'He has work there.'

'Right. Arab. So he's not coming back anytime soon, is he?'

Putali looks away, back up the hill towards the settlement. No, her father isn't coming back soon. And her mother isn't getting any better. She feels a hand on her shoulder. Meena. Hope is sparkling in her eyes like the bangles on the wrist of a dancer. Putali feels the excitement catching, even over her own sadness.

'Are you interested?' Santosh pushes. There is something unreadable in his expression.

'What about my *aama*? My mother? Who will care for her, if I have a job? Or do the washing?' Putali waves a hand towards their clothes, flapping along the wire.

Meena leans closer. 'Your *bajai-aama*, she can help. And your little brother——he's almost six now. That's much bigger. A job will change everything——just imagine! Enough money for proper medicine and *masu*, meat, to make your *aama* strong ...'

Putali frowns. She is thinking.

The boys are impatient to get going. Rajit stubs out his cigarette and they climb back onto their motorbikes.

'Think about it,' he says. 'But don't tell anyone. You know how hard it is to find work these days. You don't want someone hearing you talk and snatching your spot on the bus.'

'B-b-bus?' Putali stammers.

Santosh almost rolls his eyes but he catches himself and

instead bends as far over the bike's handlebars towards Putali as he can. His face is so close, Putali can smell his dry breath and the aftershave he wears. 'The interview's in India' he whispers.

'Interview? India?' Meena squeals. 'Like a real job? In Kolkata? Or Delhi?'

'Why not?' Santosh flashes her a grin. 'We'll come back tomorrow and pick you up, if you're interested that is. But remember—don't tell anyone.'

Meena nods and grips Putali's hand. 'We won't tell a soul,' she says, beaming. 'You can trust us.'

A strange expression flicks across Rajit's face for a second, but then he pulls the visor on his helmet down and kick starts his motorbike.

As the boys ride off in the dust, Meena gives another squeal and spins on the spot. Putali watches her and can't help but laugh. A grey roller bird swoops low over the rice fields, the blue underside of its wings brilliant in flight. Meena runs ahead, up the dirt paths between rice fields, towards the settlement. Then she spreads her arms, just like the roller bird, and swoops back to take Putali's hand.

Part One

One

Meena leaned over the plastic bowl. Her head ached. Her eyes stung. She retched one more time.

'Is that all of last night's dinner now?'

The voice was Meena's roommate, Sarita. The older girl clicked her tongue and entered their shared room before kicking off her thick heels and pulling the unused condom packets from her bra. Meena could see the shoes over the bowl's rim—black platforms, sparkling with plastic diamonds. She groaned and held out the bowl. Her hand was trembling. She felt the spit hang from her lips and attempted to wipe it away. Sarita muttered something under her breath about losing income while Meena was sick, then took the bowl and disappeared from the room to empty it. Meena lowered her aching self back onto the hard mattress that was their bed. Even with the bowl gone, the room smelt like vomit and sweat. There was only so long Madam put up with girls in Meena's condition before they disappeared. Meena wasn't sure where to. She pushed the thought away and curled her body, staring at the poster hanging on the wooden partition that was the wall between their room and Deepa and Devi's. Muffled noises from the other side told her Devi had a client. Meena's stomach threatened to heave again.

Sarita returned with the now empty bowl. She dropped it on the floor beside the bed and shook out their blanket to rearrange it over Meena. Meena felt the warmth of it, distant over the false cold of her fever. Somehow, after all her years in Madam's hotel, Sarita still knew how to care. Meena felt as uncaring as the cardboard they used under their mattress for extra padding. She groaned involuntarily.

'You've been throwing up too much. It's disgusting.' Sarita scolded without venom. She felt Meena's forehead. 'You're not pregnant, are you? I've heard of girls getting pregnant in the wrong stomach. Maybe that's your problem?' A flash of concern crossed Sarita's face, contradicting the businesslike tone she used.

Meena winced as she shook her head. Although she'd barely had a period since coming to the brothel, she knew she wasn't pregnant. Devi had been pregnant three times. Deepa at least five times and Sarita more than she admitted. But Madam was quick to organise abortions and the girls were back working a week later. She knew the procedure.

'I'm not pregnant.' Meena fumbled over the side of the bed until her fingers felt the bowl's wet plastic. 'It's my gut. I ache ... I get fever, and I'm weak, so weak I feel like ... I'm ...' She stopped. A distantly familiar tinge of emotion was holding back the truth. She snapped it away. She couldn't admit to fear, not here, not in front of Sarita. That was the rule. The only way to survive. When she finally let the words out she had herself back under control. The words sounded like someone else's: 'I don't want to die.'

'Psshiit, you won't die!' Sarita stalked away, a sudden anger tensing her shoulders. It was the same restless anger Meena had noticed increasing in Sarita over the past few months. Something was bothering her roommate. And nothing ever bothered Sarita.

Meena willed herself to watch as Sarita dragged a comb

through her thick hair. The repetition of the action seemed to shelve the older girl's restlessness. Meena didn't know Sarita's story, only that she'd worked for Madam longer than any of the other girls in the hotel. Sarita was one of Madam's privileged working girls—privileged because she was technically free to leave. At almost thirty years old, she was no longer indebted to Madam. Sarita chose to make a living from what Meena and the other young girls were forced to do. And she contributed to the running of the hotel, which kept Madam happy.

'You're not grateful enough,' Sarita lectured without turning around. 'That's always been your problem. Sure, you don't cry all the time like you used to three years ago—lucky for you, you learned that lesson quickly—and you don't gouge the eyes out of your clients anymore.' She laughed at a memory Meena could no longer place, like so many memories she refused to consider.

'But, you never did learn to be grateful, did you? I know better than anyone that it's not paradise here. But if you work the system—'

Meena stopped listening and allowed the words to sink into the anaesthetic-like fog she'd constructed to survive. She willed her mind to absorb only the immediate: Sarita eyeing her reflection in the tiny mirror pinned to the wall. Sarita's pink fingernails moving swiftly on her hair, changing the style, pinning half of it up and pulling loose strands down either side of her face. Meena's own hair felt like her soul: dry and flat.

'Will you die here too?' Meena asked.

'What?!' Sarita spun round to glare at her. 'No one's dying! Look, I'll be back in an hour. I'll try and get Madam to come up and see you. Maybe she'll call a doctor—'

'*Nain*, no. She won't.' The fog was thicker now.

'I'll make her. You used to bring in good money ... before you got sick. You're too valuable to lose, she'll see that.'

'But I'm ... older now ...'

Sarita spat onto the floor. 'You're so ungrateful, you know that! One of your clients brings in twice as much as one of mine! Do you think I like working here? Do you think that's why I stay?!'

Sarita snapped her mouth shut, as if she'd let out a truth she hadn't meant to. For a moment her eyes glared a strange mixture of emotions Meena had never seen before, and then it was gone. Meena felt her stomach tighten but Sarita just clicked her tongue, back to normal, and deftly reapplied the dark *kohl* to her eyes. Once she had finished, she ran her fingers slowly down the scarf that hung beside the mirror.

'I'll never wear this scarf here,' Sarita had announced to Meena after she'd received it from a regular but cruel client. 'I'll never give him the pleasure of seeing me wear it. But when I'm rich, and have my own beauty parlour, and do the hair and nails of movie stars—then I'll wear it. I'll wear it every day so that when he sees me he'll know who I am, and he'll know that I know the animal he really is.'

She'd never spoken of it since. But Meena had been noticing, as she did now, that Sarita's fingers were lingering longer and longer on the scarf. Its purple-and-silver threads almost begging for Sarita to carry them into the sunlight.

Sarita sucked a quick breath before she turned and held out an open palm. 'I'll buy you some medicine.'

'I haven't got any money.'

'What? None at all?'

Meena tried to shake her head. The action made it throb. 'I ... gave the last bit to Bala ... to buy antibiotics ...'

'So where are they? Why haven't you been taking them?' Sarita demanded.

Meena cringed. Her gut was cramping again. 'I did ... they

didn't work. Nothing's worked.' She squeezed her eyes shut.

Sarita sighed in irritation. 'I'll talk to Madam,' she huffed, then left the room.

Meena listened to Sarita's flip-flops on the stairs. Meena didn't trust Madam like Sarita did—or at least, like Sarita said she did. Madam only showed kindness when she expected something in return.

'You weren't cheap. I paid a lot of money for you,' she'd heard Madam say to the new girls just as she must have once explained to Meena. 'I can't just let you go home because you don't like my business! I've got financial problems now, and if you continue to act like a baby they'll get worse.'

Meena must have fought the system once, she had scars that told her so. But that was a long time ago, before she moved downstairs, before she had shut down her memory and the ability to feel. She had become just like the rest of them; working like she was told to. Every day. No weekends. No holidays. No time off for cups of tea, or watching TV, or recovering from rough clients.

But lately Meena's health had deteriorated past the point of faking it. She was taking fewer and fewer clients, and those who did agree to follow her up the stairs were rough with her weakness and refused to leave tips. Then yesterday, Meena slept in. She woke just before the evening meal, rushed through her dressing, and make up, ready for work, then collapsed beside the squat toilet, leaning in her own vomit. Vishnu, the male guard in charge for their floor, must have carried or dragged her back to bed still dressed, still wearing her *sari* blouse, skirt and vomit. Meena did the slow calculations: if Sarita had taken off her work shoes and had left with casual flip-flops, then Meena had been in bed, alone, all night. That meant only one thing— Madam had given her time off. Madam had been kind.

Two

There was a tapping of long fingernails on the partition wall.

'Ehh, Meena? Are you there?'

Meena rolled onto her back and lifted the edge of the poster to reveal a round hole in the plywood board. Devi's stained teeth grinned through the hole. Her mouth was smudged with lipstick.

'I'm here,' Meena forced the response Devi was waiting for. She could now see the dark lines of kohl around the younger Nepali girl's eyes.

'You look terrible.' The dark lines squinted closer to the hole. Devi spoke fluent Hindi. 'Are you still *bimara*? Still sick? At least you're getting time off. Madam's being kind to you—'

'Kind?' The word shuddered through Meena like something she was not allowed to remember.

'Oh, I'd give anything for time off,' Devi laughed. 'Well, almost anything, not that I have anything left, but you know what I mean.'

Meena's head hurt. Devi talked too much. Even with clients she talked too much. Elaborate conversations with men who didn't come to talk. Meena used to listen in, to focus on Devi's ramblings instead of the movements of the man on top of her. Devi prattled on asking about world news, about clients' families, about whether they'd arrange a police raid, and tell them how many minors she thought Madam kept. Once Meena had heard Devi caught mid-conversation with a client, by Madam herself. If Devi had just been speaking Hindi she would only have received a light beating, three bruises to the face perhaps. But she'd been talking Nepali. And Madam forbade it. Devi had disappeared for almost two weeks that time. After she returned, she didn't talk so much, for about three days, then she was back to normal—though always in Hindi.

'So, where's Sarita?'

'Out.' Meena's head pounded. She wanted to sleep. To sleep without dreaming like she had before she'd become sick …

'Good, *aacha*, listen up!' Devi's face drew closer. A cigarette rested on her lips for a moment, then she spoke, letting the smoke push itself through the hole into Meena's room. The smell wrestled Meena's stomach and tried to dig up a memory. *A father …*

'There's this man, Kamal,' Devi's voice continued.

Meena struggled with the image from the past and by weak force, focused on Devi's words instead. She couldn't remember. Not here, not now.

'Are you listening?' Devi squinted through the hole to make sure, before she continued. 'Anyway, Kamal was here earlier. The one before the one before the last one. He says he knows someone in the police department. He says there'll be a raid soon!' Devi's voice sounded like a child chasing a kitten. Meena had felt excitement like that once. Somewhere … but it had been a lie … somehow …

'The police know they're here, under sixteens. So that's me and Sita, and Lalita and Little Sita, and Manisha and—how old are you?'

Meena looked away, a sudden numbness surrounding her soul. She'd lost count. She'd been a minor last year. She'd been hidden with the little girls during a violent raid. But this year? She was older. Her breasts were almost full. Her *sari* size hadn't changed for a long while. Was she fifteen? Or sixteen? Was she still hidden property or old enough to be open and counted? Like Sarita? Or Bala?

Devi gave an impatient sigh and continued. 'This time Madam won't know anything. It's going to be a real police raid, with police doing what they are supposed to do. Think of that, Meena. And Kamal said he'll make sure the leak at the police station—don't you like the way they call it a leak as if men have nothing else to do? Anyway, he'll make sure the leak doesn't find out. It's really happening this time. We're going to be free. We'll go home and ...'

Devi's voice ran off. Meena opened her eyes. The girl on the other side of the partition sat further back now. Her eyes lost in a far off dreamland of people and places that for Meena no longer existed. Meena let the poster drop back in place. Raids were a farce—something the police did and Madam navigated. She wouldn't bother remembering the number of raids she'd been through, even if she could; jammed into hiding spaces, silent on the threat of beatings. All raids did was guarantee tighter restrictions, especially on the valuable girls—the ones who brought in the most money, the youngest Nepali girls.

***

Sometime in the early evening, judging by the sounds in the hallway, Meena drifted awake from a clouded, fevered sleep. Her mind filled with scraps of memory, like shreds of torn paper blowing on a breeze. She forced her eyes to stay open, to take in the sights and sounds around her. To concentrate. Concentrate. No memory. No fear. Just the present. The hotel preparing for an evening's work.

Meena knew the routine without thinking. The girls who were allowed out of their own rooms would all be in the kitchen, buying food with tip money. Then Sarita would go to the sitting room and switch on the flashing lights while flirting with Garud who was the guard on that level. She would pump the cushions, letting foul phrases drop from her tongue, then turn on the radio loud enough to drown them out. She'd tidy the younger girls' hair next, as they came in after eating. Then she'd assign everyone a seat. Meena's normal seat was three away from the door. Madam would come in and lay down the rules for the day. Threats for the stubborn ones. Debt reminders for the lazy ones. Together, they'd wait for the customers. And when they came it was like a show:

'Look at me, *kancho* boy,'

'Are you feeling sexy ...?'

'*Oh-ho*, I can make you feel so good!'

But Meena knew none of the girls ever felt anything close to good. Some of them moved into automatic once the lights went on. Meena had tried to have a conversation with Priti once, but the girl was oblivious to anyone who wasn't a client. She was like a machine who took men upstairs and bought money back down to Garud, who sorted out what belonged to Madam and what Priti could keep. She didn't even realise Garud sometimes kept more than he should.

'Hurry up!' Meena heard Vishnu shout from the hallway. She struggled to a sitting position. Her head spun. A sudden glimpse of green hills and dry rice fields flicked through her mind. She held herself steady. Focus. But the mental lock-down was breaking. Cracks were appearing. Cracks Sarita had warned her about.

Meena lunged over the side of the bed and vomited again, just as Sarita reappeared around the curtain.

'*Ghinauna!*' Sarita let out a stream of curses, some Hindi, some in her mother-tongue, Tamil, and some English that she'd learned from TV.

'I can't ...' Meena tried. But Sarita just swore again and covered the bowl with a piece of newspaper. 'I'll empty it later.' She tilted her head towards the business already beginning beyond the curtain. She propped her hands on her hips, barely tucked into the low sitting skirt she wore. She was already dressed for work, the black heels on, her face made up, her hair shiny with oil. She must have come in and got dressed while Meena was sleeping. 'I'm guessing you won't be working tonight, either.'

Meena stared at the ceiling. She had a vision of red ribbons laughing. The bumps on the roof curved into each other, pretending to be hills from somewhere long ago. A flicker of pain rose in her chest. The fragments were chasing her.

'Where are you?' Sarita pulled the blankets up roughly, a wary concern flickering in her voice. 'Are you delirious?'

Perhaps. Meena cringed from a beating she knew she deserved. She couldn't afford to remember. And yet she was no longer strong enough to fight it ...

Sarita studied her for a moment longer then sat beside her, resting a hand on Meena's knee. 'I went to the bazaar again today,' the older girl spoke softly. So softly Meena had to strain to hear. 'They have medicine. Free for girls like us, and oranges, so I brought you some.' She laid the round fruit in front of Meena. They glowed through her daze.

'The medicine is just Cetamol. The nurse said it won't fix you, but would be good for pain and fever. Take two capfuls, three times a day.'

Meena watched Sarita dig through a plastic bag for the bottle of medicine. She heard the seal break.

'Smells nice,' Sarita commented then held it out. 'Drink

this, and promise me you won't vomit it straight back up again.'

Meena tried to sit up again. Sarita held the plastic cap to her mouth and poured the yellow liquid in. It was sweet and powdery on her tongue.

'Now, go to sleep. I'll work in Jameela's room again and make sure Vishnu keeps everyone out of here.' She paused as if weighing up her words. 'I asked Madam to call in a doctor for you. She won't. She says you're behind payments on your debt. There's only so much I can do to distract her from coming to check on you.' Sarita swore, her eyes flicking ever so briefly to her leaving scarf. 'How far behind are you? Really?'

Meena laid back. She looked up at Sarita, the girl she had hated for so long until she'd realised she wouldn't be alive without her. She tried to answer, to say she was fine. That she'd be better in the morning. That the images, the memories that were hounding her could be kept at bay. That she'd be back working, paying off her debt before Sarita could say 'Namaste!' But her head spun. Grunts rose from Deepa and Devi's room and her answers dissolved into nothing. There was a noise—fist against face—from the room next door, but no one cried out. Sarita stood waiting, an unexplained emotion across her face. The fluorescent light shone too bright. Like the sun that defied a cage, and Meena heard laughter, young nervous laughter from the back of a motorbike. Laughter that wasn't Sarita's or Devi's or her own.

'Is there ... a bike?' she asked. But Sarita was already gone, and the only noises now were those that came from the hotel. Meena closed her eyes, succumbing to dizziness. Laughter rang again. She knew it wasn't real, and yet it was. It came from long ago, long long ago, and someone she had tried to forget ...

She is on the back of a motorbike, side-saddle behind Rajit, one arm around his waist the other gripping the back of his bike. Meena's ridden with the boys before, many times, but never like this. Never so fast or with such purpose. Never with the exhilaration of dreams coming true! She lets out a laugh, excitement bubbling like a spring in monsoon. She can feel Rajit laugh too, the trembles of it rippling his stomach and making her blush. She is glad he can't see her. Glad he can't read her thoughts. But there is someone else sharing her laughter. Someone on the back of Santosh's bike. Someone little, whose nervous delight carries over the noise of the bikes.

Three

'Where is she?' Madam's bark ripped Meena from the dream—if that is what it had been. The images had been so clear. A scent of motorbikes and dust lingered in a memory she couldn't have. There had been a girl ... younger than Lalita ...

'Why is she still in bed?!' Madam's anger jolted Meena's consciousness back to the present. She heard Sarita's answer from the hallway, beyond their curtain door: 'She's unwell. I'm worried about her.'

Madam huffed. 'I'm worried too! I can't afford for girls like her to be too sick to work. You should know that better than anyone!'

'Yes, Madam,' answered Sarita.

The curtain lifted as Madam hustled her generous curves inside. Behind her crowded Garud, Madam's son and accounts manager, and then Sarita. Meena tried to sit up in acknowledgment of the hotel owner but her head pounded and she felt the room begin to tilt. '*Nain!*' Madam made a flustered motion with her hand. 'Lie back down!'

Madam frowned, hands on her sari-clad hips, and studied Meena quickly, careful to remain as close to the door as possible. 'So? What's wrong?'

'I'm not sure, Madam.' Sarita spoke with full respect. 'She's been sick for several days now, with fevers, vomiting and delirium. She worked as long as she could, but now I think she may have something more serious. The fever doesn't even respond to Cetamol.'

'Cetamol?!' Madam spat the word in disgust at Sarita's efforts. 'I've told you before, if you're going to waste money on medicine, get the strong stuff. The antibiotics kind.'

'She's had them. They didn't work.'

Madam took a step back at this piece of information and frowned. 'Vishnu!'

Vishnu appeared, his fists twitching for work. Meena felt her mind begin to shut down ready for a beating, a waft of motorbike exhaust filled the room but seemed apparent only to her. Sarita stepped forward as she had so many times in the past.

'No, Madam, she doesn't need what Vishnu can do. I'd know. I'd tell you if it was disobedience, or laziness—you know I would.'

Madam untucked the end of her red cotton *sari* and wiped the sweat from her forehead. She kept her gaze on Sarita; measuring her. 'Vishnu's good for other things. He knows where to get stronger drugs. I've had a request for Meena. Her *babu*. Tonight. She needs to work.'

Meena felt, rather than saw, something in Sarita snap. She'd seen defiance in Devi before, or Bala or Krishni, but never in Sarita. Sarita never flinched, never disagreed. Not when it came to Madam's will. But something was different. The subtle change Meena had felt in Sarita, the change that had something to do with the leaving scarf, made Sarita's eyes flash. Meena felt her world, small and reeling as it was, begin to tremble. Vishnu sensed the change too and took a slight step back, a ripple of respect softening his fists. Madam, however, didn't notice, or if she did, she chose to ignore the tremor.

'Will you order a doctor? A doctor for healing?' Sarita

spoke her request in sharp pronouncements.

'No, I will not, she owes me too much money for that.' Madam turned to walk out. 'Vishnu, go see about something stronger than Cetamol.' She spat the name of the medicine in Sarita's direction. 'I do not intend to keep our clients waiting. Meena's *babu* will be here at nine. Get her ready to work.'

The simmering in Sarita rose to a boil. 'No!'

Madam may have paused midstep but Meena wasn't sure. The curtain lifted and then they were all out in the hall again. An ugly silence settled over the floor of the hotel. Even the chatter from Devi's room stilled.

No one said 'No' to Madam. Not unless they were willing to pay the consequences.

Meena could no longer see the glare in Madam's voice, but she felt it. 'You whore! You know very well who is in charge here, and it is NOT you—no matter how useful you think you are. If I say she needs to work, then we make sure she can work.'

'She needs more time, not drugs. She'll improve with proper care and time.'

'Which would be fine if we were a *hospital*!' Scorn dripped from Madam's words. 'But. We. Are. Not. Vishnu, why are you still standing here? GO!'

Meena heard Vishnu hesitate briefly, then hurry down the stairs. 'Garud, take over watch duty on this floor until Vishnu returns. Get back to work, Sarita. I should not have to remind you that your accommodation and employment in my hotel is a privilege I can easily revoke.'

There was a brief silence. Then Meena heard Sarita's voice again, forcibly respectful this time but no less stubborn. 'Madam, she is not like Fatima. Please let her be. Give me one more night to care for her. She will not need the expense of Vishnu's drugs. Can I trust on your kindness?'

Meena cringed. *Kindness?*

Madam must have had the same thought. 'Kindness?! This is a brothel, Sarita. We sell love, not kindness!' And then in a much lower voice so only snippets could be heard, Madam continued. 'She's going to … it's obvious … a Madam doesn't get attached … be careful … drugs ease the pain … he buys them … the heart and such, whatever is still healthy … I'll split the profit if that will keep you quiet … twenty percent for you.' Madam's voice sunk beyond what Meena could hear and then rose again in response to something Sarita had said. 'For the last time, *stop telling me what to do in my hotel!* I don't even remember this Fatima you keep raving about—little Bengali girl, you say? So? They are all little! Some grow up, others move on. When business is difficult we must do difficult things! She owes me money. They all do. If they can't work to pay it back, I find other means. It's what I do. It's why my hotel is as successful as it is. One day you will understand … You cannot get attached to the workers … No, we will not discuss this anymore … Get back in your place before I forget how useful you've been!'

Meena heard Madam turn on her plastic slippers and tread heavily down the stairs. Garud made a crude comment to Sarita and there was the sound of a quick scuffle before Sarita lifted the curtain and stood—a hollow replica of her usual self—just inside the doorway. It took a few seconds before she even seemed to see Meena.

Meena felt her gut clench, but not because of the illness. This time it was fear tightening its belt around her—deep fear that whispered of loss and death and panic.

Sarita saw it too and Meena felt ashamed. But the older girl didn't scold her this time. She didn't remind Meena of how fortunate she was or how she should be grateful for surviving. She just looked away, away from Meena's eyes, and wandered over to her scarf. The purple-and-silver one hanging on the hook. Her leaving scarf. Sarita wove her fingers into the fabric and held it tight. 'How much did you hear?' she asked, keeping her eyes away from Meena.

'Not everything,' Meena admitted. More afraid now by the distance Sarita was creating between them than anything Madam may have said.

'It's not safe for you here,' Sarita seemed to be whispering the words to herself. 'Once Vishnu comes back ... Your *babu* ...'

'He's not my *babu*.'

Sarita turned now and looked at her. A single line of wetness slid slowly down her cheek. 'You shouldn't be here. You should never have been here. I won't let them inject you. I won't let them.'

'But Madam ...' Meena tried to argue, almost willing things back to the way they had been before she'd become sick. Sarita wiped a hand across her cheek and came to sit on the edge of the bed. She brushed the wisps of hair back from Meena's forehead and quickly poured her another dose of the orange Cetamol. 'Go back to sleep,' she said. 'I'll figure something out.'

'I don't want to ... my dreams ... I can't remember ... I don't want to ...' Meena felt the belt of fear tighten even further.

'Shhhh.' Sarita laid a hand on her forehead, clicking her tongue at the feel of it.

Meena let her eyes close but wouldn't allow herself to sleep until she'd found and gripped Sarita's other hand. And for the first time that Meena could remember, Sarita didn't shake it off.

The two bikes swerve in unison, missing pot holes and taking the widest route around the bends from the settlement towards the city. They are like two birds on a wind current: swooping, diving, free. Meena glances across at Putali, smiling now, enjoying her first ride on a motorbike. Brave little Putali. Her best and only friend.

When the boys had first mentioned the plan, Putali had been nervous. Meena saw it, in her hands as she made tea, or collected scraps of wood for the fire. But Meena had whispered long into the night, explaining how Rajit would smooth everything over. How Putali's *aama* would be proud, not frightened, when she learned about the new jobs. Jobs in India. Jobs that could open new possibilities beyond the settlement. They would have a new life, Meena had whispered to Putali confidently. A new life where Meena's drunk father could no longer reach her. Where rock-chipping bosses would no longer skimp on pay, where they had time and uniforms—with bright red ribbons—for the very best schools, and there would always be medicine to heal beloved mothers. Holding hands in the dark and safety of Putali's one-room home they had dreamed and wondered and imagined together until even the settlement bottle shop fell silent. Then Putali finally agreed.

'*Pir na-garra*, don't be afraid.' Meena had whispered as Putali's head grew heavy with sleep against her shoulder. 'We won't be gone long.'

Four

Sarita was gone when Garud and a girl from the lower floors yanked Meena from wherever she had been into a sitting position.

'What ...?'

'You've got to get ready, Madam says,' Garud stated as the girl undressed Meena roughly. He muttered something about Meena needing more than drugs to turn him on, but the girl just ignored him. She took a towel, wet with water and something sweet smelling, and wiped Meena down, lifting her arms to wash armpits, circling her breasts and cleaning sickness and sweat from her neck and back. Then she dressed Meena again, this time with a gaudy pink skirt and top that looked like it belonged to Devi.

'Make up?' she asked Meena without emotion. Meena couldn't will herself to point, but the girl found what she needed on Sarita's shelf anyway. She didn't even bother asking if Meena could apply her own makeup, she just gripped her tightly by the chin and got to work.

'Sarita?' Meena managed to ask before red lipstick was applied.

The girl just shrugged. Garud smirked in the background.

Meena lowered herself back to the mattress and closed her eyes. The girl was fast. The *kohl* lines swift and confident. Soon she was made up. Ready. A lie of desirability painted on her face. Then the fussing stopped. Meena opened her eyes in time to see Garud nod in approval. 'She's ready. Go get Vishnu'.

The girl disappeared.

'Where's Sarita?' Meena tried again, her heart rate increasing at the mention of Vishnu's name. But Garud turned and waited, holding the door curtain open.

Pir na-garra. Don't be afraid. The Nepali words sounded louder than memory in Meena's mind. She tried to sit up again, unsuccessfully. She knew looks wouldn't be enough to entertain tonight. Not enough to warrant a client's payment and tip.

She felt sick again. The perfume on her skin suddenly sour. 'Sarita?!' she tried to call.

Footsteps rose on the stairwell. Not Sarita's. The girl was back, with Madam in the lead, followed by Vishnu carrying a small plastic vial and a single syringe.

'Give her enough to get working. The dog, Waman, will be here soon. Once I receive payment from him, we'll decide whether to keep her.' Meena dropped her eyes, the memory of Sarita's surprising concern flooding in and colliding with the evening's expectations.

She knew who Waman was. He called himself her *babu*, her favourite client. He showered her with gifts and tips and exclusive attention whenever he visited the hotel, which was frequently. Sarita said she was stubborn for refusing his gifts, she said Meena could do well with a *babu* like Waman. But Meena couldn't stand him. She gave all the gifts he left away.

Vishnu snapped the top off the vial and approached her bed.

'Give me your arm.'

Meena didn't move. She knew what Waman was like. She knew what he would do with her weakness and knew that what

Vishnu offered would make it easier to bear—but she also remembered everything Sarita had been telling her lately about clean needles and staying safe and AIDS. The needle Vishnu held might give her the strength and enthusiasm to get through the evening, but it didn't look clean.

Madam strode across the short distance of floor and slapped her hard across the face. 'Do what he says, or you'll pay more than your debt!'

Meena's face stung. Madam rarely struck her girls, she usually left it to Vishnu or the other men. But in this instance, Vishnu was in charge of the needle. He tapped it like Meena had once seen someone else do, somewhere ... a long time ago, in a place that ached with betrayal—No! She forced her mind back to the room in front of her. She wouldn't remember. She couldn't. Not here. No matter what happened.

'Get it done,' Madam barked and marched from the room, taking Garud with her.

Vishnu waited until she was gone then grabbed Meena's arm and pulled it out straight.

'Please ...' Meena managed. 'A clean needle.'

But he just held the syringe between his teeth, tied his grubby handkerchief around her upper arm and began feeling for her veins. He had obviously done this many times before. Meena felt the world begin to spin. Against his strength and Madam's will, there was nothing she could do.

'Now hold still.' He drove the needle into her vein and was about to inject what he'd been ordered into her when Garud clattered up the stairs.

Meena recognised the urgency even before he spoke. The hushed tones, the way he tried to move without thudding the concrete floor. Something wasn't right. Something was happening.

'Forget about her! Get the little ones away—someone tipped off the police. It's a raid.'

Vishnu swore. He stood up and moved quickly from the room, leaving the needle hanging in the crook of Meena's elbow. She could hear Garud telling him of the police breaking through the lower floor guards. Of the police knowing they had little ones, illegal ones. Of Madam trying to block them, stall them from coming upstairs, but it wouldn't be long. Meena heard the panic in Garud's voice. This one was serious. Vishnu took charge.

'You do upstairs.' His volume was carefully monitored. 'I'll do this floor.'

Meena's mind struggled for clarity. It must have been Devi's Kamal. He must have told the police about the little girls. Hidden, secret girls. Girls who'd once had dreams that swooped and dipped over rice fields. Meena felt the panic rise. Madam showed no compassion to girls who resisted being hidden during raids. She willed herself to the edge of the bed but her arm jabbed with pain. The syringe! It hung on an angle, the needle still injected, the plunger only partially depressed. A dull coolness was spreading around the entry point, a peculiar light headedness gathered around her. Must get it out ... Meena trembled, but she gripped the needle and pulled it free. A line of blood trickled from the wound and she held it tight.

Noises from the hallway increased. Vishnu turned up the radio but it didn't drown out the desperate shuffling as girls were herded from their working rooms to the hiding place. He'd be counting the girls now—counting little girls pressed between the false wall and the mildewed concrete. There were six of them on this floor. Lalita was the youngest. She still had a flat chest and barely spoke. But she never needed to win customers. Even without any fancy tricks, she brought in the most money. She had only been three weeks out of the special rooms upstairs.

'Where's Devi?' Vishnu's voice seemed slurred, or was that the effect of the drugs? She felt slightly better, somehow. Stronger, though still nauseous. She could hear a scuffling from the room next door. Devi's room.

'No, don't go, there's no need. Stay, stay with me ...' But the bed creaked and a client hurried into the hall. Vishnu's boots drew closer. Meena could hear them now, in Devi's room.

'Get!' His tone was low but furious. Devi began to whimper—a strange brave whimper—and then there was a struggle as the silly girl tried to fight the inevitable. Meena tugged herself, dizzily, to the edge of the bed. She tried to pull herself up, to swing her legs down, but her muscles weren't responding fast enough. She'd be next. Vishnu would come and grab her, squishing her into the hidden space; body against young body, the air thick with sweat, perfume and urine. She'd felt what Vishnu's beatings were like for those who were too slow.

'I won't go! Not this time. Kamal's coming for me. He said he loved me—' Devi's words were cut short as the sound of her head hit the partition.

'But Kamal said—'

'Shut up!' Vishnu's boots slammed against a tin box. Devi let out a desperate scream and then there was a deep whack. Meena could hear Vishnu back out in the hall, his feet heavy as if he was carrying something, dragging someone. She heard the click of the false wall as it slipped into place. There was no time now. Madam and the police were almost on their floor. She'd have to hide somewhere else.

Meena scanned her room, the drugs making the place look brighter and her mind believe there was a hiding spot she hadn't seen before, even though she knew no such place existed.

The sound of hurried footsteps rose from the stairs. Madam's voice came with them—she was hoarse from shouting. Meena struggled to sit up, to hide. Hide anywhere. Maybe under the bed ...

She could feel her heart beating, as loud as the police baton striking doors. She was too late for the false wall but if she made it under the bed, perhaps Vishnu would not beat her so hard. He'd see, Madam would see, that she had tried. She groped the edge of the bed and stumbled forwards. But her legs buckled, not living up to the strength Vishnu's drugs had promised. Concrete hit her face.

'Out of the way!' a police officer shouted. Madam protested. Meena looked up. She tasted blood—oddly sweet—and the police officer's baton caught the curtain of her room and tugged it aside.

Five

'What about this one?' The policeman stepped into the room and glared at her. 'How old is she?'

Meena lowered her eyes. A warm wetness spread from between her thighs and with it the smell of urine. Shame sat like a vulture in the room.

'Her?' Madam spat in frustration. Meena could tell the woman was trying to think fast. 'She's obviously of age, like all my girls. She's just sick, bimar.'

'And the syringe?' the officer demanded.

'Diabetic.' Madam tossed the explanation aside as if irrelevant. A large frowning man in a suit came into view.

'She fell off the bed. What's the problem? Let's leave her to clean up in privacy, ehh?'

The officer strode past Madam and prodded Meena's side with his baton. Meena cringed.

'Roll over!'

She forced herself onto her back. The sparkled skirt stung, tangled and wet, against her legs. She was the skinny goat left over at the end of a festival; far, far away from the hills it had grown up in. Two younger police officers peered past the suited man into the room. They all eyed Meena with disgust. She stared at the ceiling.

'She's too skinny. She looks too young,' the officer growled, his words like the prods and squeezes of a greedy rich woman. 'How old are you?' This last question was directed at Meena but Madam hurried in. 'Old enough! Can't you tell what a woman looks like? She's just sick and skinny. Am I not allowed to provide employment for sick women? Is that a new law? What next, no women at all? Then what would you do when you need some comfort ehh!?' Madam laughed for the officers but Meena didn't miss the cold, cruel glare aimed in her direction.

The officer prodded Meena again, this time in the breasts.

Madam tried again, 'I've told you before, we have nothing to hide. But if you'll follow me we can let this girl get cleaned up and I'll show you the real loveliness on offer at my hotel, so that if you do visit here again, it will be for much more enjoyable reasons!'

'I don't see anything lovely here,' one of the men at the doorway commented. Madam retucked her *sari* in frustration. She was losing control. 'We have others!'

'Like me,' Sarita's voice rang into the room. It was slightly puffed, as if Sarita had hurried up the stairs, but it was still her working voice, dripping with sensuality. Meena stared at Sarita as she squeezed between the onlookers to take in the scene before her; Meena on the floor, syringe on the bed, officers poking, prodding, sneering. Then Sarita made eye contact and Meena began to beg … silently. Sarita's eyes read the slightest flash of agreement, then she turned to lean against the peeling door frame as if she had all the time in the world.

'Do you find me lovely, officer?' Sarita asked, suggestively. 'Although, I don't have to be lovely all the time ...' Her words hit their mark. The policemen couldn't help but look at her. Even the man in the suit stared at the flesh oozing from Sarita's *sari* blouse. She grinned at them all, one by one, as if they were the only men on earth, then glanced at Meena again. A peculiar expression flickered across her face for the quickest moment. Her unspoken questions louder than any protest Madam could have made. Why are you on the floor? Are you alright? Did they inject you? What with?

Meena groaned. I don't know. I'm afraid. I know I'm not allowed to be. I know they'll beat me. My mind feels funny. I don't know ... She willed Sarita to read her thoughts. But if Sarita understood she didn't show it. Instead her eyes shifted, almost hesitantly, to the wall where her leaving scarf hung. Its silver threads wishing for sunlight. Promising something different. Sarita clicked her tongue. Meena saw her take a deep breath as if about to dive into the dark, then she slid her tongue provocatively over her moist lips. She was really working now and Madam was beaming in triumph.

'I'm going upstairs,' the man in the suit announced after a cough and a struggle to avert his eyes from Sarita's charm.

'Certainly.' Madam preened. 'The girls upstairs are more suited to your tastes.' She smiled showing her crooked front teeth. The suit man spun on his heel with a glare at the moustached officer Sarita was working up to. 'Stay here,' he spat. 'But watch her.' He jabbed his finger in Madam's direction. Madam made a face of offence. The officer kept his eyes on Madam as instructed until the boots of the suit man and the younger policemen could be heard upstairs, and then let his eyes wander back to the curves of Sarita's body that stretched up the door frame. Madam leaned forwards. 'We normally charge extra for takeaways, but in your case I can waive that fee ...'

Meena gagged. Her stomach threatened to heave.

The officer made a face and stepped back, towards the door. 'We were informed you had minors,' he mumbled to Sarita, almost as if apologising. Sarita giggled, then darted Meena another look. One that was laced with meaning Meena couldn't understand. I don't know. I don't know ...

Sarita nodded ever so slightly, then tugged the police officer towards her fiercely until there was no gap between their bodies. She pushed herself against him until his face flushed.

'I'm not a minor,' Sarita whispered in the man's ear. Then she leaned even closer and began to speak so softly that no one else could hear. The officer blushed again, desire almost choking him. Madam nodded and mouthed some instructions. But Sarita ignored her. She said something else. The police officer glanced briefly at Meena and then back to Sarita. He nodded. 'I knew it!' Sarita said, and she poked the policeman playfully in the chest. Meena was confused. She wasn't the only one. Madam was glaring for an explanation, but before she could say anything the man in the suit and the other policemen returned. The officer quickly pulled himself from Sarita to stand alone in the hall.

'Who told you we were coming?' the suit man demanded, glaring at Madam.

Meena watched Madam scowl like a stray cat.

'Where have you hidden them?' He came as close to Madam as his disgust would allow. She just sneered back at him, 'I hope you're happy, wasting our time and yours!'

The suit man swore in a language Meena didn't understand, then spun in his boots down the stairs.

Sarita's police officer eyed Sarita again, hungrily. Sarita tilted her head towards Meena in a question. Madam eyed her in simmering distrust.

'Let's take the sick one, at least,' the police officer called down to the man in the suit. The response was tangled in echo and curses but the officer cocked his head to one side at Sarita. She flashed him a wide smile, reached up and kissed his jaw, then skittered back to kneel beside Meena.

'What are you ...?' Meena tried to ask.

'Shhhh.' Sarita lifted Meena's head off the ground and wiped the side of Meena's mouth. 'Listen, I'm getting you out of here.' Her voice was hushed and strained in a way Meena had never heard before.

'I tried, I tried to get under the ...' Meena whispered feeling strangely distant. Sarita seemed to notice the change. She stood up, busied herself with something Meena couldn't see, then dragged the blanket from the bed to lay it on the dry bit of floor next to Meena. 'You were always so little,' she whispered as if admitting something she never wanted anyone to hear. 'But I won't let them do to you what they did to Fatima.' She leaned down. Her forehead pressed against Meena's for the briefest second. Meena could smell her cheap makeup, and the coconut hair oil and the remains of aftershave from several clients. 'I—' Sarita started.

'She'll get better soon, no need to panic!' Madam's words interrupted.

'We're taking her,' the police officer snapped with sudden authority, and then to Sarita, 'Hurry up. Boss is waiting.'

Sarita nodded. She bundled Meena into the blanket with a dazzling swiftness. It felt as if someone else was being wrapped in the coarse fabric. Someone else was having a small plastic bundle shoved into their chest. Someone else listening to the gentle tone of Sarita's words: 'They'll take you to the hospital. He promised. Get better. Stay safe.'

'What—?' Meena tried but no one answered her. She felt herself being lifted. It was Sarita's shoulder her head rested on; Sarita's breath she felt over her ears.

She tried to clear her mind. She tried to think: about the rules of the hotel, about what Sarita had said of the tiny girl called Fatima who'd been her roommate long before Meena, about how often Madam let her girls go to the hospital—which she was sure was 'never'. Confusion danced with fear over the wasteland of her life.

'Let's go,' Meena heard the officer order. She felt the brush of the curtain over her face. Dust, lust, stale perfume. Madam was shouting now, 'My girls always use condoms. It's not my fault she's sick.'

They moved down the stairs, past the waiting room. Sarita's fingers dug into Meena's body as they squeezed through the grill gate that kept customers from the lower level. Meena could smell the dried meat and burnt oil of the kitchen, the strong soap and bleach of the lower bathrooms. Then they came to a corridor Meena didn't recognise but her stomach twisted in fear at the sight of it. She felt the world spinning and she clung to Sarita's neck. Something akin to panic rose in her chest like a scream she'd started but never finished. A doorway swung open and a breeze—dusty, urgent and free—wove its way up the hall towards her. Meena cringed. She couldn't look away.

'Sarita!' Madam's threat was low and barely heard, but Meena didn't miss its meaning. She felt a hesitation ripple through Sarita's body, and then a fierce determination.

She was aware of the approaching doorway; the night scents of an unwashed city blew over her, air stirred by the wind, whispered to by sunrises and sunsets, travel-weary from plains and *himals*.

'It's time to leave' Sarita murmured. The door frame passed overhead, as did the short concrete awning, and Meena gazed up—past the leaning, crowding buildings held up by age or scaffolding—and saw, for the first time since long, long ago, a sad and stubborn moon.

It is several moments before Meena's eyes adjust to the shadows of the tea shop. A girl her age—dressed in an immodest, sleeveless shirt—approaches with a tray of tea cups.

'Have some tea,' Rajit instructs as he motions for Meena and Putali to take seats at one of the timber tables. 'I'll go tell *Baa* we're here.'

The serving girl hands the friends two hot cups of sweet, spiced tea. Santosh pays and orders himself a small golden bottle of *roksi*. Meena doesn't recognise the brand; it isn't anything her father can afford to drink.

Eventually Rajit comes back. He mumbles something to Santosh, then sits spread-leggged on the end of a spare bench and waits. It's only when the tea leaves and other brown dregs are left in the bottom of her tea glass, and Meena is just about to ask for a plate of mo-mos, that Rajit speaks again, 'Here he comes.'

Meena looks up to see Rajit's father, her uncle, step into the shade of the tea shop. He walks with long strides and a dark expression—the same dark expression he wore when he helped Father home after he'd found him out too late drinking. Meena's never been terribly fond of this uncle, never really spoken to him. But perhaps he is kinder than she thinks? He must be, if he's thought of her for a job. He knows how tough things get when *Baa* takes to drinking all his earnings.

Meena puts on the widest smile she can manage, nudging Putali to do the same. '*Namaste*, Uncleji,' Meena greets him formally, her palms pressing together at her chest. Putali only hesitates briefly before doing the same.

Rajit's father tilts his head in recognition of Meena but doesn't move to join them. 'Who's this?' He points at Putali, directing his question to Rajit and Santosh.

'Ahh.' Rajit grins as if he were very clever knowing Putali. 'That's the little one I told you about. They're friends. Always together. Two is better than one, you always say.'

Meena's uncle shoots a glare at Rajit as if he has said

something rude.

'Her name's Putali,' Santosh explains. 'She's younger than Meena even.'

Rajit's *baa* stares at the girls. It is as if he can't see them properly in the dim light of the tea shop, as if he wants to make sure they both have two arms and two legs and necks that join their heads to their bodies at exactly the right place. His studying makes Meena feel uncomfortable.

'How old are you?' he suddenly asks Putali.

Putali stammers, then blushes with embarrassment, not used to the attention of a strange man.

'She's almost eleven, and I'm twelve,' Meena speaks for her. 'We might seem young but we're really hard workers. We're strong and sensible, and trustworthy.'

'Good,' he nods. 'That's what we want.' Then he turns to Rajit. 'Bring them to my tailor, you know the place?'

Rajit nods.

His *baa* studies Putali a moment longer, a glimmer of satisfaction deep in his eyes.

'Would you like some new clothes?' he asks her without any particular kindness.

Meena almost laughs. New clothes? For them? How ridiculous.

Part Two

Six

Meena's head spun. The street was crowded, surging. Down the front steps she went, still hefted in the blanket in Sarita's arms. Her head brushed against a group of watching women— old women in their thirties with dark skin, cheap lipstick and crooked noses. They were watching her, staring at her, talking amongst themselves about disease and karma and bad types of drugs. Panic rose in Meena's chest and she gripped Sarita closer. But Sarita was prising her arms free. She was putting Meena down.

'Let go, let go now,' Sarita said gently and Meena tried to get her bearings. She was being placed on the rough and hard floor of a waiting jeep. A police jeep, by the sound of the murmuring comments.

'No!' Meena tried to hang onto Sarita; to grip her arms to stay, to force her.

But something was hardening in her roommate's expression.

'What's happening?'

'They'll take you to the hospital. I made a deal.'

'A deal?' Meena scanned the night street scene and found the officer Sarita had bargained with waiting, perched smugly on his motorbike. Madam smouldered from the door of the hotel and Vishnu watched on in distaste.

Sarita stood up and straightened her hair and outfit—as

she did 15 to 20 times a night. Meena tried to sit up, to get herself from the back of the jeep, to make Sarita explain. But she couldn't. Her limbs weren't responding, her mind kept threatening to slip into memory.

'Just lie still,' Sarita said, like she'd said so many times in the past. But this was different. This wasn't on a bed, or on the floor. This was a jeep. And there were no walls. Madam wasn't in control, and Sarita ...?

Sarita took a step back.

'No ...' Meena clung to the door frame, trying to pull herself out. 'Sarita?'

One of the younger policemen whacked the side of the jeep with his baton.

'Don't lose my scarf!' Sarita called out suddenly. And then the door of the jeep slammed closed.

Panic swelled. 'Sarita!'

She heard the men laughing, she heard Sarita's working voice, strained now, but still effective, and the moustached officer's replies. Then everything else was swallowed up by the sound of the jeep's engine starting and its tired siren working up to alarm.

Meena gagged as dust and fumes seeped under the red lit gap under the jeep's back door. She groped for the blanket's edge and tugged it upwards, as far over her mouth and nose as it would reach. All around was noise: horns, motorbikes, engines, shouting, cursing, laughter. They were taking her somewhere. Taking her through streets so crowded with people she could hear them slap the sides of the jeep as it passed. Her head bumped against the metal floor as the jeep picked up speed. Whatever the minute effects of Vishnu's drugs were, they were wearing off now.

She hugged the bundle Sarita had thrust at her a little

tighter, as if to hold back the stabbing pain of her stomach. What had Sarita meant about the scarf?

With aching fingers, she felt in the darkness for the contents of the bundle. There was something soft—thin threads of fabric caught on her fingernails. A small bottle was tucked in there too, and something that rustled under her fingers like paper. Meena twisted the bundle around, groping for an opening, but the movement of her elbow dragged the blanket down from over her nose. Air, choked with thick exhaust, swamped her. She dropped the bundle against the jeep floor as she retched yet again.

On and on the jeep went until it stopped with a jolt that sent Meena's body back and her head hit the metal. The jeep's passenger door opened and someone climbed out. Boots approached the back door and it swung open to show one of the young officers standing in the night. He swore and covered his nose with his sleeve.

'A dog in her own vomit!'

The others inside the jeep laughed. 'Get her out then, and clean up her mess.'

Meena attempted to wipe the spit from her face. The policeman growled in disgust.

'Get out!'

She tried to obey, but the blanket was twisted around her legs. She struggled to get them free, but didn't have the strength. The young man swore again. 'Look, we're at the hospital!' He motioned towards a tall, grubby walled building behind, boasting an illuminated red cross. Meena stared. She'd only seen one hospital in her life—it hadn't been night time, and it hadn't looked like this. The police officer clapped his hands under her nose. 'Get OUT!' His face was red. He must have been shouting at her.

Meena forced herself forwards, but her legs were still stuck. 'I can't,' she whispered.

'What?! Just get out, you whore!' The officer struck her on the face.

'Not so loud!' one of the men inside called back. 'They won't take her.'

The young officer ducked his head, humiliated. Meena flinched.

'I'm not going to hurt you! Just get up.' He tugged at the blankets until Meena's legs fell free against the hot metal. She felt his hands tug her shoulders upright. The ground wobbled below her. The cement rolled.

'Get down!' The policeman tugged the blanket until she tipped off the jeep's end. Her feet hit the concrete, then her legs crumpled after them. The policeman shoved Sarita's bundle out after her; it hit the ground with the crack of breaking glass. Something soft and pretty sparkled under the street lights from the bag's opening. It was Sarita's scarf, her favourite one, her leaving scarf. The one she had never ever let Meena touch. Meena felt her breath catch somewhere in her chest.

She heard the policeman yelling something to the men in the jeep. Something about Meena not being able to walk and the other men replied, ordering him to carry her. But all she saw was the scarf. She dragged herself forward to grasp the bundle and pull it closer, but the policeman got there first.

'What's this?' He kicked the rest of the bundle lightly with the toe of his boot, causing the contents to come free of the bag, all sticky with the remains of the Cetamol bottle. Beside Sarita's tightly-knotted scarf, there were one of Meena's *kurta-suruwals*, an orange and three notes of dirty money. Money that had this morning been in a man's wallet, then tucked down Sarita's blouse, now buried in her bundle. It was hers. Unearned. Another gift, but what for? Meena reached for the notes but the policeman was faster. He snatched them up before her fingers even touched the *kurta-suruwal*.

'My fee,' he chuckled and wiped the notes carefully on his trousers before folding them into his shirt's top pocket. Then he looked at Meena again and kicked her knee. 'Get up.'

She pulled the knotted scarf and *kurta-suruwal* to her chest, watching as the orange rolled away. Then she tried to scoop up the filthy blanket. The Cetamol was sticky on her fingers, the glass sharp and caught in the threads of Sarita's scarf.

'Take her to Emergency,' one of the men in the jeep called.

The young officer swore in displeasure. His rough hands dug under her armpits as he tugged her upright. It took all her strength to hold the remains of her bundle and not to drop them. Her legs felt like carrots.

'Walk!' he commanded. He smelt strongly of cheap aftershave.

Meena forced one carrot leg after the other. The blanket dragged, the glass in Sarita's scarf pricked her fingers. The policeman steered her towards the hospital building and to a wide ramp leading up to a well-lit doorway with big red lettering above it.

A woman wearing a white *sari* and holding a broom met them at the top. She eyed Meena without smiling then held the broom across her body blocking the way.

'Outpatients is that way.' The woman's voice was dark like her skin.

Meena's head spun. Outpatients? What was that?

'She's Emergency. We found her in The Cages,' the policeman snapped.

The woman took a sharp look at Meena and shuffled backwards, making a way for the policeman to half-guide, mostly drag, her under the red lettering and through the doorway. Then the policeman withdrew his support and the cold hard floor came up to whack hard against her joints. Her fingers slid into the slimy wetness of someone's spat *paan* but she struggled to remain upright. Her eyes clouding, like the blackness that came when Vishnu beat too hard.

'I don't know what's wrong with her,' she vaguely heard the policeman talking above her. 'She's obviously sick, so go find someone to— I don't know, do something with her. She's not my problem.'

Meena tried to lift her head, to make the blackness recede. But the policeman was gone; she was conscious of the sounds of jeep doors slamming and engines starting up again. And then there was silence.

'You should be in Outpatients.'

Meena turned, barely able to keep her head upright. The woman with the broom glared at her. Meena let her head sink. She had no money to pay for anything, and no strength to leave. But the woman didn't speak again. She didn't beat her with the hard end of her broom. She didn't bolt the doors and tie Meena to a bed. Meena could just see, through the fall of her own dirty hair, the very dark-skinned Indian woman step backwards three times. Then the straw broom began to move, brushing and brushing, further and further away until Meena was alone.

Meena felt herself slide down the wall until she lay against the cold hard floor. With shivering fingers she wrapped her *kurta-suruwal*, the broken bottle and Sarita's scarf into the blanket and hugged it to herself. She felt tired, so tired. Her head pounded. From where she lay she could see the doorway she'd come in by. The ramp led out into the night. Street lights and night smells—some sour, some spiced—floated in. And no one came to close the door. No one came to lock it shut, or lock her in. Meena hugged the sticky bundle closer to her chest and lay aching, unable to do anything but watch the open door.

Seven

It was early morning when Meena opened her eyes to the polished black shoes clacking on the hospital floor in front of her. The space in the doorway was grey now with the city dawn, and the silence that had been the Emergency room was replaced by a soft murmuring of people in pain and being attended to.

'What's this?' The Hindi voice belonged to the shoes. Meena forced herself to look up, twisting her aching neck. The shoes were worn by a tall man in a white coat.

'Well?' The man asked again.

A young nurse in a crisp white *sari* answered, 'I don't know, Doctor Sir. She was there when I came on duty.'

'But why is she here? We can't have people squatting in Emergency.' The doctor sounded angry. Meena felt her fingers go cold. The *sari*-clad nurse ducked her head.

'Get her on a bed. The ambulance is due back soon!'

The black shoes clacked away and the nurse called one of her colleagues to help. Gloved fingers dug into Meena's ribs as they first dragged, then lifted her up. The mattress was cold and vinyl-covered. It wore wide silver tape like a scar over a tear. Meena tried to pull her *sari* skirt down, to cover her now exposed legs, but her arms wouldn't cooperate. Her breathing was coming too fast, like a man with a heart condition. She thought she heard the wailing of an approaching siren. The room suddenly filled

45

with white coats and trolleys with screaming bodies. A little girl lay curled under a pile of pink, sparkling fabric. She was crying—no, she was sitting up. Staring at Meena with dreams too big to be anything but lies. Meena's mind reeled. Vishnu would be coming. And the broken bottles. She clawed out in panic. But then there was blackness.

***

'How old is she?' A different doctor stood beside her bed now with a chubby-faced nurse. Meena blinked. The room was quiet now. The doors to Emergency pulled closed. All evidence that an ambulance had come and gone had been cleared away. She was the only body on a bed.

'Does she have a file? When did she arrive? Who brought her here?'

The chubby nurse hurried to check the end of the bed. 'No file, sir.'

Meena heard a familiar voice crack and then lift, 'Excuse me, sir. The police brought her, sir.' It was the woman with the broom.

'When?'

'Last night, sir. I told them to take her to OPD, but they said she was Emergency. They said she came from the … The Cages, sir.' The cleaning lady faltered.

Meena's mind struggled to understand. Cages? Trapped birds were kept in cages. She had come from Madam's hotel.

The doctor folded his arms, his eyes locked on Meena's face. Her vision of him shifted. He wobbled and grew transparent before her eyes. Would he buy them new clothes? She didn't want new clothes. No new clothes. No jewellery … she flinched.

'I'm not going to hurt you,' the doctor spoke too loud. He reached his cool ungloved hand against Meena's cheek and gently pulled down her eyelid with a finger from the other hand. 'She's malnourished. And dehydrated, on top of whatever else she's dealing with. Has anyone given her anything to drink?'

The nurse remained silent. The sweeping lady mumbled something about being paid to sweep. The doctor shook his head. 'She's a sex worker, then?'

Meena stared at his shiny face, clean shaven, nick-free. Sex worker? But she hadn't had a choice. Not like Sarita, who had paid back her debt and chose to stay. Not like Madam, who had made enough money in her younger years to run her own hotel. Not like Ganga. Ganga? Something in her chest pounded panic. She crawled as far away from the doctor as she could.

He frowned. 'Make her a file. Do a basic examination, then send her over to OPD. They can see if there's a poor bed for her. She can't stay here any longer.'

***

The nurse returned sometime later with a thermometer. 'Open your mouth,' she said. Meena obeyed without thinking.

'Now, hold it still,' the nurse instructed.

Meena forced herself still. Reality seemed thin. Memories tiptoed at the corners, threatening to barge in, to wake something she couldn't stop.

The nurse bustled about her. She wrapped a thick black band around her arm, then tightened it, making Meena's hand ache. She took the stick of glass from Meena's mouth and listed a series of numbers to another nurse to write down. Then she stretched Meena's body out flat on the plastic mattress.

'I'm going to check your stomach,' the nurse explained as she pushed the grotty blanket bundle aside and tugged Meena's skirt down to sit low on her hips. She poked Meena's belly with cold gloved fingers. 'Tell me where it hurts. Here? Here?'

Meena gritted her teeth. Her gut ached everywhere. Around her middle it was sore from constant vomiting. Lower, below her belly button, it burned with pain that swelled and sunk, but that pain had been around for months. Acute pain always came before she had diarrhoea, and now as the nurse prodded, her intestines churned and made her wince.

The nurse made several comments and the other nurse wrote them down.

'Lift your skirt,' the nurse instructed.

Meena blinked. Her stomach was still sore from where the nurse had been poking. 'Your skirt. I need to check between your legs,' the nurse said.

Meena fumbled for the damp fabric. The nurse made a loud sigh and pushed up the entire weight of the dirty *sari* skirt, exposing her knees, her thighs, her pubic hair. Meena shut her eyes. She was worse than a cheap goat today. The nurse poked around Meena's vagina with her cold gloves and spoke some words Meena didn't understand. Long words. Words that didn't sound pretty in any language. Words that burnt like the gloves did on the tender flesh. Eventually the nurse snapped Meena's legs back together and pulled the skirt fabric back down to cover her pelvis. Shame stank all around her. She tugged at the skirt and struggled to make it lie lower, but the nurse told her to hold still and placed the glass rod under her tongue again.

More words were written as the nurse changed gloves. Then came the questions. How long had the pains been in her abdomen? How long had she been aware of sores between her legs? Sores no one could see? How long had the diarrhoea been coming? What about the nausea and vomiting? What about the fevers? Then the metal clipboard was hung on the back of a wheelchair and Meena, along with her dusty, sticky blanket bundle, was lifted into it.

They wheeled her down the hall, then another. Faces swam past her. Sick. Desperate. Concerned. The Outpatients Department heaved with people. She heard them say something about sex workers, and beds for the poor, and not being 'Emergency' and she was left waiting. It must have been several hours later when her wheelchair jolted forwards, down a different corridor, into a small metal room with doors that shut by themselves only to open again later to another view.

Along another hall and to a nurses' station. She heard herself being discussed and the older nurse behind the desk waved towards the left saying, 'poor beds'. Yet another nurse appeared and ordered whoever was pushing Meena to follow her, down one final corridor to the very last room on the floor. A room with a door that hung crooked on its hinges.

There were sick bodies on all but one of the six beds lined up under the fluorescent tube lights. Each body clung to a blanket that looked only slightly better or slightly worse than Meena's own. None of the beds had visitors beside them, and all of them held women.

The nurse wheeled her to the first bed on the left. The mattress was brown vinyl that had split and been patched repeatedly. The nurse from the desk and a new one wearing gloves lifted Meena onto the bed. The sudden coolness of plastic shocked Meena's body to shivering. She didn't want to be here, not with these cold hands, these cold people.

'Give me your blanket.' The desk nurse tugged Meena's blanket away.

'No—' Meena tried, but her hands were too weak even to reach out after it. The nurse scowled. She shook out the bundle. Meena watched Sarita's scarf, the *kurta-suruwal* and the final shards of the Cetamol bottle fall to the ground again. The nurse spread the sticky, smelly blanket over Meena with a look of

49

disgust then lifted the *kurta-suruwal* and scarf from the floor.

'What's this?' The nurse held up the knotted scarf. 'What's inside? Drugs?'

Meena blinked, confused. Drugs? She remembered Sarita's final urgency: 'Don't lose my scarf!' And she wouldn't. 'It's nothing,' she stammered. 'Just a gift. It's mine—'

'And inside?' The nurse's eyebrows raised. 'I know your type.' She began unravelling the purple threads of the scarf, un-knotting it.

My type? Meena reached for the scarf. The leaving scarf.

'Oh,' the nurse's tone changed. She tossed the scarf to Meena and held something up for the other nurse. Meena tried to see too, but her head pounded and dizziness threatened to overwhelm again. It seemed to be a card, a business card. From Sarita.

'Little Sister Rescue Foundation,' the nurse read. She looked at Meena with renewed interest. 'Really? Well this will make Matron happy. They can pay for you. Where'd you get this card? Kamathipura? A drop-in centre?'

'I don't ...' Her gut cramped in warning. 'It was a ... It's mine ...' She squeezed her eyes shut as pain overtook her abdomen.

'I wonder where she got it. Madams don't let the young ones outside, let alone visit a drop-in centre,' the second nurse whispered as they moved away.

Meena's stomach twisted around itself. She needed the toilet. Another stab of pain wrenched her gut then the foul warmness sank into her skirt. Shame. There was nothing left of beauty now. One of the nurses turned around. The stench of her was spreading. Meena looked away. The nurse called an aide in from the hall. 'Clean her up.'

'Which one?'

'The skinny one,'

The aide glanced wearily around the room. 'They're all skinny in poor beds, Nurse.'

'Ahh. *Ek-dum dublo*,' the woman in the fabric shop murmurs. The measuring tape runs around Meena's waist and then under her arms, across the new bumps of breasts. 'Very skinny.'

Meena laughs. Her uncle had been serious about the clothes. Two sets each, he'd said. So Meena has chosen the blue swirly one and the pink fabric with shiny silver patterns. Putali decides on a very traditional *dhaka* pattern, then umms and ahhs over lengths of green or turquoise.

Meena takes the fabric from her friend and holds it up against the sunlight streaming across the shop floor from the open doors. Then she does the same to the turquoise.

'Choose *hario*, green,' she advises with a cheeky smile. 'It's not so see-through in the sun.'

'And you can always have another later,' Rajit suggests from where he sits with Santosh on stools by the door. Santosh winks over his cigarette.

Putali blushes, then holds her arms out so the woman can measure her. Putali doesn't have any bumps yet. She is still a child really, but Meena is impressed with her courage. She hasn't complained once since they'd made their decision to go with the boys. She just trusted, like Meena did, that this was going to work out brilliantly.

Meena lets her eyes run along the rows of coloured fabric. They are beautiful, but not as lovely as what Meena has seen on TV. One day they'll have enough money to buy the very best, and won't have to rely on the kindness of uncles and cousin brothers.

'*Bahini!*' Santosh calls, interrupting Meena's dreaming. 'Come on, we're finished.'

She quickly stands as the store woman ties her bundle of fabric together and tosses it with Putali's to land in a pile beside the tailor and his pedal-operated sewing machine.

'When will they be ready?' Rajit asks the tailor.

'The day after tomorrow,' the tailor says as he turns the hem on a business shirt.

Rajit glances at Santosh, then shakes his head. 'No. We need them tomorrow.'

'We're very busy at the moment. Festival time,' the tailor explains.

'Can you have them ready by tomorrow, or not?' Santosh's tone is condescending.

'150 rupees,' the tailor mutters.

Rajit snorts. '*Haus*, okay. 150 rupees. But I need them in the morning, not the afternoon,' Rajit clarifies.

The tailor scowls, but agrees. He pulls the white thread from his machine and begins winding on a bright green cotton. Meena grabs Putali's hand excitedly and follows the boys out.

Eight

'Awake now?' The white-hat nurse was barely older than Meena. She lifted Meena's wrist with a cold hand and squeezed it as the nurses in Emergency had done earlier. Meena stared around the room, taking note of the occupants with more clarity than she had the day before. Some of them returned her stare. Others had their eyes closed or were turned away. The room was too bright for all of them. The light, cold and artificial, exposing their shallow cheeks and sallow skin. Somehow, looking at them, Meena knew she'd been cleaned up—roughly, inadequately—but enough. Her legs felt bare under the blanket; the only clothing remaining was the glittery *sari* blouse.

'Your clothes are being washed,' the nurse clipped, answering Meena's unasked question. 'And your blanket. You soiled them. Remember?'

Meena didn't answer. The weary familiarity of shame wrapped itself around her. She stared at the bag of water hanging from the metal pole beside her bed. The nurse was checking it now, adjusting the speed at which the water dripped through a clear cylinder into a thin tube that ran down past the edge of the mattress and back up again to disappear under the blanket. Meena pulled her arm out from beneath the blanket. The tube was attached to the back of her left hand. A pale, sticky plaster fastened something to her skin and Meena could feel the movement tugging gently at the tubing.

'What is it?' Meena watched her hand shake weakly, as if it wasn't her own. 'I don't want it. Take it off ...' She moved to peel the sticky plaster free but the nurse hurried forwards and pushed Meena's arm back to the bed, holding it firm against the mattress.

'Settle down!' the nurse snapped, the aniseed on her breath clashing with the smell of bleach and sickness in the room. 'You mustn't fiddle. You're sick. The IV will give you strength. Lie still!'

Meena felt her body go limp by automation. The nurse frowned, a strange expression flashing across her face. A soft, unarticulated groan came from the next bed, taking the nurse's attention. Meena blinked. Her mind fighting memory, fighting emotion. The sound came again, weak. Too weak. Meena tried to roll over, to pull her back to the sound. Hadn't she heard a sound like that before? Long ago, when she had been very small. It had been a hospital then too, but she hadn't been the patient. Or had it been someone else ... someone more recent? Meena's mind tangled the images, now swirling with the scents of hospital. Her mother had died on a poor bed like this, died with a baby in her belly. And Meena had been the one to take the news home to her father, drunk in the fields by mid-afternoon. She remembered that clearly, but there was another groaning from the past too. Stronger than this one ... and a petite sparkled *sari* set stained with blood ... No! She wouldn't think of it. She couldn't. Not when Madam could come and collect her. Force her back to the hotel. To Vishnu. To Waman. Not when she didn't understand what Sarita had done.

***

It was several hours later when the nurse returned, this time with a doctor. Meena didn't bother to watch them, but she heard them move bed by bed around the room; asking questions, supplying answers, requesting medications, taking notes.

'How old's this one?' the doctor asked in crisp Hindi when they reached her bed.

'She won't say,' the nurse replied.

The doctor stepped closer. Meena could see the folds of his neck crease as he spoke. 'Dehydration decreasing. Good. How much fluid has she had?'

The nurse rattled off some numbers, almost confident.

'Tell me your age, *bahana*, little sister.' The doctor used a voice for children. 'Age first and then your name. This isn't a police station. We won't arrest you. We just want to make you healthy again.'

'Tell him,' the nurse snapped. 'Your blanket and clothes have been washed. I'll bring them once we finish the rounds, if you cooperate.'

The doctor pursed his lips, waiting. Meena turned her face towards him.

'I am fifteen ... maybe,' her voice was soft.

The doctor passed the clipboard to the nurse who hurried to write down Meena's answer.

'And your name?' The doctor continued.

'M ... Meena.'

'Are you Nepali? Were you trafficked to India to work in the sex trade?'

Meena didn't answer. The doctor was using words she didn't understand. He tried again, 'Trafficked? Sold? Were you sold to the brothel by someone? A relative maybe?'

Meena ducked her head. The memories continued to struggle forward. Memories she didn't want. Buffaloes were sold. Or goats. Or a piece of tin from the roof of a slum home. Her father said they didn't need it after mother died. He said if they slept close to the wall they wouldn't get wet. He would find rice bags to patch the hole later. It wasn't long after that Meena had begun sleeping somewhere else. Somewhere safe, with someone small—

The doctor broke through her thoughts. 'You'll need your blood tested, so we can find out what diseases you may have. An HIV test would be good too. Have you heard about HIV?'

Meena shook her head but she pulled her arms under the blanket. Blood tests were something Sarita had told her about. Needles and blood spread AIDS, Sarita had said when she'd come back to the hotel late one afternoon. Her voice had been dull, matter-of-fact and tinged with an uncharacteristic defeat. AIDS, Sarita had said, would make you die.

But the doctor was still talking. 'There's high exposure to HIV in the red-light districts. Have you had your blood tested before? At Little Sister'—he paused and checked something from the file the nurse held. 'At the drop-in centre?'

Meena shook her head again. The nurse spoke for her, 'We think the card was a gift. This girl probably never went there. She's too young. They don't let the young ones out.'

The doctor considered this then asked the nurse, 'But you called Little Sister Rescue anyway? They've agreed to pay for her treatment?'

The nurse nodded. 'Twice.'

'Good,' the doctor checked his watch, then began talking to the nurse as if Meena was no longer there. He spoke with complex foreign sounding words all of which the nurse wrote down in her file. Then the two of them left the room. The nurse returned several minutes later with a trolley and began giving medicines to some of the patients. The girl in the bed next to Meena received no treatment. Her eyes were now mostly closed except for the thin stripe showing the whites.

'I need to give you an injection,' the nurse explained when she reached Meena's bedside. Meena watched as two new syringes were popped out of plastic packets and filled from separate canisters. 'Roll over.'

The nurse shoved one syringe into each bottom cheek, like she was jabbing a stake into the ground to tie up a goat. Meena cringed but didn't cry out. The nurse returned the blanket, placed a bottle of water on the bedside table and tipped a sachet of powder into it. The water turned orange.

'Rehydration fluid. Drink it whenever you can,' she said, as if she didn't expect Meena to understand. 'Once you can keep that down, we'll order some rice from the cafeteria.' She handed Meena a cup. Meena took a sip, the fluid tasted of foul mandarins. She handed it back.

'And here are your things.' The nurse reached for a bundle from the lower level of the trolley. Sarita's scarf was folded neatly on top of the wrinkled *kurta-suruwal* and blanket.

'My skirt?'

'They probably burnt it. Don't complain.'

Meena pulled the bundle closer, it no longer smelt of Sarita's old perfume or the accumulated sweat of bodies. Dust, sickness and age had been washed from the blanket but not its memories. Nausea rose around the unwelcome orange liquid in her belly. The sparkled silver threads of Sarita's scarf shone under the fluorescent lights. She didn't understand what was happening. From what the doctor had said, Madam wasn't funding her hospital treatment. Someone called Little Sister was. Who were they? What had Sarita done? The only thing Meena fully understood was that Madam wouldn't let go of what she was owed. Either Meena would be returned to the brothel to work off her debt in whatever way Madam felt was fair, or someone else would have to pay. Someone always had to pay.

Nine

For three days the nurse forced the foul orange liquid and bright blue tablets down Meena's throat. The fevers came less frequently, and the nausea almost completely subsided. Eventually the nurse came in and removed the tube and bag of water, and placed a sticky plaster over the prick mark on Meena's hand. The next day a young boy, who said he was from the cafeteria, arrived with a small tin bowl of rice and watery lentil *dal*. He put it on the cupboard beside Meena.

'Who's that for?' Meena asked, making herself sit up.

'Nurse said first bed to the left. That's you, isn't it?'

Meena eyed the meal in disappointment, a familiar pang of hunger stirring in her stomach. 'I haven't got any money.'

The boy shrugged. 'Already paid for.'

'By who?' Meena glanced towards the door.

'I don't know. I just deliver it. Wouldn't complain if I was you. None of them get anything.' The boy motioned with his head at the other women in the room, two of whom were watching the bowl of food with interest.

Meena lifted the bowl onto her lap. The boy turned and left, his flip-flops scuffing the floor softly. The scent of the food spread into the room—cheap, warm but food. Meena ate with her fingers. Two mouthfuls, three, then she put the bowl back on her bedside cupboard and laid down again.

***

The woman in the bed beside Meena died the next day. Her body was rolled away on a thin trolley covered in a sheet. Then a cleaner came and wiped down the brown plastic of her mattress with something containing bleach and a nurse wheeled in another patient. Another woman with sunken cheeks and a bag of water attached to her arm. The new patient grunted as she was lifted up onto the bed but Meena didn't see her face. It was bandaged severely.

Several hours later a young Indian woman in jeans and a deep orange *kurta-suruwal* shirt was led into the room. The woman's eyes seemed to scan the room with familiarity before approaching Meena's bedside. The nurse who had led her in stood at the end of Meena's bed.

'There are chairs in the hall,' the nurse said.

The woman in the orange *kurta-suruwal* just studied Meena.

'She says she's fifteen,' the nurse read details from the metal clipboard. 'Admitted last week, hasn't agreed to a blood test yet. Do you need a chair?'

'No.' The new woman pushed Meena's blanket away to make space to sit on the bed, then she placed the palms of her hands together and smiled showing wide white teeth Devi would have been jealous of.

'*Namaste*,' she said kindly. 'My name is Sharmila. I work at the Little Sister Rescue Home. We've been paying for your food and medication since the hospital contacted us. Apparently you had our details from the Kamathipura Drop-In Centre? But they have no record of a girl called Meena on their visit list. Did a friend give you their card? Or are you using another name now?'

Meena didn't speak. This drop-in centre—was that where

59

Sarita had gone when she wasn't at the hotel or soliciting clients from the street? Is that where she had learned about clean needles and AIDS? Is that why she had begun to change, becoming increasingly agitated with Madam?

Sharmila continued to talk, ignoring the fact Meena hadn't answered. She explained how Little Sister Rescue Foundation had several drop-in centres in red-light districts, a child care facility in one, and almost three homes for girls who had been rescued from brothels. Meena didn't really listen. She just studied Sharmila silently. She was just the type of girl Madam liked to keep on the lower floors; pretty features but not too exquisite. Affordable but still reliable as a steady income for the hotel.

'You are from Nepal, no?' Sharmila asked.

Meena didn't answer.

'We have a few girls from Nepal at Little Sister,' Sharmila continued. 'Some from Bangladesh and even one from Myanmar. Our aim is to rescue as many girls as possible, and to provide care for those who escape the brothels. After a period of rehabilitation and re-skilling, we support reintegration of survivors to their home communities.'

Meena didn't understand. She knew Hindi fluently now, but these words were unfamiliar.

Sharmila kept talking. 'The nurse on the desk said you don't answer their questions. You must feel very worried. Are you afraid of being sent back to the brothel?' Sharmila laid a hand on Meena's leg. 'You don't have to be afraid. You can talk to me. I know how you feel. I can understand.'

Meena shifted her leg and looked away.

'I do understand,' Sharmila lowered her voice. 'About five years ago. I came to Mumbai when I was fifteen. "Mumbai city, the land of dreams", ehh?' She quoted a pop song. 'I was in the brothel for four years.'

Meena narrowed her gaze. Brothel? Hotel? Sharmila kept talking. Softly, gently. 'I was almost fifteen. I stole my step mother's money and ran away with a boy. He said he loved me, so we caught a train from Rajasthan to Mumbai. He said we'd find good jobs and get married, but he left me at his "Auntie's house" which turned out to be a brothel.'

Meena pulled her legs further away from Sharmila and stared at the end of Sarita's scarf poking from the bedside cupboard. She clenched her teeth together then asked without looking for the answer, 'Do you know Sarita?'

'Sarita? No. Was she your friend? Did she give you Little Sister's business card?'

Meena didn't answer. She pulled the scarf from the drawer and wrapped it around her hands.

'You don't need to be afraid,' Sharmila said softly. 'I'm here to help you. I'm not working for a madam.'

Meena eyed the woman at the end of her bed. Sharmila wore tight jeans, but her shoulders were covered. So was her middle. She wore makeup, but it wasn't working makeup. Not like Sarita had taught her to apply several times a night.

'I ended up in a brothel, just like you,' Sharmila spoke so quietly. 'I was sold, by the boy who said he loved me. But Little Sister rescued me. They've helped me so much. And now I help other girls. Like you. Tell me your story. Where are you from? How old were you when you left home? And who is waiting for you to come home?'

Meena stared at the orange top. It was embroidered around the neckline with tiny mirror inserts ...

'I was twelve ...' Meena whispered, but only partly to Sharmila. The gap between memory and reality was closing and it ached. 'There's no one waiting for me.'

Sharmila smiled like she was trying to be kind. 'I'm sure

there is. A friend, maybe?'

Meena shook her head. She felt her throat constrict but framed the sounds anyway. 'I don't know where she is.'

'Who?'

'Pu ... Put ...' Meena couldn't say it. She waited for the slap, the cursing, the scowl. The past mingled with the present—aching, spitting, fighting—and she was afraid. But Sharmila didn't flinch. There was no anger on her face, no anticipation of punishment and in its place a silent searing pain began to build in Meena's chest. The type of pain medicine could only look at. The pain Meena had locked away deep, so deep she thought she had forgotten it.

'Tell me ...' Sharmila said.

But Meena rolled to the wall and waited, without speaking, until she felt Sharmila rise from the bed and leave.

They ride quickly up Old Bazaar Road to Uncle's house, Meena behind Rajit again, Putali behind Santosh. Zipping in and out of local taxis, motorbikes and the occasional *bhaisi*, buffalo, without stopping to look at any other fancy shops. Uncle's house is tall and skinny, the concrete painted apricot orange.

'We'll stay here tonight,' Santosh explains as he holds the front door open and then locks it securely behind. He introduces Meena to his mother, a woman she has only heard about but never met. She sits thin and pock-faced in a dark room with Rajit's baa. The air is thick with cigarette smoke.

Meena presses her palms together at her chest and greets her aunt formally. Putali does the same, but the woman barely nods in return. She eyes the girls suspiciously from her narrow face then sends them to the bathroom to wash. 'Use lots of water!' she calls after them as they hurry in the direction she's instructed.

Meena and Putali push the bathroom door open and gaze in awe. Putali's father had built a tiny hut of old rice and grain bags to cover their family's pit toilet. The roof leaks but at least it's private and tidy. Meena's *baa* has never been bothered to dig a proper hole after the old one was covered by a mini mudslide four monsoons ago. So, she and her father just use the ground a little way away from the house. For clean water, both Meena and Putali's family access a common tap morning and afternoon, and all laundry or body washing is done by the river.

But Rajit's father's house is pretty fancy; there are taps inside! Meena saw two in the kitchen on their way in, and now there are several in the bathroom—the same room as the toilet! The toilet itself is shiny blue crockery, like the stuff posh tea cups are made of. There is a small blue sink with a tap hanging over the top of it and another tap sticking out of the wall that must be used for washing. Meena fiddles with the main taps. 'Do you think there will be hot water? Like on the soap ads on TV?'

Putali shrugs her shoulders.

Meena tries the taps in the other direction. Putali lets out a brilliant shriek. Cold water streams like messy rain from a shower spout above their heads. Poor Putali is saturated. Meena laughs as her friend hurries out of the rushing water, anxiously wringing her sopping shirt. Her face in panic.

'Don't worry. We get new clothes tomorrow!' Meena chuckles.

Uncle's wife opens the bathroom door and growls at them. She tosses two sachets of shampoo under the shower's stream. 'Don't play,' she scowls. 'Just get clean.' Then she shuts the door again.

'Don't play, get clean,' Meena mimicks between giggles. Putali ducks a hesitating hand under the stream of water to retrieve the shampoos. A soft smile creeps onto her face like sunshine on wet rice fields. 'It is warm!'

Jen

Sharmila and the nurse were both frowning. The nurse waited impatiently beside a small hospital trolley and Sharmila sat on the end of Meena's bed.

'*Suno*, listen, Meena.' Sharmila leaned forwards trying to replace the frown with a look that resembled kindness. 'A blood test doesn't hurt much, just a little sting. The blood is collected in tubes and taken to the lab. It won't take long, and you'll get your results—'

'I don't want it,' Meena repeated. 'I'm feeling better. I don't ... need it.' Her voice wavered, it sounded too weak to agree with her.

The nurse sighed and rolled her eyes. 'They're all the same. Ignorant. Uneducated—'

Sharmila's frown deepened and shifted direction briefly to the nurse. The nurse shrugged and pulled on a pair of new gloves. 'There's only so much we can do for patients who refuse to be tested. We don't know what conditions they have without a thorough investigation.'

'I know.' Sharmila interrupted firmly. She turned back to Meena. 'The doctor is already treating your dehydration, typhoid and dysentery. You're obviously improving and gaining strength. And you have been eating the meals we've organised?'

Meena tilted her head slightly in agreement, not taking her

eyes off the nurse and her needles and tubes.

'Good. But it's time now to check for other diseases, so you can get back to full strength—'

'For what?' The question was out before Meena had intended it.

Sharmila looked confused. 'So you can be healthy again, of course, and get on with the rest of your life.'

Meena felt her chest constrict at the statement. The rest of her life? What did that mean? The nurse took her silence as agreement and stepped forward, a small damp wipe between her fingers.

'*Nain*,' Meena said, pulling her arm out of reach. 'I don't want it. The doctor said I didn't have to if I didn't want to, he said I have a choice.' Meena heard herself repeating the ridiculous claim. No one would ever say such a thing to her. They would hold her down. They would force her and draw the blood from her arm. Then they would test it and when they found disease, they'd throw her out and let her die on the street, or worse ... Is that what had happened to ...? Meena couldn't finish the thought. She jolted backwards. The bars at the end of the bed pressed into her back. Her head shook like Devi's under Vishnu's beating. The other women in their beds turned to watch. The woman down the end with dyed red hair was laughing. Meena could hear her words. Whore. Bitch. Slave. Filth. The nurse grabbed at Meena's arm.

'Stop,' Sharmila said suddenly, reaching out to hold the nurse at bay. 'There's no rush. If she's not ready, she can wait.'

The nurse scowled. 'And the longer she'll stay sick, wasting a bed with her waiting.'

Sharmila's face surged with colour. She stood so suddenly the bed shook and a brief look of shock swept across the nurse's face. 'Wasting a bed?' Sharmila's voice rose. 'Really? Is that because she's poor? Or because she comes from the brothel?'

The nurse didn't answer.

'I thought hospitals were supposed to care for the sick. Any sick! Well you write on her file that Little Sister Rescue Foundation will follow up the blood tests. You don't have to wait any longer for your silly bed. All you have to do is get her healthy enough to leave. Whenever that is, call me, and we'll come and pick her up.' Sharmila swung her handbag over her shoulder and waited, hands on hips, until the nurse returned her gloves to the trolley and wheeled it away. The room was silent, but for the soft sound of the woman in the next bed trying to breathe. Even the woman up the end had stopped laughing. Sharmila stepped closer to Meena. She spoke softly now, gently.

'If she brings you medicine, accept it, but don't let them take your blood. We'll worry about testing later. You don't belong in a brothel,' Sharmila went on. 'But you don't belong in hospital, either. At Little Sister, we'll help you, and when you're ready you'll be able to go home. You're free now.'

Meena kept silent. The bars from the bed pressed into her back, accusing her of the past. Sharmila patted her knee. 'Don't worry, you'll be home soon.'

Meena looked away. It was as if the stronger she got, the weaker her hold on the lid of the past. She could almost smell it: the wind from a bus, the hot air of the Terai, the sickly scent of a frowning man's aftershave. Where was home? And who would be there ready to blame ...?

***

It took a few more days before Meena could manage to walk, one foot after the other, on the elbow of a nurse's aide to the toilet. She entered the stagnant room and squatted over the white porcelain hole. Then the aide came to scoop Meena up again.

The medicine Sharmila had spoken about was delivered as expected. The blue pills had to be taken twice a day for another week, the orange pills three times a day for two weeks, and the thick white cream applied regularly to her vagina. Meena ate what was delivered by the cafeteria boy and managed to keep it down. But she didn't get her blood tested.

Eventually the day came when the doctor asked no more questions and gave no further instructions to the nurse.

'She's ready for discharge,' he said without looking up. 'Get the bed ready for someone else.'

Meena pulled herself into a sitting position and stared at the other women in the room after the doctor had left. The bed next to Meena held the bandaged-head woman. On the bed next to that lay a woman who'd been beaten by her husband's other wife. Beside her lay a middle-aged sex worker with a pelvic infection like Meena. On the other side of the room were a skinny, long-legged girl with a fever, a woman who continued to bleed after a still birth and a girl with a complicated broken leg. They were all like her: poor, used, alone, and yet Meena now realised they were different too. Of all the girls in the room, she was the only one who'd received daily meals, the only one whose condition had improved since the day she'd arrived. The others were growing weaker, talking softer, moving slower. They were waiting to die. A sick taste rose in Meena's throat. She lay down and rolled over, so she couldn't see the others anymore.

Sometime that afternoon the noise of heels woke Meena from a dreamless sleep. Sharmila was standing triumphantly at the end of the bed. She wore a bright pink shirt that laced up at the neck and long black trousers. A dozen pink bangles glimmered on her wrist. 'Are you ready to go?'

'Where?' Meena watched Sharmila carefully.

'To catch a taxi. You're ready to go home!'

Home? Meena studied Sharmila's face. If it had been Sarita, Meena would have been able to tell if the words were lies. Even Devi, or Vishnu, or Madam showed their lies on their faces. But Sharmila was a stranger.

'Come on, get up.' Sharmila laughed at her.

Meena fumbled under the blanket until she found Sarita's purple scarf and wrapped it round her shoulders.

'You won't need those old things anymore.' Sharmila dropped a plastic bag onto Meena's lap. 'Here, have a look.'

Meena glanced through the bag's opening. A T-shirt and trousers lay folded together. She shook her head. 'I don't want new clothes.'

Sharmila's thin eyebrows crossed slightly. 'I thought you might like to get out of your old stuff and leave in something fresh.'

'*Nain.*' Meena pushed the bag away. 'I don't want the clothes.'

Sharmila hesitated for a moment, then tilted her head in agreement. 'Okay. No new clothes. You'll have to wear your old stuff then. Get in.' She pointed to an empty wheelchair. Slowly, Meena lifted the blanket and slid her legs over the side of the bed. Her old *kurta-suruwa*l barely disguised the thinness of them. She felt weak, like a too thin twig holding up a leaf.

'Do you need help?' Sharmila leaned forward, her pink bangles jingling.

Meena shook her head. She eyed the navy-blue vinyl of the wheelchair seat, then dropped her feet to the cold hospital floor and twisted to sit in it. Sharmila pulled the blanket off the bed and gathered it into a bundle, handing it to Meena before collecting the bag of medicines from the bedside cupboard.

'What about this?'

Meena looked up. Sharmila was holding the old *sari*

blouse—the sparkled, sequined one from Madam's hotel.

'This yours?'

Meena nodded. Hers. She had bought it with a collection of tip money. Money she could have paid to Madam to lower her debt. But girls out of the little rooms had to provide their own clothes.

Sharmila dropped the blouse to land on the blanket in Meena's lap. Meena pushed it away. The sparkles dropped to the floor.

'Don't you want it?' Sharmila asked.

'*Nain.*' Meena looked away.

'It's quite pretty—'

Meena pulled the blanket closer. She kept her eyes from Sharmila's. If she was expected to go back to work, then she'd need the blouse. But if she wasn't ...

'*Thika*, okay,' Sharmila said as she positioned herself behind the wheelchair. 'You ready?'

Meena fingered the scarf on her shoulders watching the faces of the other women in the room. What had Sarita done when she had made the bargain with the police? If it hadn't been for the card in Sarita's scarf, would she still be lying here with these women? Was there really no Madam waiting to collect her? Waiting to collect her debt?

The wheelchair began to roll towards the door, leaving the sparkled *sari* blouse on the floor. Sharmila chatted as she pushed, describing trees and lawn and flowers of the Little Sister Rescue Home. Down the hall they went, Sharmila stopping only briefly at the nurses' station, before continuing down a ramp, and then another. Finally, Meena saw the doors of the hospital—the ones she had seen that first day from the outside. Sharmila pushed Meena between struggling patients and a cross-looking woman, to a queue of waiting taxis. Meena stared upwards; she couldn't help herself. The open sky was a grey blanket above the buildings.

'Out you get.' Sharmila jiggled the wheelchair outside a waiting taxi. The door was open, the seats inside were red and shiny. Meena hesitated. Shiny seats. Bus seats. Jeep seats. Rickshaw seats. She glanced back at Sharmila.

'Don't worry.' Sharmila smiled. 'I'm coming with you. You won't be alone. Not anymore.'

And Meena ducked her head, despite herself, and slid into the taxi.

'Putali, ehh, Putali!' Meena nudges the sleeping green shoulder. Her little friend wakes, snaps her mouth shut and wipes the wetness around it, embarrassed.

'Look,' Meena points to a frantic butterfly butting against the inside of the bus window.

'What's it doing here?' Putali asks.

Meena shrugs. 'I'll let it out.' She shoves hard against the stubborn glass and forces the grudging window open. A gust from outside the bus tumbles against the butterfly's wings. They watch it fight forwards and then fall outside, quickly disappearing behind the bus. Meena pulls Putali closer so they can lean together and take in the view. They both smell of shampoo and new clothes now. Their wrists jingle with glass bangles. Putali has even managed to get Santosh to buy her some earrings by smiling shyly at him. The small dangles of green glass beads hit the sides of her neck. She looks much older than eleven now, especially with the dark make up they have both drawn around their eyes. They look like fashionable young women!

Meena points out the bus window to the tumbling river far below the cliffs. 'See how it winds like an angry snake?'

'Oohhh, I hope we don't crash.' Putali grips Meena's shoulder. Meena laughs. The water shines bright turquoise, like the *kurta-suruwal* fabric Putali had almost bought. It pounds the boulders that bars its way down the mountains, leaving little sand banks on opposite bends. *Himal* water, rushing down, down, down to freedom. Just like them.

The bus is noisy and full. It is so full that Meena's uncle had only been able to buy three tickets. The boys were so brave, hiding their disappointment. But now it is Putali and Meena, side by side, two rows from the back of the bus. Rajit's *baa* sits across the aisle beside an old man wearing traditional *Newari* dress: skinny trousers, long shirt, vest and *topi*. Meena's uncle sits with his face forward and mouth tightly shut. He probably doesn't like the music. It is loud and western in style, the Nepali language scattered with English words like, '*cum an pardi*' or '*aye luv yu*'. Meena has no idea what the English words mean but the music is fun. Right now, everything is fun, and so far away from chipping rocks or cutting grass.

The woman sitting in front of Putali is rich. She has hill-tribe-style gold hanging from her ears and chats constantly to the young man carrying a chicken who is sitting beside her. Constantly, that is, until she suddenly leans across him and shoves the window open to vomit outside.

'*Chhya*! Disgusting!' Meena swears as the huge splats of vomit fling through her newly opened window and land across the top of her pink *kurta-suruwal*. She tugs the window pane back in place before the rest of the vomit slides across the glass. The woman has obviously drunk a Mango Frooti with her meal at the last stop and it now blurs the view of the river to a lumpy, sickly sight.

'Uggh,' Meena grimaces, taking in the disgusting mess across her chest—across the only beautiful, new thing she has ever worn.

Putali reaches into her plastic bag of belongings and pulls out her old shirt. 'Here. Use this to wipe it,' she offers.

Meena takes the shirt. 'Next time throw up in a plastic bag!' Meena shouts as she tries to wipe the vomit from her.

She looks across at her uncle, appealing to his kindness

and help, but he scowls at them. Before they boarded the bus, he'd warned them to be quiet. 'Don't talk to anyone about why we're going to India. There isn't enough work in Nepal these days. If everyone finds out where we're going and why, they'll hurry ahead and take your jobs!'

Meena glances around the bus. Several passengers are watching her now, her and Putali. Their faces are blank, staring, but the girls have been noticed. Meena ducks her head to hide her shame. She doesn't smell like shampoo anymore, and Rajit's *baa* seems annoyed.

'How much longer, do you think?' Putali asks softly as she puts an arm around Meena. 'It's not your fault she vomited on you.'

Meena shrugs. There are hills all around them. The bus is speeding down a road that hugs the rock on one side and teases a cliff to the river on the other. All she knows is that their destination is somewhere flat. Close to India. She holds up Putali's old shirt, now stained with vomit. 'What will we do with this?'

Putali pinches two fingers on a clean edge and drops it to the floor of the bus. 'I won't need old rags like that now, will I?' she grins shyly and leans back to rest her dark head on Meena's shoulder.

Part Three

Eleven

Meena snapped her eyes open as the taxi horn belched once more. The sprawl of Mumbai flickered past her window. Traffic swarmed: trucks, taxis, double-storey buses. Buildings changed personalities like the sets on movies, some looking so old and foreign, Meena felt like she was watching a film. Sharmila smiled as Meena straightened up, her fingers pausing as she typed something onto the screen of her mobile phone. Meena didn't smile in return. She just turned back to the window to watch the city. At one point, Meena was sure she saw an endless break of sky and an enormous expanse of water. The ocean. She'd seen it only once before, with Putali. Meena felt a sob rise but forced it back, forcing her focus, like Sarita had taught her, on what was real: the buildings, people, buses and cars. Eventually the tight-packed city breathed a bit more space. Shorter apartment blocks became more common, scattered among large private houses with high walls and big iron gates. Finally, after driving through several choked intersections, the taxi heaved to a stop at the top of a narrow road.

'Keep going'—Sharmila leaned forward—'Little Sister Rescue Home is just down the road.'

'You can get out here.' The taxi driver dropped his hands from the steering wheel.

'But she's sick. We came from the hospital, remember? She can't walk that far. You keep driving, I'll keep paying.'

'Taxi'll get stuck.'

'No it won't. Many taxis come here, and trucks too. It's just down the road, behind the old house. Keep driving.'

The taxi driver didn't speak. He tipped some tobacco out of a small sachet and popped it in his mouth. Meena could see his jaw in the rearview mirror. It ground lazily.

'Ugh!' Sharmila snapped the taxi door open and gathered Meena's blanket and bag of medicine with her. 'Here!' She dropped the taxi fare ungraciously in the driver's waiting hand then marched around to Meena's side.

'Out you get then. I'll have to get the girls to come help you.'

Meena swung her legs out of the taxi and onto the gravel track. She wobbled to stand up. Sharmila propped her arm under her shoulders and helped her over to the side of the road, where a large block of concrete—presumably left over from some long ago road works—waited. The taxi backed up and drove lazily away to find new passengers. Sharmila swore under her breath.

'You wait here.' She deposited Meena on the concrete block along with her blanket. 'I'll go and get someone to help you to the home.'

Sharmila marched down the road she had tried to make the taxi go. One of her heels twisted in the gravel and she let out another curse. Meena tugged gently on Sarita's scarf. Sharmila was acting more like a hotel girl now. Maybe her story had been true?

But Meena didn't have time to consider it any further. A small cluster of girls soon strolled from the gates Sharmila had disappeared into. These girls wore plain *kurta-suruwals* and flip-flops. There were four of them. The tallest appeared about twenty, but the rest were maybe only slightly older than Meena. One girl had her hair cut short, so it hung cropped under her ears. She walked with a limp.

'*Namaste*,' the oldest one said as they approached. 'Welcome to Little Sister.'

Meena didn't reply.

'I'm Manju.' The girl continued as if Meena had introduced herself. 'This is Asha, Kani, and Nahita.' On the last name, she pointed to the girl with the short hair. The girls gathered comfortably around her. There was no urgency or secrecy in their manner. Asha and Kani latched their arms together to make a carry seat.

'Sharmila said you're not so strong,' Manju commented. She lifted Meena up and placed her on Asha and Kani's waiting arms.

'My blanket—'

'I've got it,' the short-haired Nahita spoke up. She fixed a grin to her face and picked up Meena's blanket as if she had other things she'd prefer to be doing.

The girls carried Meena down the road, through the black gate and past a small guards' hut. Manju closed and locked the gate behind them. Meena heard the latch click and tightened her grip on the shoulders of the girls carrying her.

'Don't worry,' one of them laughed. 'We lock the gate to keep people out, not in.'

Meena couldn't speak. She gripped their shoulders and let her eyes take in the new surroundings. Nothing felt like a hotel. The property was a large rectangle, fenced with high yellow rendered walls. There were two large, flat-roofed yellow concrete buildings and a smaller brick residence to the left. Between the buildings was a strip of grass big enough to park two mini-buses, several tall, though scraggly trees and a water tap. There was a sound, too. Chickens?

But the girls didn't stop long enough for Meena to be sure. They carried her up the steps of the first yellow building and into a small office to the left. 'Sharmila will be back soon,' one of them said, before they left her sitting in a chair in front of the wide desk.

Meena stared out the window. The curtains, though dusty, were tied back to let in sunlight and air. Meena could see the girls who had carried her. They were walking, laughing now, towards the second large building at the back of the property. One by one, the girls disappeared through a doorway leaving the garden empty. Even the girl, Nahita, limped up the stairs with Meena's blanket, taking it away. Meena's chest constricted. But the air here was moved by breeze, not bodies. The trees outside were real, with real leaves, and there was a clothesline on which clean, dry clothes flapped in the sun: *kurta-suruwals*, underwear, trousers. A fancy *kurta* top hung on the line beside a long deep-orange shirt Meena recognised. It was the shirt Sharmila had worn on the day she had first come to see Meena in hospital. Sharmila must live here.

'Taxi drivers make me so angry.' Sharmila entered the room just as Meena turned away from the window. Her heels were back on her feet and her face held some form of composure. 'I heard there's a Mumbai taxi service driven by women for women nowadays. They have magazines to read in busy traffic, and mirrors for reapplying makeup. How I wish I had the money to afford that!' Sharmila said. Behind her an older woman entered the office. This one was short and dark-skinned like a southern Indian. She wore a simple *sari* that contrasted with the weighty gold bangle around her wrist.

'So this is Meena, another Nepali girl come to stay with us for a while?' The older woman seated herself in the large office chair and wheeled herself forward awkwardly, until she could lean her elbows on the desk. She opened a cardboard file and took a shiny pen from a wooden pencil holder. Meena had never seen hotel managers use a pen like that. The woman wrote something at the top of a page, then leaned forward to study her. Meena stared back. The woman had skinny lips that were barely coloured. It looked as if she had applied one layer of lipstick at the beginning of the day before her morning meal and not touched up since. Her eyes were small but her nose, which stood proud without a nose ring, was long.

'Welcome to Little Sister Rescue Home. The girls here call me Maa. You can do so also. My role here is to facilitate your recovery. We have a daily schedule of activities that you will be expected to participate in once you are able, but for now we will be working to bring you back to full health. Sharmila has been bringing regular updates from the hospital, so I am aware of the treatment you have received so far. But how are you feeling, really? It must feel very different to be away from the brothel, no?'

The woman didn't really give Meena enough time to form an answer. She just smiled kindly and then proceeded to read from her paperwork. 'Sharmila also mentioned that you are feeling apprehensive about your blood tests? We hope once you are settled with us, you will feel confident enough for it. Blood tests can give us a clearer understanding of what your body is dealing with. It helps us help you. HIV is only one of the things we test for at Little Sister.'

'Do you have HIV?' Meena heard the question escape before she was ready.

A peculiar expression skittered across Maa's face for a moment. Then the older woman smiled. 'No, I do not have HIV. But I did not work in a brothel. HIV is a virus that is commonly spread through unprotected sexual contact. Some of our girls here are HIV positive, but we treat everyone the same. We cook together, and wash our clothes together. There is no discrimination.'

Meena heard the words, but her mind was thick. She couldn't understand. Sarita had told her about AIDS; she'd said that condoms trapped the disease and kept you healthy, but she had said nothing about HIV. Were they the same thing? But Maa had moved on. 'I just need some more basic details for my file today, then Sharmila will settle you into the dorm with the other girls. Now, where are you from, *bahana*, little sister? Sharmila said you come from Nepal—is this true? Were you born in Nepal?'

'Western district, Nepal.' Meena stared out the window again. A girl was taking clothes from the line. A blouse. A skirt. A colourless handkerchief ...

'Do you have family at home?'

How old would Putali be now? Fourteen—almost a woman—except ...

Maa continued speaking. Meena tried to concentrate, but it was becoming harder to keep her mind clear. It hadn't been like this in the hotel. She'd been able to steady herself, like Sarita had taught. She'd been able to forget. There'd been nothing else to do. Nothing else ... Her fingers clawed the arms of the chair. The room began to spin. She heard Maa's chair roll back and Sharmila's heels clatter forward. Away. Away. Meena pushed the images. Her head hit something hard and someone took her hand. But she couldn't pull herself back. She had seen pink— perhaps it was just Sharmila's top? But once, once it had been her own. Her new *kurta-suruwal* bold against the dust of the Terai. Bold and brave like a butterfly about to be hit by a train. And then blackness.

The movement of the bus ceases just before the golden Terai sun meets the flat horizon.

'Isn't it beautiful?' Putali breathes.

Meena looks and smiles. They have made it to Bhairahawa. All the way down the mountains to the plains, just across the border from India. Together.

Meena follows Putali and Rajit's *baa* from the bus station to a nearby street. Her legs feel wobbly at finally being used again. She clutches their one bag of belongings, as if to steady herself. They only have one bag between them now, her clothes stuffed in with Putali's. Putali hadn't coped well with the final stretch of winding road and they had to use Meena's bag as a sick bag, then tossed it somewhere in the gully before Butwal.

'*Chitto-chitto*,' Rajit's *baa* calls. 'Hurry up!' He leads them through crowds of people, darker skinned and more pointed in features than back up the mountains. They hurry past snack vendors and tea shops, down a street of hotels until Uncle chooses a tall, thin one painted pale orange—almost like his house. Inside, a greasy-haired young man shows them upstairs.

'Toilet's in there.' The man pushes a tin-panelled door open to show a grimy floor toilet that doesn't smell as clean as the one in Rajit's home. 'There's no lock, so use the brick.'

Meena scrunches her nose up. It would be cleaner squatting in the empty block near her house, or over one of the drains near where the rock chippers work, than to use this filthy toilet. She doesn't even bother considering the likelihood of hot water.

'And this is your room.' The man twists a key in the padlock of a room further down the hall and then hands it to Meena's uncle. The girls follow him inside. The room is small, its one window offering a view of the paintwork on the building next door. Rajit's *baa* allocates them one bed and dumps his bags on the other. Meena sits on the mattress and tries to bounce without success.

'I'm going to buy tickets for tomorrow.' Rajit's *baa* says. 'Stay here until I get back.'

The girls wait until he's locked the door behind him and his footsteps have disappeared down the hall. Then Meena removes the soiled pink shirt and replaces it with the swirly blue one. She lays back to stretch out on the bed. It smells musty and the pillow is hard, but at least the ground doesn't move.

'Have you ever been this far from Pokhara?' Putali asks, climbing onto the bed, beside Meena.

'No, never.'

'Me neither. It's very flat here.'

Meena nods, but she shuts her eyes in contentment. Hills mean walking up and walking down and walking back up again. 10 rupees a load is what she could get for carrying things up to the settlement from the city. 10 rupees. That is enough for one packet of two-minute noodles, or two cups of tea. She isn't going to be walking up hills anymore—unless she wants to.

Putali tucks her warm hand into Meena's. 'Where do you think we'll go tomorrow? Will we get to the new job place?' Putali murmurs.

'Maybe,' Meena answers. 'I imagine we just have to get across the border. I don't think it'll take long, not like today. Uncle said India has lots of jobs for people like us. We should be able to send money home to your mother by next week if we work hard.'

'What will we be doing?' Putali asks.

'I don't know. Probably something easy, like working in a shop or a factory. There are lots of factories in India.'

Putali lies quietly for a while.

Meena rolls over and props her head on her hand to look at her little friend. 'What are you thinking about?'

'My mother. We won't be away too long, working in our factory or shop, will we?'

'No.' Meena squeezes Putali's hand. 'Don't worry, your mum will get better real quick once she gets the proper medicine.'

She watches a small smile rise on Putali's face.

'I wouldn't have been able to do any of this if you weren't my friend,' Putali says. 'I'm not brave like you.'

Meena smiles and lies back again. A single light bulb hangs

from the middle of the room. Spider webs lace it to the roof and build a shade of dust. Later, after her uncle returns and they've had something to eat, someone will flick the filthy switch and the room will be blackness. Total darkness.

Meena snuggles closer to Putali. At least she won't be alone.

Twelve

The chattering of girls pulled Meena from sleep or dream or memory. She groaned and rolled over, her forehead pounding. Memories tripped over each other, threatening to tie her in knots. The blanket over her body was Sarita's. But the roof wasn't Madam's hotel, or the hospital. The air here smelt like perfume, marigolds and curried okra. The wall nearest her was pale yellow. A spot of mould grew near the floor.

The room held eight beds, most of which had a girl seated on them. All but one of the girls turned to look at Meena as she pushed herself up to sit. Some of them she recognised from yesterday, most she didn't. A bell rang from somewhere else in the building and the girls started moving towards the door.

'*Bhojana*? Are you hungry?' one of them asked as she walked past Meena's bed. It was the twenty-year-old girl who had lifted her from the rock. Meena managed a nod, unsure what was expected. The rest of the girls traipsed from the room, disappearing into an unseen kitchen. The short-haired girl hesitated by the foot of Meena's bed. 'I'm Nahita, I carried your blanket yesterday, remember? And that was Manju. The bell means it's mealtime,' she explained.

Meena eyed the distance between the bed and the door.

'I'll bring you yours.' Nahita sighed. 'I feel like that some days too.'

Meena waited in the empty room. She felt tired. Not sick—the cramps had gone—but so tired, and confused, like she should be asleep, resting before the evening arrived. But what was this place? Really? It was full of girls, but the windows were wide open and beams of sunlight sliced the floor into segments. Meena reached out her fingers until they entered the nearest stream of light. Bright, clean light. When was the last time she'd touched the sunlight? Sarita and her room hadn't even had a window. Deepa and Devi's was boarded up with painted plywood. Something inside her melted, like *ghee* beside a stove. Meena pulled her fingers back.

There was no chattering coming from the unseen kitchen anymore, only the occasional sound of a spoon scraping against a cooking pot. Meena turned from the sunlight to see Nahita limp back with a plate of food. She laid the plate on the mattress beside Meena. Rice, thick lentils, spinach and potato curry. The girl placed two chillies beside the rice. Then she held out an empty bowl and a jug of water.

'Wash your hands.' Nahita spoke with a Bengali accent. Meena held her hands over the bowl as the girl poured the water and washed.

'I'll leave the water here for after. Enjoy Manju's curry.' Nahita slid the jug under the edge of the bed then returned to the kitchen.

Meena ate, slowly, feeling the sting on her tongue and lips as she bit through the chillies. It was reasonable food; better than the hospital kind, not as greasy as the food at Madam's hotel, but even so, Meena couldn't eat it all. She piled what she couldn't eat onto one side of her plate and licked her fingers. Then she leaned over the bed, pushed her plate out of the way and rinsed her hands.

Eventually one of the girls returned from the morning meal. She stood close to the doorframe for a few moments, staring at Meena. Her face was wide and fair—Nepali. She moved her lips, but didn't speak. Something that looked like fear entered her expression and she hurried past Meena's bed to the one opposite, huddling on the mattress as far away from the other girls as possible.

'That's Purna.' Nahita returned and answered Meena's unspoken question. 'She doesn't talk much. And this is Leela, your neighbour.'

She waved her hand in vague introduction to the calloused girl who'd returned with her and now lay across the adjacent bed. This girl's face was heavily made up, her eyes hard under the eyeliner and colour she wore. But her skin was pale and her features were almost Mongolian. She was obviously from up north, though probably not a true Nepali.

'I guess I'm supposed to say a nice *Namaskar*?' Leela muttered, after Nahita had taken Meena's plate away. 'Another poor girl trafficked from Nepal? Don't expect any sympathy from me.' She rolled onto her side, obviously ending anything that may have been a conversation.

Meena pulled her knees to her chest. How old was Leela? Older than her, older than Manju even, but it was hard to tell with hotel girls. And she could easily imagine someone like Leela working years, maybe as long as Sarita, in a hotel. Meena turned her attention to the other girls. They each seemed to have a small cupboard up the end of the room, in which they kept their belongings. Several of the girls began getting dressed. Meena watched simple *kurta-suruwals* come out of the cupboards, or ordinary T-shirts. There were no sexy sparkled saris, no sleeveless blouses. Meena glanced back at Leela. She was lying on her stomach and had pulled a mirror out from under her pillow. She pouted her lips in the reflection, before winding up a stick of lipstick. It was full red—thick and glossy. She caught Meena watching and gave her a glare. 'I'm not letting myself go just because no one's paying me for sex anymore,' she snapped, daring Meena to contradict her. From across the room, Purna whimpered and Asha, one of the girls who had carried Meena in from the road, let out a sigh. 'You know, Leela, sometimes you should just shut up.'

'Why?' Leela asked. She had a look on her face like she was teasing a kitten. 'You know I'm right. No one wants an ugly girl. Not in the brothel, not on the street and certainly not back home. Didn't anyone tell you that?'

'Oh, shut up!' Asha spat back. Her eyes darted in quick, hot anger, like this wasn't the first argument the girls had had. Leela smirked, but shut her mouth and shoved the lid back on her lipstick, before winding it down properly. The tip of red squashed into the clear plastic lid. She pushed the mirror and the make up back under her pillow and stalked out of the room.

Asha's small face flushed. She pulled the ties of her trousers and knotted them. 'It's not true, what she says,' Asha said, looking at Meena. 'We're valuable as we are, not because of how we look.'

She paused, as if waiting for Meena to respond. But Meena had nothing to say. Madam had always insisted they look their best. She beat girls for not applying enough makeup. Men treated girls kinder if they looked better. Paid better. And the fair girls, the little girls ...

Asha was staring at her. Purna began rocking. Meena wanted to block them all out.

'Maa says we have rights. She says we're beautiful because of who we are—'

'Maa says?' Nahita limped back into the room. 'Are you

86

lecturing the new girl before she's had a chance to settle in?'

'No.' Asha looked even more flustered. 'It's just that Leela was spouting off all her stupid "you've got to be beautiful" garbage and I didn't think the new girl had to put up with it. Leela thinks she is better than everyone. She thinks just because she was sold the youngest, she has the right to treat everyone else terribly, especially if they come from Nepal, but really she's just … just …' Asha searched unsuccessfully for words.

'A bitch?' Nahita put in with a grin. 'Don't listen to her, Asha. She couldn't even be kind to her reflection. As for the new girl, she looks like she can take care of herself—even if she is from Nepal.'

Nahita cast Meena something of a smile, then picked a bundle of washing from the last bed and placed it on the windowsill at the end of the room. She climbed up after it and sat there for a moment, before dropping both legs to the other side of the window. 'I'll see you at lectures, if I can bear hearing any more of it …'

Nahita dropped out of the window. Asha sighed. She didn't look at Meena again, or speak to her. She gathered a green-covered booklet from her cupboard, and a pencil, and left the room. One by one, the rest of the girls left as well. Even Purna crept past Meena's bed, her arms tight against her chest. Soon the room was empty. Small sounds came from other rooms in the buildings, and from traffic in a distant street. She could hear a dog barking. A crow calling. But no one came back into the room to talk to Meena, or take her to the 'lectures' Nahita had mentioned. The doors were all open, and no one was coming to lock her in.

Carefully she shuffled to the edge of the bed and dropped her feet onto the floor. Then, listening for anyone coming, she reached over the gap to Leela's bed. She groped under Leela's pillow until her fingers hit the cool glass of the mirror. She let her breath out slowly and lifted the mirror to find her face in it. She was thin. Not as thin as she had been when Sarita had last shown her a mirror, but her skin was still pasty. Her lips were colourless, her hair dry and wiry. She looked old. She slipped the mirror back under the pillow. Her fingers hit something else— Leela's lipstick. She darted a look over her shoulder and then pulled that out as well. Leela had made a mess of it. The dark glossy red Meena had once thought was so elegant was now crumpled and moist. She shoved the lid back on and replaced the lipstick under Leela's pillow. Outside someone laughed. Meena stumbled backwards to her bed. It was becoming harder to hold back the pain. Groping for Sarita's scarf, she lay down and curled herself into a ball.

Thirteen

It was a week since Meena had arrived at Little Sister—a week of restless sleep and wobbled journeys to the toilet. Now, Sharmila stood at the end of her bed with her painted nails resting neatly on the curve of her hips. Meena drew herself up to a sitting position.

'There's a seminar this morning you might like to attend,' Sharmila said. 'Shall I take you over to the meeting room?'

'Seminar?' Meena asked. 'Like a lecture?'

Sharmila sighed, an echo of frustration in her voice. 'That's what Nahita calls them.' She sat on the edge of the bed, taking care not to touch Meena's feet. 'We call them rehabilitation seminars. Regardless of what Nahita thinks, they are a very important part of what we do here at Little Sister. We're here to help girls grow into full health and some of that health includes teaching ideas and values. You know, things like that.'

Meena didn't know. Sharmila kept talking. 'Some seminars focus on women's issues and rights. Sometimes we do role plays. It is important to understand our place in the world. Just because we were forced to work in the brothels, doesn't mean we are useless. And that's why we have so many options for learning new skills too. Vocational classes are available for everyone—you can learn sewing, knitting, tailoring, beading, candle making. You can even learn to read too—'

'Did you?'

'Did I what?'

'Did you learn to read?'

Sharmila folded her hands almost smugly. 'I knew how to read before I came to Mumbai. And Little Sister has just sponsored me to complete a business certificate. There are many options available for me now.'

Meena didn't say anything. If there were so many options, why was Sharmila still at Little Sister?

'Come on. I'll help you walk to the meeting room.' Sharmila held out a hand with each fingernail painted a different colour. Meena left the offered hand empty and stood up by herself. She followed Sharmila across the garden and to the main building where Maa's office was.

'That's the nurse's office.' Sharmila pointed to the locked door opposite Maa's office. 'Upstairs is Didi's office and the accounts team. There is a toilet under the stairs.' Meena took note of the small, closed door Sharmila pointed to.

'And this is the meeting room,' Sharmila announced with pride. The room they'd entered faced the street, though the view beyond the window's decorative wrought iron bars showed only the stained brick wall surrounding the Little Sister property. The floor was carpeted wall to wall with two large woven rugs, dedicated as seating space. Maa stood up the front, beside a desk and free-standing white board. She wore a floral yellow *sari* and smiled in approval at the sight of Meena and Sharmila. Most of the girls from Meena's room sat on the rugs, waiting for something. Leela and Manju were leaning on the far wall. Asha sat with another group of girls Meena hadn't met. They chatted and plaited each other's hair comfortably, as if they had lived in the home forever. Purna and Nahita weren't among them. Sharmila deposited Meena against the side wall, then strode to the front of the room to meet with Maa.

Meena let the coolness from the wall soak into her back and focused on slowing her breathing from the walk across the yard. Maa and Sharmila whispered a bit more before Maa took a seat beside the desk. Sharmila flicked a switch on some sort of projector and a picture of a rickshaw landed on the wall.

'Welcome to this morning's seminar,' Sharmila began. Her voice was loud and overly confident—similar to the tone she'd used with the staff at the hospital. The girls on the carpet stopped their chatting and plaiting hair. They each laid their hands calmly in their laps and fixed their eyes on Sharmila. Meena tried to do the same, but her mind seemed to jitter each time Sharmila changed the photo up on the wall: a woman carrying water, a woman carrying a baby with several toddlers gathered at her feet, a young girl washing dishes for a rich family. And then there was a logo. Pale blue. Something Sharmila called 'the yu-enn'. Meena couldn't understand.

'Rights.'

Meena turned to see Nahita sink down beside her. She was late. Maa frowned from her seat at the front, but Nahita didn't flinch, she just leaned back against the wall and tucked her crooked leg away. 'She is telling you about your rights,' Nahita explained.

Meena turned to the front and tried to listen again. She searched for a link between Sharmila's words and the photos she was flashing onto the wall. The photos could have come from Meena's settlement. But the words Sharmila used were hard. She used foreign words with her Hindi, and used long words Meena had never heard before—not at home, not in the brothel. She looked away.

'Don't worry. I didn't understand anything when I first came, either.' Nahita leaned closer to Meena, her dark hair swinging forward. 'It is all just blabber until they tell you what each word means. A "right" is something you are allowed to expect. It's like what someone high up in a foreign office says you should always get. Like food. Sharmila says it is our right to get enough food to eat. That means we're supposed to get enough rice each day. If we're not getting it, someone's doing wrong by us, and we're allowed to get cross.'

Maa stood up briefly to glare at Nahita.

Nahita chuckled under her breath. 'So much for my right to speak.'

Meena rewrapped Sarita's scarf about her shoulders and tried to look like she was listening to Sharmila's speech. Maa nodded, pleased.

'The rights of a child are similar.' Sharmila flashed another photo onto the wall: a small girl child carrying two old oil tins of water from the local tap. 'Every child has a right to play and to have a safe place to live ...'

Meena glanced at Leela. The older girl sat with her head down. Nahita noticed her looking.

'She's from Assam,' Nahita explained in a whisper. 'Her father sold her to work as a domestic servant when she was five. 'I doubt she had many rights as a child. But rights or not, safety is all relative. I hate this crap.' She stood up and walked out. Sharmila barely paused before continuing.

And then she was finished.

Meena's mind ran off again. She could see Sharmila answering questions, see Leela's face red and angry, and see Maa gently restoring peace. Safe? Had Meena been safe as a child? Before Madam, before Rajit and Santosh?

She could see the tin roof of her father's house. The rain pelting through the gaps. She could see the smoky fireplace. The steep embankment that led to the water tap. The face of the drunken neighbour peering inside. Safe? No. She hadn't been safe. Not at home. But she'd been safe in someone else's home, curled under a blanket, sharing stories and dreams and ... Meena choked back a cold, hard sob. She couldn't cry. Not here, not now ...

'Aren't you glad you got out of bed to listen to such an encouraging morning?' It was Maa, standing in front of her, the dust stained hem of her *sari* almost touching Meena's knees. Meena couldn't bring herself to agree, or disagree. She just waited until the *sari* had swept away. Her thoughts battled. Her chest tightened. Her throat ached from the weight of holding everything in. And then, Nahita was there again, squatting in front of her, her head tilted matter-of-factly to the side.

'Stuck?'

Meena nodded.

Nahita sighed. 'Don't worry. You won't find all the lectures that boring or confusing.'

'How many of them do we have to go to?' Meena asked. Her voice small and tight.

'They like us to attend every "rehabilitation seminar" while we're here. But Sharmila gets so repetitive. I attend as many as I can to keep Maa quiet, and skip the rest.'

'And then what do you do?'

Nahita eyed her, as if weighing up how to answer. 'Stuff,' was all she ended up saying.

'How did you get here?' Meena asked Nahita.

'Me? You mean was I rescued in a brothel raid? Or how'd I end up in Mumbai?'

Meena tried to sort her question out.

'They found me in a brothel raid last year,' Nahita answered anyway. 'I was at Hotel Happiness before this place.'

Meena's mind spun. She didn't even know the name of

Madam's hotel. How was that possible? For three years she had been there, done everything Sarita had told her, everything to keep her from Madam's wrath and Vishnu's belt. But did the hotel have a name? She'd never asked. Had Sarita known? Deepa? Devi? And what about the hotel before that one, where she'd left ... Where she'd been taken from ... Where ...

'Were there Nepali girls in your hotel?' Meena asked suddenly.

Nahita scowled and stood up, 'Are you that stupid? There are Nepali girls everywhere in Mumbai. There's even a whole red-light district where Nepali girls and women are the specialty.'

'What do you mean?' Meena's mind fogged up.

Nahita tilted her face away from Meena, her hair swinging to the front, hiding her features. 'You have no idea, do you? No wonder Leela hates your type so much.'

'My type?' Could Leela know about what she'd done to Putali? Meena tugged at the scarf around her neck again, her fingers trembling. Nahita sighed and sat down, taking Meena's hands in her own.

'Nepali girls: expensive, innocent, pure, manipulative.'

'But I'm not—'

'No, probably not. But Leela doesn't see that. All she sees are the Nepali girls who tricked her—Nepalised her after her boyfriend ran away, sold her for a high price to the brothel and then, just when she thought she was going to be free, told her *babu* she wasn't really from Nepal and made him fall in love with them instead. Nepali girls are everywhere, Meena. Everywhere.'

'But they're not the only ones *babus* fall in love with, or the only ones who sell girls into ... into ...' Meena couldn't say the word.

'The brothel? No. They're not the only ones. I'm Bengali. I was expensive once too.' She lifted the hair from the side of her face, letting the sunlight shine on her right cheek, revealing a burn scar running from her right ear to her chin. She continued, 'I refused an abortion once, in Kolkata. They let me give birth. I held my baby for one day: perfect, tiny, beautiful. But it cried, bothered a client, so they took it away.' Nahita paused. Meena could hear the girl's breath. 'I refused clients then, thinking I was smart enough to make them give my baby back. Thinking I had a right to my own child. But they didn't, of course they wouldn't. And my refusal to work just made them mad. They scarred my face, and broke my leg with rods from the fire. The next time I was sold, down here to Mumbai, I wasn't worth as much. In the brothel, no matter their race, girls lose value the older and uglier they get.'

Meena stared at the scar on Nahita's face. It wasn't wide, but it twisted and discoloured her skin. It would have been agony to heal. Meena didn't want to think of the injury that had caused her limp. 'Was your baby a boy or a girl?' Meena finally asked.

'I named her Iraira.'

'A girl,' Meena whispered.

'Yes, she was,' Nahita said, and she dropped the hair back over her face.

'Now listen,' Meena's uncle explains early the next morning, after the girls have dressed and done each other's hair. 'We'll take rickshaws over the border. I'll go in one, and you two can travel in another.'

Meena can't help but giggle. Now that the night is gone and she feels pretty again in her new clothes, familiar bursts of excitement tremble to escape like steam in a pressure cooker. Rajit's *baa* has explained the jobs they would be interviewing for; hotel jobs, like waitressing, cleaning or kitchen duties. They are important, steady paying jobs the girls could learn easily.

Meena just hopes she looks professional enough to make a good impression.

'Do you understand?' her uncle interrupts her thoughts. 'We will take two rickshaws.'

'But we'd all fit on one, Uncleji. Putali can sit on my knee; she's only little. We don't mind squishing to save money—'

'No!' He snaps, then takes a deep breath and smiles. 'We'll do it my way. I know what works best. We travel separately. We keep our mouths shut. Understood?'

Meena nods politely to show she won't question anymore and Putali does the same, keeping her eyes down.

'At the border, the police might ask you questions. Tell them you're going to visit Meena's father's mother. If they ask more questions, explain that you won't be away long because you need to help plant rice. I'll meet you at the other side. Then, we'll travel together to the big city. From now, until we meet again, you do not know me. Do you understand?'

Putali opens her mouth and shuts it again. Meena squeezes her hand, feeling the uncertainty in it. 'We understand, Uncleji,' Meena speaks for both of them.

They catch their rickshaws just outside the hotel. Meena helps Putali up first, then climbs onto the shiny red seat beside her. Rajit's *baa* watches their every move, so Meena tries to smile to let him know he can trust them, but the man doesn't smile back. A small breeze blows up the street, bringing the scents of snack vendors and dust and rubbish. From somewhere a bird calls out, as if in warning. Meena grips the rickshaw arm rest and they jerk into motion.

'I wonder if your grandma is expecting us,' Putali mumbles without enthusiasm.

'Don't worry, I'm sure my uncle knows what he's doing,' Meena returns, but when she sees his cold, hard stare disappear into the rickshaw in front of them, she feels a nagging discomfort. 'It'll be fine,' she says, more to herself than to Putali.

The rickshaws travel one behind the other to the busy

intersection leading out of Bhairahawa, then they swap places almost as if following previously arranged instructions. As the road nears the border check-point at Sunauli, traffic slows. Rickshaws, full of goods or passengers, jostle for road space. Stalls selling fruit or ice cream or drinks of crushed cane sugar fill the roadside. Meena even sees a few white-skinned tourists trudging under heavy packs—it isn't even mid-morning and they are wet with sweat. The police are busy too, checking passengers on motorbikes or rickshaws, sometimes questioning, sometimes frisking. Gradually, Meena and Putali's rickshaw creeps forward, closer and closer to the police check-point. Meena glances back to see where Uncle is, but he glares at her so severely she doesn't do it again.

'We'll be next,' Putali whispers as they roll to a stop behind another rickshaw. They watch the police call a female passenger down from the rickshaw, leaving the man she has travelled with alone. The woman is directed to the side of the road and questioned. The woman gestures and argues and finally opens her handbag to display its contents. The officer seems satisfied and lets her return to her ride.

'I hope that doesn't happen to us,' Putali croaks.

The police officer beckons to their driver to move forward and they roll up slowly beside the check-point.

'Where from?' The officer in blue camouflage asks the question in a bored tone.

'*Bhairahawa*,' the driver answers.

The police officer's eyes dart from Putali's face to Meena's. He is more handsome than Santosh. Much stronger too. Meena can't help but smile.

'Where are you going?' The officer directs the question to Meena.

'We're going to visit my father's mother,' Meena answers as instructed.

The man looks lazy, but he studies them a bit longer and then glances at the traffic behind. Meena can't help herself, she looks back also, but Uncle is nowhere to be seen. 'We're going for a week,' she explains quickly. 'But we'll come back soon, to help *Baa* plant the rice.'

The officer nods and waves them on, already turning his attention to the young men crowded in the rickshaw behind. Meena feels Putali relax, and lets out a sigh. Up ahead, a huge signboard blocks the view to India. It is a painting of a man, a girl and a bag of money. Under the illustration are the bold black letters of words Meena can't read. Her uncle is right; there are a lot of people trying to make money these days. Great big signs are even made about it.

Fourteen

'Meena? Are you still in bed?' Sharmila woke Meena the next day. It was mid-morning as far as Meena could tell.

'Maa sent me to look for you. She said she'd asked Kani to tell you to come to the office. I guess you didn't get the message. Have you been here all morning?'

Meena remembered a shorter girl coming now, telling her to go see Maa. But she hadn't really listened. She hadn't wanted to move.

'Come on I'll take you,' Sharmila offered, taking Meena's hand. 'You'll get used to things in time.'

'Some things you never get used to,' Meena whispered, but she dropped her stubborn legs over the side of the bed anyway and followed Sharmila from the room.

Maa's office door was open. The dark-skinned Indian woman sat hunched over a desk full of paperwork. Her shiny pen moved over a form in one of the open files until she noticed Meena waiting.

'*Aacha*, good. Come in.' Maa pointed to an empty chair with her pen. 'Sit down.'

Meena obeyed. The shutters were closed today, probably to keep the hot air out. Meena glanced up at the non-functioning air-conditioning unit attached high on the wall behind Maa's desk.

'Warm, isn't it?' Maa acknowledged Meena's observations. 'We don't spend our donor's money on luxuries here. There are more pressing needs. But ... it's good you're with us, Meena. How are you feeling now? Are the girls taking care of you? Are you comfortable? Is there anything you need?'

Meena didn't answer. She wished for the window shutters to be open again, so she could see outside. Maa checked her paperwork briefly. 'I see you've only attended one of our educational seminars so far. How did you find it? Sometimes it feels a bit much at the start, but you will get used to it and find Sharmila's sessions very helpful. Now, let's see ...' Maa checked a list on the paper in front of her, ignoring the fact she'd just asked a question. 'Our nurse comes twice every week. It will be good for you to have a check-up soon.'

'Why? I'm taking my medicines from the hospital. I'm getting better,' Meena interrupted.

'I know, you are doing everything correctly and we are pleased. But we need to monitor your progress and make sure you are being properly treated for whatever your body is dealing with. Have you been experiencing much abdominal pain?'

'I told you, I've been taking the medicines.'

Maa took a deep breath. She made some marks on the paper in front of her, then pulled open a grey file. 'I want the nurse to speak to you about your blood tests,' she said. 'One of the reasons you may not be gaining strength as quickly as you'd like could be that there are conditions we are not treating. Conditions we can only know about once we take a sample of your blood. Syphilis, for example, needs a blood test to be properly identified and if left untreated, can have serious implications—sterility for one. It would be good, if you are feeling comfortable, to have your blood tested as soon as possible.'

Meena stared at her hands.

'You don't need to worry. At Little Sister, we follow strict pathology standards. HIV testing is recommended, especially if you have been exposed to unprotected sex. Did you use condoms in your brothel?'

Meena nodded. She suddenly felt too hot, Sarita's scarf too tight around her neck. There had been many, many times without a condom. In fact, it wasn't until she had moved from the rooms upstairs that Sarita had taught her how to use them. Too many men trusted sex with a young virgin to cure infections. And others became dangerous at the suggestion of protection. Meena's mind crowded with images she didn't want to see. Her stomach churned. She lifted her gaze to Maa, unable to answer the woman's question, her mind spinning back to the hotel where she'd left Putali. Had anyone taught Putali to ask clients to use a condom?

'Never mind,' Maa continued gently. 'Even if your test comes back HIV positive, we won't treat you any differently.' Meena watched the Indian woman's thin lips move as she talked. She was speaking about counselling, craft groups, literacy programs, bundles of sanitary pads available in Didi's office upstairs. Meena took some of it in and let the rest of the words fill the room. Finally, Maa leaned forward on her desk until her bosom almost fell out the top of her *sari* blouse. 'Routine is good, Meena. It will help you recover. Don't be afraid to begin again.'

And then, as if on cue, Sharmila appeared.

'Take her to Didi, she can begin her chores today,' Maa said, closing three of the files open on her desk and dropping them into a tray.

Meena pushed her body upright. She looked at Sharmila, her pretty make up, her styled hair. Sharmila was smiling, with her hand out again to help. Meena pulled one foot after another. She walked past Sharmila, out to the office and then down the stairs. The sun was warm on her hair, just like a memory. Warm sun above, cool mud around the ankles. The pleasant feeling at the start of rice planting before your back got sore and the mosquitoes made your legs itch. Who had planted rice in their place the year they'd disappeared? Would Putali's mother have been strong enough to work the days required? Meena felt the familiar rise of frightening emotion.

'Didi's over here.' Sharmila's directions interrupted Meena's thoughts, and she blindly followed where the older girl led, ducking the clothesline full of dripping shirts and unwelcome thoughts. A woman Meena now knew to be Didi hovered near a group of girls chatting as they pulled weeds from between the bricked paving. Didi was tall and broad shouldered. She wore her hair cut short, even shorter than Nahita. Her T-shirt was baggy and modest over her rear, her legs in old, unshaped jeans. The woman glanced at Meena and flashed her large teeth. Her smile was full of something Meena couldn't read.

'You must be Meena. I've been looking forward to meeting you. Come and join us, we need another gardener this morning.'

Meena stopped walking. Some of the girls, Asha and Kani included, waved. Sharmila returned to the office and Didi placed a kind hand on Meena's shoulder. 'How strong are you feeling? Would you like to work with the others on the bricks, or should I find you something to do, so you can work seated?'

Meena eyed the other girls. They girls pulled weeds in a squatting position, shuffling forwards and sideways to reach more of the stubborn plants, their faces bright and open in easy conversation. Meena wobbled slightly.

'Sitting perhaps?' Didi chuckled. Her laughter wasn't unkind. 'Come over here. The girls forgot to weed the garden bed near the stairs before they moved to the paving.' Didi held Meena's elbow and guided her across the bricks to the small flowerbed she spoke about.

'Maa probably told you how strongly we believe in keeping busy, yes? Staying in bed all day doesn't help a mind heal, but gardening seems to. It's funny that, isn't it?' She didn't wait for an answer, but lowered Meena onto the cool, prickly grass. Meena's knee knocked the garden's brick edging. She swore under her breath.

'Just work on that little patch for today. Pull out the weeds and pick off the dead marigold tops—it encourages more growth.'

Meena didn't move. She felt Didi rub her gently on the shoulders before returning to join the other girls working on the paving. 'You are a strong girl, Meena. I can tell.'

Meena watched Didi squat down with them. The older woman joined their work and conversation as if she were one of them. Meena turned back to the garden before her. It had been planted with flowers: wide-mouthed petunias and yellow marigolds, but their colour was choked by weeds. Like a fat man on a little girl. She hesitated to touch the plants, to feel the cool flesh against her fingers. She looked back at Didi. The woman laughed at something one of the girls said. Meena reached out, gripped the base of a thick weed and pulled. A tiny grey butterfly escaped from the leaves and brushed her fingers as it flew away. Something in her chest began to hurt. She tugged at the weed again, pulling it from the damp soil, and accidentally catching a new, unopened bud of a marigold between her fingers. A forbidden sob rose in her throat as the butterfly darted away and the marigold bud fell to the dirt. Something hot ran down her face. Meena brushed it away. Her hand was trembling, her shoulders tense. Meena forced her eyes open, willing them dry. She hadn't cried. No, she hadn't.

'Meena?' The quiet voice was Didi's. 'Would you like to pull weeds with us instead?' Her words were gentle.

Meena looked away. She reached frantically for her tough face. The one Sarita would be proud of. The one Madam expected. The one Vishnu wouldn't laugh at.

Didi squeezed Meena's shoulder ever so gently. 'It's alright to cry, Meena. Alright to cry here,' she whispered. Meena shook the woman's hand away. She glared at the weeds and the garden and the glowing marigolds.

Didi squatted by Meena's side, she began to pull weeds. Slowly. Talking softly as she worked.

'Did Asha tell you she's made contact with her family again after five years away?'

Meena shook her head. She kept her eyes averted but sensed the calming presence of the older woman beside her. She could hear the light, cheery conversation of the other girls over the pounding in her head now.

Didi kept talking. 'Yes, Maa is arranging for Asha and her parents to meet soon. If that meeting goes well, Asha will be able to return to live with them.'

'But she is a whore,' Meena croaked.

'No.' Didi paused her work briefly. 'Asha is not a whore. Neither are you.'

Meena felt her chest grow tight again.

'Sometimes people need to be re-educated, to learn how to love again,' Didi continued softly. 'Asha's parents may have old and restrictive ideas, they might not know how to care for a girl who has been trafficked, but if they are not comfortable taking Asha back this time, we'll keep trying. She's their daughter and regardless of what they think or understand, I know they truly love her.'

The older woman didn't say anything else for a while, but then she leaned close enough that Meena could smell the cloves and cardamom on her breath. 'You know, Meena, sometimes it's ourselves we have to re-educate. It's ourselves we need to learn to trust again.'

Meena and Putali barely speak as the rickshaw carries them across the border and down a long stretch of Indian road. They just hold hands, and hold on, soaking in the sights. Eventually their rickshaw stops by a greasy tea shop and bustling jeep station, where Meena's uncle waits. He hands a wad of dirty rupees to the sweating rickshaw driver, then beckons for the girls to follow him to a crowded jeep nearby.

'Climb in,' he directs.

The girls squeeze into an empty space and lean as close to the window as possible. In many ways, India feels just like Nepal, but it is also very different. Women wear longer *kurta-suruwals*, faces are narrower, noses longer, skin darker. As they travel further, fields become less frequent and buildings more common. Little stalls grow into stores. Then, stores change to fancy arcades. Their jeep weaves its way between rickshaws, taxis, buses and private cars, until it stops outside a cluster of hotels and restaurants deep within a city. Meena and Putali climb down and follow Rajit's *baa* into another hotel where he books them a room and orders three plates of food in the downstairs restaurant. Rice, vegetables and chicken curry arrive and they begin to eat hungrily. Then, Meena's uncle hands them each a tall glass of cold, freshly-crushed cane sugar juice. 'You've been very good,' he says.

Meena grins and sips her juice, savouring its super sweet taste. Her uncle nods, obviously pleased with them, and sits back to eat his meal slowly.

'When is our interview, Uncleji?' Meena asks. 'Is it this afternoon?'

Rajit's *baa* shakes his head. 'No, not yet. I have to meet an acquaintance first.'

'Can you trust him?' Putali asks in a small voice.

Meena's uncle almost frowns, but quickly checks himself. 'I only make acquaintances with people I can trust. Finish your food, then go upstairs to rest. I'll come back once I've found my friend.'

The girls drain the rest of their juice and finish off their rice, nibbling the chicken right back to the barest bones—it is so tasty.

'I am soooo tired,' Putali mumbles as the two of them stagger up the stairs to the room Meena's uncle had reserved. Meena agrees. She follows Putali into their room and only just manages to shut the door behind them before her knees buckle and she crumples onto the closest mattress. She didn't think travel and chicken would make someone so sleepy.

***

Sometime near midnight, Meena awakes. She stares with groggy eyes around the room. Putali is asleep, her mouth slightly open in soft, sour snores. Her uncle sits with his back to her on the edge of the second bed, and there is another man; a stranger with arms crossed over his chest and gold on his fingers. They are talking in whispers. Gesturing sharply. Meena tries to sit up. She tries to make her hands into a greeting, to be polite to her uncle's acquaintance, but her arms will not respond. Her mouth refuses to shape the words she is already forgetting. The two men turn around to watch her. She blinks. Again. Then the sweet sleepiness closes the room from sight.

Fifteen

The nurse's office was clean and neat. Two posters with captions Meena couldn't read hung on the wall. A measuring tape was stuck beside the door frame, and a set of scales lay on the floor beside it. Along one wall stood a long, thin bed with a skinny white mattress, on the opposite wall stood a tall metal cupboard with one door slightly ajar. In front of the cupboard was a large desk, identical to the one in Maa's office, and sitting at the desk was the nurse.

Meena lingered by the door as Sharmila introduced her to the nurse, handing over the grey file that had been on Maa's desk the day before. The nurse motioned Meena inside with a wide, toothy smile and opened the file. 'You can go now,' she said to Sharmila with a voice as bland as salt-less *dal*.

Sharmila closed the door behind her, leaving the nurse and Meena alone. Meena propped herself on the arm of a waiting chair. She stared at the nurse, who stared at the words and boxes in the folder. The woman was young, but old enough to be married. She wore no nose ring and had very little jewellery.

'Okay,' the nurse said finally, using the English word Meena recognised. 'Climb up onto the bed and I'll take a look at you.'

Meena did as she was told. The nurse began checking her eyes, pulse, blood pressure, all the while talking. The nurse had cold fingers. Her questions repetitive of those asked by Maa and the hospital staff. She took Meena's height and weight and commented on small improvements since the details written in the grey file.

Then she turned to gather some supplies from the metal cupboard. 'Do you like it here?' the nurse asked.

'It's okay,' Meena answered. In Hindi. She could see the other girls doing exercises on the pavement between the two main buildings. They looked ridiculous, copying Didi's actions like clumsy, disconnected dancers.

'Do you understand why I need to take a blood test today?' The nurse returned to Meena's side. She had a curved bowl now with a packeted syringe, a length of rubber tubing and several clear test tubes lying in wait.

Meena hesitated. She rubbed her arm where she knew the needle would be placed. 'You want to see what diseases I have. If I have HIV or AIDS.'

'Well, HIV is the virus, AIDS is the illness. A person can have HIV without being sick with AIDS,' the nurse explained briskly. 'And we'll test for other conditions too and get some basic blood counts. Do you have any questions?'

'When will I ...' The words were getting stuck in her throat. She felt dumb, uneducated, but she needed to know. 'How long will ... until I d ...?'

The nurse looked up startled. 'Die? How long until you die?' She shook her head and pulled on some gloves. 'I don't know. We're all going to die one day, but I can't tell you when. You certainly won't die from a blood test!' The nurse almost chuckled.

Meena tried to re-frame her question. 'What about AIDS, I mean HIV? Maa said if we hadn't used condoms ... but Madam said if the customer says no condom, it's no condom ...'

The nurse let out an impatient sigh. 'Listen, a diagnosis of HIV doesn't mean certain death! We test today, and again in three months. If the results are negative, that's a good thing. But a positive result is also a good thing because it teaches us how to look after your body, how to keep you healthy for as long as possible. Yes, an HIV positive person will most likely die of AIDS, eventually, but there are very good drugs available now to control the condition. Death is a long way away if you are committed to being healthy. Look outside. I can tell you that one third of the girls doing aerobics this morning is HIV positive. But, at the moment, they are perfectly healthy. HIV isn't everything, Meena, no matter the result. It doesn't define who you are.'

Meena just sat. She could feel the thin mattress beneath her. Could hear Didi's instructions from the yard.

'Stretch deep, girls. *Aacha*, good. Now lunge. Lunge.'

The nurse pulled Meena's arm out straight. She tied the rubber tubing round Meena's upper arm until the veins inside her elbow stood out. Then, with gloved fingers, she pushed the needle into Meena's vein. The blood flowed fast and red—deeper than the red of Leela's lipstick—into the glass tube. One by one the nurse filled the tubes until she pulled the needle out and passed Meena a ball of cotton wool to press on the tiny hole.

'Well done,' the nurse said. 'I'll see you again when we get the results, okay?'

Meena tugged the scarf at her neck. Her body felt heavy, her arms thick. The nurse replaced the cotton ball with a tiny sticky plaster, then waved at the door. 'You can go now,' she said.

***

Meena shuffled down the office steps. The paving rose uneven beneath her feet. Her head felt light and foggy. Didi rushed over from where she had set the girls to jogging. She put a firm arm around Meena's waist, steadying the wobbling world.

'Are you feeling alright?' Didi's voice was soft. Meena attempted to raise her arm.

'Did you have your blood test?'

Meena just wobbled in answer.

'Don't worry. Come with me. I'll get you into bed for a lie down and organise someone to bring you a drink. You probably just need a little rest.'

Meena leaned on Didi's arm as she struggled up the four stairs to the dorm room. Didi lowered her onto the waiting mattress.

'Will you be alright in here, with just Purna to keep you company?' Didi asked.

Meena nodded. She unwound Sarita's scarf from her neck and drew the shimmery purple to her chest. What would Sarita say about blood tests? Had she ever had one? At the drop-in centre? Had Putali?

She was vaguely aware of Didi softly leaving. Of Kani coming in with a cold glass bottle of soft drink. Of Purna rocking herself on her bed across the room. The other Nepali girl mumbled sounds that were more animal than human language.

Meena squeezed her eyes shut. Didi said she needed rest. But there was no rest where her mind was racing to. For three years she had hidden the truth, hidden from the memories that accused her, blamed her and filled her with fear. But now? Why now?

Meena dug her face into the Little Sister pillow, but the images merged even faster. Flashes from a consciousness she'd avoided: walking the streets, herded along by the man, Mohan; a girl with a twisted hand applying too much make up; blood; and a feeble frightened voice calling her name ...

'Meena?!'

She snapped her eyes open to the blackness of the dorm's

pillow, her breath coming in panicked spurts. Suffocating in the darkness. She sat up. Her heart pounding. The dorm room empty now. Even Purna had gone. The yellow walls mocked emptiness. Pain. Guilt.

'Meena?!'

She crushed her face into Sarita's scarf. Faces flashed through her mind. Devi. Deepa, Lalita, Zeshaan. Zeshaan?

Meena's chest tore with the agony of unreleased tears.

'You don't cry about it,' she could hear Sarita's voice, loud in the silence of the empty dorm. 'Tears won't change fate. They just keep you weak.' In her mind, Sarita leaned forward, her lips bright, her eyes painted, a large round blood stain on her neck from yesterday's business. 'You put tears away, or you'll never leave.'

But Sarita's voice faded to the past and before Meena could stop them, the tears came. Screaming from wherever she'd buried them. Tears burning of shame and stinging with humiliation. She choked over them. Catching as they came from deep within her, mingling with anger; a deep, wretched anger that pointed fingers and called names and declared hatred of herself. Meena flung her pillow as far as she could. The bottle of soft drink thrown against a wall. A voice grew inside her. A scream. The cry of someone broken.

'I told her I'd come back!'

She tore the sheets beneath her.

'Bastards!'

She stood and kicked the leg of Leela's bed. The yellow wall shouted back at her. The calm, closed wall. She beat her fist into it. Again. And again.

'Bastards!'

Grief welled. Her face was against the wall now, her fists tight against her chest; her head slamming against the yellow concrete wall. Over and over again, beating the wall with her head until it hurt similarly to the tears in her throat and the ache in her chest. 'Bastards! Bastards! Bastards!'

The floor crumpled up to her. Her shoulders heaved. If only she could close her eyes. If only all there would be was blackness. Nothing. Not the past. It was too hard to see. Too hard to feel, even in replay. If only she could curl in the lap of her mother like she had so long ago. To be rocked, and stroked by fingers soft from spinning wool ...

But mother was gone. And the wool spinner had been splintered many, many years ago. And there was no one left to rock her, and no one who ever would. Not if they knew.

Meena opens her eyes to see Putali on the end of the bed, tugging a comb through her rumpled hair.

'I think we're traveling again today,' Putali says wearily, pointing to Uncle's bag already packed near the door.

Meena groans and sits up. Her head feels thick, her tongue dry. 'Where is he now?'

'He said he was going to order *khana*, food. Have you ever eaten so much?'

Meena shakes her head and scratches her flea-bitten stomach. She hasn't felt hunger for days now, ever since they'd hopped on the back of the boys' motorbikes.

Putali passes her the comb. She's just finished braiding her hair when Rajit's *baa* appears at the doorway. 'Come downstairs, I have someone I'd like you to meet. Bring your bags.'

Meena and Putali follow him down the dusty stairwell to the hotel restaurant. A man sits at one of the tables in front of two uneaten plates of food. He seems oddly familiar to Meena.

'Sit down,' Meena's uncle instructs.

The strange man pushes a plate of food——rice, *dal*, chicken curry, vegetables, pickles—towards Meena and indicates for her to start eating. He does the same for Putali. 'We've already eaten,' he explains softly to Putali's raised eyebrows. Meena's uncle nods his agreement then begins the introductions: 'This is my close friend, Mohan. He has been living in India for ten years now. He has found you some very good jobs, and you won't even need interviews.' He talks as if he has been practising. 'He'll take you after you have eaten, so be as obedient and helpful as possible. Make me proud.'

'But ... aren't you coming with us, Uncleji?' Putali frowns and lifts her hand from her plate of food.

'No. I got a call on my mobile,' he pulls a new, slim phone from his pocket. 'My mother's very sick. *Ke garne?* What to do? I need to return to Pokhara. But, Mohan is more than capable, and I believe I can trust you girls to make the most of this opportunity, can't I?'

Meena nods around a wonderful mouthful of chicken and potato, even if it isn't as tasty as yesterday's meal. Putali looks to her for reassurance.

'We might have time to go shopping,' Mohan suggests, studying Putali's reaction. 'There is time, before you need to start work waitressing. Would you like that?' Putali nods shyly, but there is something cool in Mohan's voice that makes Meena pause on her mouthful.

She watches her uncle stand, and Mohan also. The men walk several steps away until they are out of hearing distance and begin to talk. Mohan passes a package to Uncle who suddenly looks like a stranger.

'Uncleji,' Meena calls out, desperate for some sort of familiarity. But Rajit's *baa* doesn't seem to hear her. He shakes Mohan's hand, strides out of the restaurant and is gone.

Meena swallows a too big lump of potato. She feels suddenly sick. But Mohan is returning to their table. His eyes are steady, his lips turned up in a smile as sweet as last night's sugar cane. 'You girls are very pretty. How old are you?' he asks after ordering them each a fruit juice. Meena doesn't answer. She watches Mohan stir the juices carefully before handing them out. Mohan's eyebrows raise in expectation.

'She's twelve,' Putali rushes and then fades off, ashamed.

Meena swallows hard. 'Putali is eleven. We might be young, sir, but we are hard workers. And strong.'

'I'm sure you are,' Mohan murmurs. 'Now, finish your drinks and we'll get going, yes?'

Meena nods. She feels bad, like she is wasting all this amazing food. But for reasons she can't understand, she no longer feels like eating. She pushes her half-empty plate aside and does as she is told. She finishes the too sweet juice and waits with Mohan for Putali to do the same.

Sixteen

Meena wasn't sure how long she lay there. How long she curled with one shoulder against the wall, her back against the bed leg. All she knew was the stinging of her eyes when she forced them open, and later—after the sun had set—the dawdling of girls returning to the room, assessing the mess she had made; torn sheets, flung pillow, the spilled drink. It was Leela who saw her first, a look of frustration crowding her wide, weary face. The older girl swore. 'What's going on? What've you done to yourself?'

Meena didn't answer. Leela swore again, then scooped her rough hands under Meena's shoulders and pulled her upright, away from the wall and the leg of the bed.

'Get up!' She dragged Meena with surprising strength onto her bed. 'Keep your head upways. I don't want your filthy blood on my pillow.'

Meena allowed Leela to lay her down. She could feel the bumps of Leela's make-up collection through the pillow. She forced her eyes to remain open.

Leela glared at her, an unreadable expression flickering beneath the open disgust. 'Sharmila!' she practically hollered. 'Sharmila, you bitch! You don't leave the new ones alone like this.'

Leela marched across the room to fetch Meena's pillow,

yelling out the doorway again until Sharmila ran inside.

'What is the matter?' Sharmila puffed.

'Matter? You left her alone. She lost it.' Leela sat down beside Meena now. She reached into her blouse and pulled out a cigarette and a squashed box of matches.

'Not in here, Leela,' Sharmila warned.

Leela lit her cigarette and sucked a few breaths, blowing smoke in Sharmila's direction. Then she gently placed the cigarette between Meena's lips.

'Leela, you are not helping her!'

'Well, what are you doing?' Leela snapped.

Nahita, Asha and Renu crowded the doorway behind Sharmila. Sharmila's face surged with colour, but she clamped her lips tight. She pulled the sheets from Meena's bed and remade it, dropping the torn one to the floor to wipe up the Coca-Cola, and using Meena's blanket as a top sheet. Then, without looking at the other girls, and ignoring Leela's puffs of smoke, she helped Meena across the gap between the beds and onto her own bed again.

'Nahita, get a washer,' Sharmila ordered. 'And gloves.'

Meena heard the bathroom door open and the squeal of water in the pipes. Then Nahita was beside Meena, holding out the wet washer and gloves.

Sharmila snatched them, frowning at Meena. 'It doesn't do any good to beat yourself up,' she muttered as she struggled to get her fingers into the gloves.

'Do you want me to do it? Nahita asked.

'It's not my fault she lost it,' Sharmila muttered, her face flushing again.

'Didn't say it was,' Nahita said calmly. The Bengali sat on the edge of Meena's bed and began inspecting her fingers, one after the other.

'Do you want the gloves?' Sharmila asked.

'No, I'm right,' Nahita lay the folded washer over Meena's throbbing head, dabbing at her forehead, wiping away the warm wetness and making it cool again. She frowned, but didn't speak. Leela snorted and dropped the half-finished cigarette to the ground.

'You're a bitch, Leela.' Sharmila trod out the cigarette on her way past.

'Aren't we all?' Leela snapped back. She reached for her pillow, and the mirror underneath. Meena heard the mirror click open.

'You'll be alright,' Nahita murmured.

Meena let her eyes close. This time she didn't see the brothel. She saw a bird: the Indian roller bird that used to dart among the trees near the fields at home. She remembered it now, through the fog and ache. The Indian roller was plain and boring and grey; Leela wouldn't like it. But when a tiny bug darted past the bird, it would thrust its wings open to fly. Blue feathers, more brilliant than the sky set against the mountain snow, revealed themselves. But the bird in Meena's mind's eye lay still, bent and twisted against the side of a cage, its blue feathers nowhere to be seen.

***

Meena didn't get up the next day. While the other girls rose and dressed and moved out of the room with bundles of laundry or sachets of shampoo, she watched them through half-open eyes. Seeing, but not seeing them. Once the room was empty, she just stared at the window at the end of the room, the one Nahita would so frequently jump from. Her head was pounding where she'd hit it against the wall, her chest aching. Every now and then another slow tide of tears would come. Sliding down her cheeks in silent lines of defeat. And no one came to beat her. Sometime mid-morning the scents of cooking potatoes and rice wafted in from the kitchen. Someone walked into the room and lay a plate of hot food on a chair beside her bed, but she didn't look up to see who it was. On and off she slept and cried, not touching the food, aware of the occasional visitor following Sharmila's new orders to make sure she was never alone too long.

Eventually the girls started coming back in for the afternoon free time. Leela and Asha were arguing again. Purna mumbled something in no particular language and began applying generous amounts of potent nail polish to her toes. The smell of it gave Meena a headache. Just before the evening meal, Nahita arrived, through the dorm door, her *kurta* shirt damp down the front and under the armpits. She glanced over her shoulder at Meena as she pulled a clean set of clothes from her little cupboard and placed them on the windowsill.

'Have you been here all day?' she asked.

Meena didn't answer.

'Hasn't moved,' Leela coughed.

Nahita limped back to Meena's bedside. She picked up the half-eaten morning meal with raised eyebrows and seated herself beside Meena. She smelt of sweat and mud and spices. Where did she go each day? What did she do? Meena asked the silent questions but Nahita didn't answer them.

'It'll get better,' was all she said. She spoke like someone old, someone who'd grown up too fast. 'But it will always hurt.'

Meena stared at the cold, uneaten curry.

'Did the nurse come see you today? To check your head?'

'No,' Meena mumbled. 'I saw her yesterday.'

'Oh.' Nahita nodded with understanding. 'Did you get your blood results yesterday? Is that what happened?'

Meena shook her head.

'Are you HIV positive?' Nahita's question was firm.

'I ... no ... I don't know. She said it takes time. She said ...' Meena looked at Nahita.

'Said what?' Nahita's voice took on a sudden harshness. 'What'd she say about me?'

'Nothing,' Meena mumbled, confused. She felt Nahita's gaze, studying, prying, waiting, but there was nothing to say. Her hand trembled, the plate tipped and rice spilled in cold, hard, curried lumps to the floor. Nahita rose, she rolled her eyes. 'I haven't got time to clean your mess.' She limped quickly to the other end of the room, leapt clumsily to the sill where her clothes waited and, without looking back, dropped herself out the window.

Leela lay back on her pillow and made a laughing sound. 'She's got more than laundry, that one. You didn't know, did you? She's HIV pos'. She and Manju, and Renu, and Laxmi, and me. Oh, and probably Purna, but no one would know because the little bitch won't talk. Will you, Purna?' Leela sat up to straighten her trousers. 'You got HIV, Purna? Are you ever going to talk to anyone? About anything? In any language?'

Purna tucked her legs up to her body, knocking the nail polish over. She watched the thick red spread and her eyes widened in panic. Nahita's voice ran shrill through the open window. 'Leela! If you don't shut up, I'm going to hit your face so hard you'll never have to apply lipstick ever again!'

Leela laughed again. 'You'd better pick up your mess before Sharmila finds it,' she said to Meena. But Meena just rolled her back to Leela and shut her eyes to the room.

Seventeen

Several days later, when Meena's head didn't ache so much and Sharmila had coaxed her from the dorm and back into the Little Sister routines of chores and seminars, Maa requested a meeting.

'I've been hearing good reports of your progress.' Maa smiled as Meena entered the office and sat in the expected chair. 'Sharmila says you are attending most educational seminars and Didi has been impressed by your diligence in gardening the flower beds. She has suggested that you may be ready to begin vocational training. Have some of the girls shown you their bead work? Do you think that might interest you?'

Meena shrugged.

'They make bracelets, necklaces and earrings. To sell. The beads and materials for starting up are a gift from Little Sister, but once they begin making income, they purchase their own materials. It's a good little business. Many of our girls enjoy doing it. What do you think?'

'*Nain*,' Meena answered. She'd seen Renu and Laxmi's beading the other day.

'No beading, then.' Maa frowned slightly. 'What about macramé? I know Sharmila would be happy to teach you how to make her bags—'

'*Nain*, I don't like bags,' Meena lied. She didn't really want Sharmila teaching her anything.

Maa's frown deepened. 'Well, the tailoring class is full at the moment, all the machines are being used, but Didi is a very good knitter. Maybe you could learn to make a scarf first? You look like you need a new one.' Maa eyed Sarita's scarf. It was knotted loosely around Meena's neck, little bits of dirt and leaves stuck in the tasselled ends from her work in the garden.

Meena folded her arms over the ends of Sarita's leaving scarf. Her leaving scarf. 'I don't want a new scarf, I like this one.'

'Well'—Maa paused, obviously thinking—'What about a cardigan then? You might find it more challenging than a scarf, but I am sure Didi could teach you? Why don't you go upstairs and see if Didi is available now? Tell her Maa sent you to learn how to knit.'

'But—'

'No buts.' Maa shook her pen in Meena's direction. 'It is important to keep busy; active bodies and minds heal faster than lazy ones.'

Meena raced her mind for an excuse, something to prevent her going and begging to Didi, but none came fast enough.

'Off you go now. Tell Didi I sent you.' Maa waved Meena towards the door.

Meena eyed the corridor and the stairs leading upwards. 'I don't know where to go,' Meena mumbled.

'Go upstairs. Then down to the end of the corridor. Didi's door is always open, unless she is outside. Off you go, hurry up.'

Meena muttered a swear word under her breath, something Sarita had taught her, a word learned from an Arab client.

The stairs to the upper level of the Little Sister office block were uneven. When she reached the top, she stopped and gripped the concrete railing to catch her breath. There were more offices upstairs than Maa had said, each with a label on the front in two languages. Inside the first office was a man dressed in a suit, with his top two buttons undone because of the heat. His brow was scrunched in concentration as he spoke on a mobile phone. The next office also contained men. Two of them. Their suit jackets slung across the back of chairs, one of them drinking tea, a wide smile on his face, the other more serious. There was a computer on the desk between them, one with a photo on the screen of the serious man and his family. The men noticed Meena at the door and smiled politely. They didn't let their eyes wander. They didn't study the curve of her body.

'Didi's office is that way.' They pointed down the hall.

Meena continued in the direction they had pointed, conscious of the noise her flip-flops made, then stopped. A framed painting hung on one of the corridor walls. It was a painting of a place she knew by heart, painted by someone just wanting to make money. She could tell which lazy strokes miss-shaped the Annapurna range, which lines made the *Machhapuchhre* mountain look crooked. But even with the mistakes, Meena felt part of herself try to stand up. She brushed her fingers lightly over the canvas, feeling the ridges in paintwork—they were dusty. How had the painting ended up down here in India, in a hall where the sun couldn't shine on the peaks? She untied the scarf from around her neck and gently dusted the mountain tops. Did the sun still set golden upon them? Would the view still be visible from the front of Putali's house? She felt her chest constrict at the longing of it, torn by a succession of painful thoughts: Who lived in that house now? Putali's *aama*, mother? Or had she died without medicine to heal her? Without Putali to care for her? And what about Putali's father, her beloved *baa*—had he come back to find his daughter gone, his wife dead, his tiny son raised by someone else?

'Meena?' Didi startled her. 'Are you feeling alright? You don't look well.'

Meena felt the blood drain from her face. The hallway wobbled. What had she done?

'Come, come, you need to sit down.' Didi hurried to help Meena through the next doorway to her office. She lowered Meena into a sagging lounge chair and quickly poured her a glass of water, waiting until Meena had taken a few sips before she sat in the chair opposite. 'Are you alright now? Do you want to talk about how you feel?'

Meena shook her head. The faintness was gone now, even if the questions lingered unspoken.

'Welcome to my office, then.' Didi waved a hand around the tidy office. Meena took in the tall, metal cupboard with a mirrored door, the desk under a window that looked over the courtyard, the pretty canisters holding pens and pencils and the large poster of two children on a swing.

Didi picked up a knitting project of bright blue. Her fingers began moving, threading the wool over the needles too fast for Meena to watch. 'Were you looking for me?' Didi asked without stopping her fingers.

Meena hesitated. 'Maa sent me. She says I have to learn to knit.'

Didi smiled. 'You don't sound very enthusiastic.'

'I probably can't do it,' Meena answered, watching Didi double loop her wool before making another stitch. 'I can't even read. I'm not clever like that.'

'Rubbish!' Didi lowered her knitting. 'You have been abused, Meena. But that doesn't make you unintelligent.'

'But if I had been smart, maybe I wouldn't have ... we wouldn't have ... she'd still be ...' Meena struggled for the words. If she had been smart, she wouldn't have convinced Putali to leave Nepal for promised waitressing jobs. She would have seen through Rajit and Santosh's promises. She'd have found a way to get medicine without running away and Putali's mother would be healthy. Her little brother clapping at Putali's class six graduation. She was stupid. Foolish and stupid, and she hated herself. A hot wet tear slid down her cheek.

Didi put her knitting aside and crossed the room. She squatted down to look into Meena's eyes and placed a hand on Meena's knee. 'One day, when you are ready, I would like to hear your story. I am sure, if you heard it told back to you, you would hear how what happened was not your fault.'

'But it was!'

'Was it? Really? Did you ask to be sold into slavery? Did you choose to be broken to the point of no longer believing in yourself?' Didi's voice was firm, steady, just like her gaze.

Meena felt the sobs heaving from her chest now. She sobbed until her throat hurt and the tears, for the moment, had finished. Only then did Didi speak again.

'Would you like to be able to knit?' she asked.

Meena nodded weakly.

'*Aacha*, good.' Didi patted Meena's knee. She stood, a little stiffly, and opened the metal cupboard. 'What colour would you like?'

Colour? Meena tried to think. Red was for married women. White for death.

'What about blue?' Didi held out a skein of bright blue, similar to what she had been working with.

Meena shook her head. Blue belonged to the roller bird. 'Black,' she offered.

'Okay.' Didi rummaged among noisy plastic bags before pulling out two skeins of thick black wool and handing them to Meena. She fished two long knitting needles from a drawer and placed them on the desk. Then she untied the first skein on Meena's lap and found the loose end.

'A skein is too hard to knit from,' Didi explained. 'You get all tangled up. So we begin by rolling it into balls. Wind it around your hand at first, then, when it is quite thick, pull it free and turn it into a ball. Once you've done that, we'll start our lessons!'

Meena wound the wool around her fingers as directed. Soon it became too tight, so she removed it and changed the lump into a ball. The thread kept slipping, the wool occasionally tangling around the skein, but she continued winding, detangling and winding again until the ball began to steadily grow.

'You'll be a good knitter,' said Didi after a while.

Meena looked up.

'Yes,' Didi nodded. 'You have perseverance.'

The sides of the streets are crowded to bursting, so Mohan hurries them into a rickshaw, all three of them this time. Putali's bony bottom digs into Meena's lap.

'What is this city called?' Putali asks shyly as they start moving.

'Gorakhpur,' Mohan answers without extra explanation.

The rickshaw weaves through the city until it turns into a wide intersection and inches its way between buses and trucks and taxis to a huge cream building, twice as big as the biggest cinema in Pokhara. Enormous pillars hold up a wide entrance. People are shouting, cars honking to get into position and rumbling behind it all is another noise, like huge machines drawing in and tugging away, unseen behind the cream walls and crowded buildings. Meena strains over Putali's shoulder to look. The rickshaw stops and Mohan climbs down. He doesn't attempt to help the girls, so they jump down on their own.

'Are there shops in there?' Meena asks, amazed at the huge cream building. Perhaps it is a 'shopping mall' like in American TV?

'That's the train station,' Mohan pushes the girls in front of their parked rickshaw and towards the gaping entrance.

'Train station?' Putali bursts in excitement, 'Are we going to see a real train?' She wobbles a bit in excitement. Mohan doesn't answer, he just keeps walking, expecting them to keep up. Meena grabs Putali's hand, more because of the gnawing, uneasy feeling in her stomach than for any other reason. They follow Mohan under the huge, teeming doorway, past many sweating people to a bustling platform. A train, a real train, with faces pushing up against windows and arms leaning out, is dragging itself along two metal tracks. It moves slowly, noisily, closer, until it almost leans over the concrete platform they stand on. The girls wobble together, Putali's mouth gapes like she has started to say something and then totally forgotten what it is. Meena isn't sure it is just the excitement that causes their jitters anymore. She grips Putali's hand tighter and staggers backwards. The train's motion stops and suddenly there are men and women and children and bags and baskets and boxes pouring onto the platform. The wave of bodies push Meena and Putali close to Mohan. A woman carrying a basket of oranges is knocked, the basket's rope slips from her head, the basket falls. People begin shouting, oranges spill out under sandals and business shoes and glittery heels. Meena watches the oranges rolling, bumping, bruising, bursting—bewildered. Men begin swearing, cursing the woman and her oranges.

Mohan's mouth is moving too, his hands gripping their shoulders and pushing them forward. A voice on a scratchy loudspeaker makes an announcement in Hindi and then in another language. Meena can't understand either of them. Mohan pulls three pieces of paper from his jacket pocket and points towards the open train carriage in front of them.

'Go inside,' he leans close to Meena's ear to shout it. 'We can look inside the train. Go!'

Putali's eyes are wide but her little legs aren't working, so Meena shoves her forwards. Now that the wave of people is rushing away, there is space to move. They climb the few steps into the train carriage and Mohan prods them down an aisle. It is narrow; seats run along each side and metal fans hang from the ceiling. Only half of them work. The seats are like those on a bus, only taller, and the windows have metal bars along them.

'Stop here,' Mohan interrupts their tour. He is only half watching them, his eyes darting over details on the papers in his hands. Putali keeps walking. Meena grabs her shoulder to pull her back. Her little friend trips a little, her face pale.

'Here, sit down,' Meena tugs Putali towards one of the seats.

'No, not that one. Here, sit here.' Mohan wears something of a smile. Putali shuffles across the aisle to where Mohan stands and sinks into one of the red vinyl-covered seats. 'Aye ... I feel funny,' she mumbles under the noise of the train. She looks up at Meena and something like fear flashes onto her face. Meena glances up at Mohan. He has tucked his pieces of paper back in his jacket and is watching them. 'She feels sick,' Meena explains, as if waiting for Mohan to offer his own explaination in return.

But he doesn't. He just watches Meena like he is waiting for something to happen. Meena shakes her head. Her eyelids grow heavy under his study. Why has her uncle left them with this man? She tries to say something, but another announcement is being made on the platform. People appear at both ends of the train's carriage. Bags are lifted to shelves above and boxes shoved under seats. Bodies find their way to seats and settle in as if waiting for something. Perhaps the same thing Mohan is waiting for ... Meena looks down at Putali for reassurance but her little friend's face has gone completely blank. Meena can't understand it: in all the busyness and excitement Putali has fallen asleep. Meena's head spins.

A Nepali voice boards the train. She hears it ask a question, a question about the train making the connection to Mumbai, but Mohan's voice is running over the top of it. His voice is close in her ear, so she cannot hear the other answer.

'We'll go shopping later. And then I'll take you to the hotel. You be a good girl now, just relax. Later, later—you can trust me.'

Eighteen

'Let's finish up for the day.'

Meena's thoughts were interrupted by Didi. The older woman smiled, as if aware of how far away Meena had been. Had she really been rolling wool all afternoon? She hurried to pack up her wool into the bag Didi had given her and together they walked past the painting, down the stairs. Didi lived on the Little Sister compound in the white building to the left of the dorms, so she didn't have far to go. Meena hesitated at the office doors and watched the men climb onto their motorbikes, a waft of regret and blame hid in the bikes' exhaust. The office was quiet now. Classes were finished, most of the girls were lingering in the courtyard, collecting dry laundry or somewhere inside the dorm. A soft rustling sound came from Maa's office.

Meena stepped back, the plastic bag holding her skeins and knitting needles gently bumped against her knee. She glanced into Maa's office. Maa was still there, hunched over the big desk. Her narrow face was deep in concentration. Her hands moving over a stack of small papers. No ... Meena frowned. The small papers were photos! Meena could hear the blood pounding in her ears as she inched forward, willing her flip-flops silent, to stand in the office doorway. Maa didn't notice, so deep was her focus on the small photos. First one, then the next—studied, perused and then moved to the back of the pile, all the while moving her lips. Moving her lips like a brothel madam doing her sums.

'Wha …' Meena stammered. She tried again, louder. 'What are you doing?'

Maa looked up, surprised. She returned the pile onto her desk. 'Meena, you startled—'

'What … are they?' Meena forced the words out.

The woman glanced down at the photos, a look of knowing spread over her face.

'These are photos.'

'Of girls,' Meena accused.

'Not all, some are boys.' Maa held up one of the photos: it was a stained picture of a small, shy-looking boy. She displayed another: a girl dressed in fancy wedding red. Meena's fingers tightened on the handles of her plastic bag. The photos were not unlike the ones Madam used to send out with the broker boys, or the older girls, to bring in clients. The brokers flashed photos in the streets to loitering men and drew them upstairs to the waiting room. Meena stared at the Indian woman behind the desk. She felt choked.

She'd posed for a photo once. Dressed in green sparkles, gold bangles too rich for her wrists, make up too bright. She'd spun as instructed, while Putali clapped. Clapped. Why hadn't they known? But she knew now. She glared at Maa.

'Exquisite?' Meena's voice was a whisper now. Of course, this was why they had fed her, nursed her under the guise of helping her recover. 'Is this how Little Sister works?' she spat.

Maa's brow crinkled with a frown, 'Sit down, Meena.'

'Nain!' Meena jumped backwards, like Devi ducking Vishnu's grasp. 'I will not work for you. Not anymore. Not now.' She pushed out the words before she could take them back.

Sharmila appeared at the doorway. Her eyebrows raised, eyeing Maa, then Meena, then Maa again. 'What's the matter?' she asked, coolly.

Meena stumbled backwards. 'Get away from me!'

Sharmila stepped forwards, her heels clacking on the concrete floor. Her hands reaching out. To grab, catch, grip.

'No!' The hall spun. The steps of the office building were under her feet before she knew it. She stumbled forward, fell, and scrambled to her feet again. The paving was still warm from the heat of the day.

'Meena!' Sharmila came down the stairs after her. 'Don't panic. Everything's going to be alright.'

Alright? Meena's head pounded. No, it wasn't.

It'd never been alright.

It would never be alright.

She started to run, forwards, sideways, away from the stares of the girls under the clothesline, away from Leela at the dorm door with a strange expression on her face. The gate was still open. Meena spun towards it. Panic filled her lungs. Familiar, sick, horrible panic.

'Meena.' She could hear Maa's voice now, calling from the office building doors. 'Come back. I can explain.'

But Meena kept running. The gate released her before the guard had staggered from his hut. Sharmila's heels clattered on the paving behind Meena. She could hear the older girl calling, but Meena didn't look back. The road was wide, unsealed and empty. Meena forced her legs to run, really run, for the first time in years.

She stumbled on rocks so small they shouldn't slow her. She ran until she reached the end of the narrow road, then turned down the main street the taxi had come the day she'd arrived. It wasn't until she had rounded another bend that she slowed enough to breathe and check behind her. No one was following. No one chasing. But neither was the road empty. People hurried along its edges, buses kept their route; no one noticed her. She sagged against a power pole for a moment, trying to catch her breath. Her chest pounded; her head full of noise from breathing and blood. She had to keep moving.

She walked down the street, almost dragging her exhausted legs, pushing herself forwards, further and further away from Little Sister. Signposts stood at intersections, telling her directions to place names she couldn't read. Something knocked her knee. She still had the bag of wool Didi had given her, one of the knitting needles now poked through the plastic and dragged on the ground. The other one was gone. Meena kept walking.

Finally, to the left of a busy T-intersection, she found herself in a busy bazaar. Stalls lined the adjoining streets selling clothing, imitation backpacks and nail polish. Men with fruit carts called out their wares to everyone but her. She stopped by a snack vendor. His bowl of steaming lentil stew reminded her she hadn't eaten since the morning. He filled a few puffed pastries with stew for a female customer, who paid her money, and then ate in front of Meena.

'Do you want some?' The man behind the stew asked.

Meena nodded without thinking. She watched the pastries go soggy as the stew went in. He held it out to her. She took it.

'Money?'

Money?

She shook her head. She had nothing, nothing but the silly bag of half-rolled wool and the lonely knitting needle.

'No money? You think I give food away for free?! You stupid girl! Give me that, thief!' The man snatched the paper plate from Meena spilling the hot lentils on her wrist. 'Go! Get away!' He shooed her like she was a stray dog.

Meena staggered backwards. The signpost above the intersection pointed in four directions. Even if she could read the words on the signs, she'd never know where they meant. She was lost. Strength drained from her legs. She wobbled, staggered forwards, then back. If she didn't sit, she'd fall, but where could she sit—without money? Without anyone? Without ...

Someone gripped her forearm and spun her around. Meena squeezed her eyes shut and waited for the blow. For the fist, or the beam of wood, to strike her face ... but the attack didn't come. Instead, there was a voice—annoyed, angry and in a Bengali accent, 'What are you doing!?'

Nineteen

Meena didn't breathe. She opened her eyes. A narrow Bengali face scowled at her. A face dotted with sweat beads and cupped on either side by strands of short, damp hair. Nahita.

'What are you doing out here like a *buddhoo* beggar? You're making everyone look. They'll start tossing *paisa* at you soon!'

Meena forced herself to focus, to see Nahita clearly. She was dressed in her old *kurta-suruwal*, rolled up to the knees and wet down the front.

'They ... they have ...' she tried to explain. 'They have ... a stash ... of photos ...' She couldn't believe Nahita, with all her sarcasm, would knowingly be working for a madam.

Nahita gripped Meena's arm even tighter. Her hand was wet. 'What are you talking about?!'

Maybe Nahita didn't know. 'Photos. They have photos. Maa is just another Madam.'

At the word 'Madam', the woman who'd been waiting beside them for the bus quickly hurried away. Nahita glared at Meena. 'Don't you know when to shut up?' she growled. 'Come with me.'

***

Meena let herself be dragged two shops away to a small restaurant that made the front of a hotel. Two storeys of windows looked down on them. The windows were all closed, their curtains drawn shut.

'Where, where are you taking me?' she pulled her arm back. Nahita rolled her eyes. 'This is where I work. You're allowed to visit, as long as I still get through all my jobs.'

Meena stepped back, almost into the path of a mini-bus. Nahita swore and tugged her out of the way again.

'What are you doing?'

Meena felt sick. 'You still work? After everything you told me, about the beating and iron rod and your little baby, Iraira ...'

'Shut up!' Nahita snapped. She pulled Meena close, her body smelling of sweat and old garlic and Clinic Plus shampoo. 'You just shut up or I will surely sell you to the next real madam I meet!' Her voice was barely audible. 'Now follow me, shut up and just sit down.'

She pushed Meena onto a bench at the back of the restaurant. Disgust and anger written all over her face.

'Don't move!'

Nahita stalked to the restaurant counter and forced a joke, making those watching turn away with a grin. Then, she poured a glass of milky tea from a saucepan on the stove and carried it over to Meena.

'Drink.' She thrust the hot glass into Meena's hand. 'Just shut up and drink.'

Meena hesitated. The milk began forming a skin on top of the tea, calm and steady. Nahita positioned herself in a squat, close to Meena, and beside a barrel of water and a bowl of dishes. One by one, she scrubbed the plates and cutlery with a piece of steel wool and then dunked them in the water to rinse. Meena watched her pile the clean dishes in a basket and then carry the basket to a courtyard behind the restaurant, where the last of the day's sunlight shone in. When she returned, she brought with her another basket, this one full of clean and sun-dried dishes. Without speaking, she stacked the clean dishes on shelves behind the counter: stainless steel plates upright along the back and cups in rows along the front. Then she collected dirty plates from tables and started all over again. Meena stared. 'Is this ... your job?'

'What do you think?' Nahita was still mad.

'What about ... at night?'

'Shhhh! No, I don't do that. You know I don't.'

Meena glanced at the restaurant owner. She was leaning heavily on the glassfront cabinet displaying cheap alcohol. Her eyes were fixed somewhat blankly on the street outside.

'Do they ... do they pay you?' Meena asked.

'I wouldn't work if they didn't.'

'And all you do is wash dishes?'

'No. I wash clothes sometimes. And remake the beds after there's been a guest. Sometimes I have to cook, but not often—they don't like what I cook.'

'Maa hasn't sold you?'

Nahita sighed and sat back on her heels. Her hands dripping suds over the basin. 'Why would she sell me?'

Meena stared at the dishes waiting to be washed. Curry scraps swirled in finger lines along them. The skin of a tomato lay like the broken wing of a butterfly.

'They have photos,' she choked.

'So what?' Nahita flung her fingers up, letting drops of water scatter over her work.

'Photos like Madam ...'

'Stop now!' Nahita growled, lowering her voice to a plea. 'My boss doesn't know about that, so hush up. If they found out, they'd get me to do other stuff. You know what these places are like.' She glanced across at her boss nervously.

'But Maa, she's got photos ... like ...'

'Broker photos?' Nahita was almost whispering, her face down over the bowl of water.

'Yeah,'

Nahita sighed again. She shook her head, barely making eye contact over the bowl of dishes.

'Maa doesn't have broker photos.'

'Yes, she does! I saw them in a file on her desk.'

'Mostly black-and-white photos? Some colour? Pitiful looking photos? The kind they take before you start school or get married or something?'

Meena hesitated. Now that she thought about it, the photos had seemed quite plain. None showing girls made up and sparkly like in a brothel waiting room. 'But if they weren't broker photos, what were they?'

Nahita dipped her hands back into the water and pulled out a clean plate. 'They're photos of missing people. When parents find out their daughter—or son—has disappeared, they can give a photo to an organisation like Little Sister. The photos get passed down until they get to Mumbai. When Maa gets a new girl, she checks her photos, sees if she has their picture from someone looking for them back home. Sometimes she gives copies of the photos to the police when they do raids, to try and find other girls. That's how she found Asha.'

'So they are not going to ...'

'No.' Nahita propped her dripping hands across her squatting knees.

Meena held Sarita's scarf over her trembling mouth. No broker photos. No clients. No beating. No pain. No more.

Nahita stood up. 'Listen, I need to finish up before the night boy comes. You stay here. Don't go anywhere. Then we can go home.'

Meena nodded numbly. She drank her now cold tea and watched Nahita clear dishes from customers, wipe down the benches and fold some laundry from the restaurant courtyard. Eventually, after Nahita's boss had switched on the evening news, a boy about twelve years old with a scar on his top lip arrived at the restaurant. Nahita stood, dried her hands on her wet top, and handed him the steel wool. She then collected her payment from the boss and offered Meena a hand.

'Let's go.' She sighed.

'Are you finished?'

'Yeah. He works nights.'

They left the restaurant and crossed the now even busier intersection. It was dark outside, but the streets were well lit and the bazaar had a sort of festive atmosphere at the end of a long day.

'What will Maa do?' Meena asked, following Nahita closely as she appeared to be taking a short cut back to Little Sister.

'To you? Not much. You might get a lecture about staying safe and not taking unnecessary risks, that's about all. It's Sharmila you need to be worried about. Sharmila's the one with a temper.'

'So, why don't we go somewhere else?'

Nahita stopped walking. 'Where else do girls like us go?' she asked. 'Little Sister is stuffy, they have too many rules and if they're cross with you, it's like living with a vulture—peck, peck, peck. But it's safe. And it's a place to stay until you decide what you really want to do. At least that's the way I see it.' Nahita started walking again.

They passed a mound of warm and rotting rubbish waiting to be collected, before Nahita led them down a narrow alley. The houses on each side rose up behind high walls topped with shards of glass.

'What do you want to do?' Meena asked suddenly.

'Me?' Nahita kept walking. They passed under a streetlight and Meena almost thought she saw the girl smile—a dreamy sort of smile, like the heroine in a movie before she bursts into song about her true love. But the light was gone before Meena could be sure.

'I'm not sure yet,' Nahita finally answered. Then she stopped at a black gate at a bend in the alley. 'Here we are.' She poked her hand through a hole in the gate to unlatch it and pushed the scraping gate open. 'Come on. Sharmila'll be mad, but she won't hurt you.'

Meena paused. She recognised the rear of Little Sister property; the old shed, the side of the chicken hut, the rusted tin bin for burning rubbish. Nahita pulled Meena through the gate and shut it behind them both. The padlock threaded through the handle and clunked loudly in the night air. Meena felt her shoulders tense.

'Nahita? Is that you?' Sharmila's voice rang across the compound. She sounded like she'd been running.

'Here she comes,' Nahita muttered, as the older girl burst, flustered and red-faced, into view.

'Nahita. Meena ran away. Did you see her in the bazaar—' Sharmila's eyes landed on Meena.

'Yeah, here she is,' Nahita said. 'You shouldn't let Maa frighten people like this.'

'Maa didn't frighten her,' Sharmila snapped back. She glared at Nahita.

Nahita rolled her eyes and stalked towards the dorm. Meena made to follow, but Sharmila grabbed hold of her arm on the way past. Her eyes were furious, something akin to panic burned in them.

'Don't you ever, ever, do something like that again!'

'Wake up. We're almost there.' Mohan's hand is on Meena's shoulder, tight and hurting.

She tries to sit up, to look awake, but she feels squashed and stale, like the oldest cabbage in the bottom of a *doko* basket.

Mohan stands in the aisle of the train. He is pulling Putali up, directing her to wait in front of him as he had done earlier that afternoon when he'd retrieved their bags from the previous train. How long have they been traveling through this city, this place where buildings never stop and fields have been forgotten? Where Meena has to crane her neck to see the tops of apartment blocks, only to marvel at buildings growing even higher? She's never had to look so high to see something man-made before.

The train is slowing now, and people stagger to stand, squeezing past Mohan towards the doors.

'Get up,' Mohan commands. He inches back against a straight-faced business man to give Meena space to stand.

'Where are we?' Meena asks.

'Mumbai Central,' Mohan answers.

'Mumbai?' Meena breathes and Putali echoes her.

Mumbai—the home of Bollywood? Mumbai—one of India's most famous and wonderful cities?

The train screeches to a stop and they move with the crowd onto the platform. Meena grips Putali tightly as they walk, almost in a daze. She can feel the distance from home in the air, in the architecture. Even the people are foreign, a thick mix of cultures, everyone focussed on their own agendas.

'Don't let go,' Putali calls as the crowd heaves together onto the platform and then disperses like ants towards uncounted ant-hills beyond the station walls. Mohan herds them forwards, never letting the girls drift too far. Meena wishes it had been her uncle, and not this stranger, guiding them through this mass of people.

But Mohan, at least, seems to know exactly where to go. He leads them confidently down the road, then weaves into a tightly packed suburb, until they reach a tea-shop between two hotels.

'I didn't realise we'd be going so far to get a job,' Putali mumbles, as she stares up at the balconies full of drying laundry.

Meena doesn't comment. She notices the colours of the hanging saris. She watches the women hanging them out, some laughing. Several of the upper floor balconies have bars over them, as if they are cages—to stop birds flying in, perhaps, or people falling out? She feels like asking, but Mohan hurries them inside, sits them down with another plate of food—some *samosas* this time with a Fanta each—and begins talking to the restaurant owner.

Something about this place doesn't feel right, but Meena can't quite name it. Perhaps it's just that they are so far from home, or the silent knowledge sinking in that, even if they wanted to change their minds and go back to how life had been, they'd have to ask Mohan to help and he wouldn't likely agree. Not after spending so much on train fares and food for them.

'I don't like it here,' Putali whispers while Mohan's back is turned.

Meena nods, but tries to force a cheerful smile for the both of them. 'It's different to what I'd expected, but it must be what my uncle had planned ...'

'Maybe.' Putali sounds unconvinced. Worry flashes across her little, round face and Meena can tell she is thinking about her mother. What is she doing now? Will she be worrying? Will Meena's father be worrying? Meena at least knows the answer to that question. She takes a deep breath. '*Pir na-garra*, it'll be okay,' she says. 'It's just new and different. If we stay together and work hard, we'll be rewarded. We'll plan a trip home as soon as possible and surprise your *aama* with the money we've made.' She gives Putali what she hopes is a convincing smile, then hurries to finish her food. The *samosa* doesn't taste so good anymore, and it's getting harder to believe the promised job will be as good as Rajit and Santosh had described.

Mohan returns as soon as their plates are clear. 'Go out the back and tidy up. Do your hair, wash your face and here'—he holds out the most unusual thing for a man; a thin tube of lip gloss—'put some of this on.'

Meena hesitates, but Mohan pushes the tube into her hand and turns her towards a doorway leading to the back of the restaurant. There is a water tap out there, and a grimy mirror. The girls do as they are told. Smoothing down fly-away strands of dark hair. Rinsing the spice and crumbs from their fingers and corners of mouths. Then, Meena applies the lip gloss first to herself, and then to Putali, just as she's seen movie stars do in television advertisements. It makes their mouths look wet, but pretty.

Mohan is pleased when they returned. 'Good, let's go.'

'Are we going shopping now?' Putali asks nervously, as if she doesn't want to be disrespectful.

'No,' Mohan answers. 'There's been a change of plans. We need to go to your hotel now, the manager wants to meet you as soon as possible.'

Meena watches Mohan's face as he answers, a familiar disbelief rising in her chest like when her father would promise to buy rice on the way home from work.

Mohan doesn't wait for any more questions. He just takes their hands, one in each of his as if they are little children, or something more precious. And despite the dreams of new jobs and opportunities, Meena feels her stomach cringe.

Twenty

Meena squatted on the concrete by the water tap and dropped her dirty clothes into a bucket under the flowing water. As she prepared her clothes for washing, she was conscious of Sharmila's unceasing gaze from the office window. Already today, Meena had endured the promised lecture from Maa about staying safe and not putting herself, or the other girls at Little Sister, at risk. Apparently, now that she knew how to get there and back, Meena was permitted to visit Nahita at work—something Sharmila disapproved of. But Maa had insisted on Meena attending every educational seminar for the next two weeks, with her permission to leave Little Sister property being revoked if she did not comply. This seemed to satisfy Sharmila, who had taken personal offence at Meena's disappearance, but the older girl continued to keep a strict eye on Meena whenever she could.

Meena pulled her new *kurta-suruwal* from the water and began to work soap into the fabric. Maa had purchased new clothes for some of the girls last week and Meena had been allocated several garments. But her period had come yesterday by surprise and the stain was thick and dark on her trousers. She pushed the bar of strong smelling soap into the stain and rubbed the fabric with her fists. The sun was cooking her back, warming it like a perfect blanket would. Nahita joined her, sharing the water as they worked together in silence.

'So, how long were you in hell?' Nahita asked after a while.

Meena stopped her scrubbing. 'Hell?'

'Working? In the brothels?'

'I think it was three years,' Meena answered. 'I was twelve, now I'm fifteen—I think. You?'

'I think I was two years at Hotel Happiness because we saw two seasons of that American show about those couples that aren't couples that live in the apartment together. I don't know how long I was in Kolkata—I wasn't allowed to watch TV there. And before that I was married for about a year to the old butcher, so I'd count that as well.'

'How old were you when you were married?'

'I'm not sure—ten or eleven, I suppose. There were too many daughters in our house and not enough food, so my parents thought they'd solve the problem by arranging marriages, one for my older sister and one for me.'

'Child marriages are illegal in Nepal,' Meena said, glancing at the office where Maa had joined Sharmila at the window.

'They're illegal in Bangladesh too. Doesn't mean they don't happen. Out in the villages, where no one cares, who's going to stop it? You can't tell me it doesn't happen in Nepal.'

Meena shook her head. 'No, it's the same.'

Nahita squeezed the soapy water from her shirt and plunged it back into the bucket. She talked as she worked: 'My father arranged my sister's and my weddings. She was fifteen. She got the handsome one with a motorbike and new clothes. I got the old butcher and his ugly first wife.'

Meena listened as Nahita spoke of beatings, of being made to do all the housework. She told of how she soon learned to cook, and that she had to wait until the entire family had eaten before she was allowed to eat; if there was nothing left, she was accused of not cooking enough. Eventually she had run away and met an old widower who promised to take care of her. But she had been sold to the brothel instead.

'How'd you get out? Did you pay back your debt? The money your madam spent when she got you?'

Nahita made some sort of snorting noise. 'I don't think anyone ever pays back their debt. They just end up older and not worth as much, so madams don't really care anymore whether they stay or go. In my case, the top half still looked young, so I still brought in money. But there was a client, a nice one ...' She looked up to see if Meena understood.

Meena nodded. She knew—nice clients were the gentle ones, the ones that said sorry, or bought thoughtful gifts or offered to help. Madam didn't let many of them into her hotel, said they weakened her girls.

'Well, he asked questions, every time he came, and eventually he said to me, 'You don't like it here do you?''

'And what did you say?'

'I told him I hated it, I said I wanted to escape. The next time he came he snuck me out the back door. When the guards saw us we started running. But he was holding onto me too tight, like he owned me or something. So I pulled away, kicked him in the groin and ran like an athletic superstar.'

'In a *sari*?'

'In a *sari*.' Nahita laughed. 'Somehow I found a drop-in centre where they hand out food and condoms, and offer free medical check-ups for what they call 'sex workers'. The people there were good. They told me about Little Sister and I've been here ever since.' Nahita sat back on her heels and stared at the water for a time. 'But one day I'm going to leave.'

'Where will you go?'

'I don't know yet. I can't go back to the village. You heard what Leela said, I'm HIV positive.' Nahita ducked her head and wrung her shirt too tight, the dye ran in a coloured stripe down her arm.

'My parents would say I am not their responsibility—they married me off, I don't belong to them anymore. I belong to the old butcher. But he'll turn me away because I've been 'defiled'. The first wife will insist on the death penalty for adultery, to preserve the 'honour' I have taken from their household and to get her own back once and for all. The community will shun me. What's the use of learning from Sharmila and the nurse how to live 'a long and healthy life with HIV' if I go back? I might as well die right now.' She paused, then tipped her water out, mixing it with what was left of Meena's.

'But you'—Nahita looked up—'unless you have an old butcher husband with a witch of a first wife, you should go back.'

Meena stared at the wet fabric under her fingers. 'I haven't got a husband,' she mumbled.

'Parents?'

Meena thought of her father. 'No, not worth counting.'

'Friends?'

Meena stood up. Three girls sat chatting on a mat under the tree. Their fingers busy making beaded necklaces to sell.

'I had one friend—she was younger than me. Her mother was nice, she made tasty pickles ...' Meena's voice caught at the memories.

'Then you should go back,' Nahita said. She stood and began hanging her wet clothes over the wire clothesline. There were no barbs here. Nothing to catch and tear their shirts. Had anyone found their clothes beside the river? Taken them back to Putali's *aama*? Is that how she found out? Or had she gone looking, seen the abandoned bowls by the stream and searched the river bank for their bodies? For Putali's body ...

'You should put henna through your hair.' Nahita fingered the end of Meena's braid, interrupting her thoughts.

Meena stared at her, forcing her mind back to the present, willing the guilt weighing so heavy to keep out of sight. But Nahita just grinned, oblivious. 'Your skin is pale. It would look nice. I'll buy you some on the way home.'

'Don't use your money on me,' Meena protested.

Nahita shrugged. 'I can if I want.' And she left Meena alone in the sun by the dripping clothes.

***

Two days later, Sharmila caught up with Meena on the way back to the dorm. 'You and Nahita seem to be good friends now.' It was more like a question than an observation. Meena tilted her head to the side.

'She's not always a good person,' Sharmila went on. 'You don't want to be too much influenced by her ideas.'

Meena shook her head, confused. 'I don't understand. We talk, but I hardly see her. I attend all your seminars and she's often in the bazaar working.' Now that she thought about it, Nahita had been attending less and less of Sharmila's talks and spending more time away from Little Sister.

'Exactly,' Sharmila agreed. 'She refuses to accept the help we offer here and at the same time, actively resists the attempts made to re-unite her with her family in Bangladesh.'

'I don't think Nahita wants to go home, she has other ideas of what she wants to do.' Meena remembered the far off look in Nahita's eyes.

'What ideas? She obviously didn't tell you that Maa has found her family. She has contacts in *Dhaka* who are willing to support Nahita's return, but Nahita won't go.' The colour in

Sharmila's face rose.

'Does she have to go if she doesn't want to?' Meena asked.

'No. We don't force people to do anything, but Nahita won't even try. She refuses to discuss it. She is stubborn and obstinate and ungrateful—'

'Ungrateful?'

Sharmila glanced across the yard at the gate. 'I'm allowed to stay here, Maa needs me. I have an important job to do. But some girls make up lies and disrespect Maa, yet take all they can, ignoring the rules. Nahita's like that, she's irresponsible.'

'But she brought me back from the bazaar the other day. If she was so bad she'd have let me keep running. She wouldn't've helped.'

Sharmila opened her mouth to say something but a car pulled up outside the Little Sister gate. The sound of its horn made Sharmila jump. She glanced at Meena, her face flushed as if she had almost said too much, then turned and hurried to Maa's office.

Twenty-one

The guard pulled open the gate and a taxi inched its way inside, then proceeded to do a five-point turn, so it was ready to leave again. The exhaust fumes admitted to bad mechanics until the driver switched the engine off.

'Meena, go tell Asha her taxi's ready,' Sharmila called from the office window. Her face was the normal colour now, but her voice still strained.

Meena obediently stepped up into the dorm. Purna, Leela and Asha all sat on their beds. Purna was rocking, her face towards the wall. Leela sat trimming the ends of her hair with nail scissors. Asha was on the end of her empty bed, gripping a bulging Chinese bag.

'Your taxi's here,' Meena announced.

Leela grunted. Asha looked up as though someone had whacked her in the stomach.

'Where are you going?' Meena asked.

Asha blinked twice before replying, 'Going? I'm ... I might be going home. That's why Maa told me to pack all my stuff. They might decide to keep me.'

'If you're lucky,' Leela said.

'I thought that was happening later, sometime next month, or something?'

'Yeah, so did I.' Asha stood up, she ran her fingers over the end of her bare mattress. 'But Maa said my parents want to see me. She said they love me. We're going to Delhi on the train, we'll meet my parents in a park, and if they want me ... Maa will come back here, and I'll go back to the village.'

Meena didn't understand. How could Asha go home, just like that, after everything? 'But what will you do? Don't they know you worked in the b—'

'They know,' Leela muttered. 'But Maa's bribed them to take her back.'

Asha's face flooded with quick anger. 'No, she hasn't!'

'No? Well what's that you were telling me about the chicken business starter loan? You think they would have been so willing to have you back if it wasn't for the chickens Maa's going to organise? "Oh no, we don't want a chicken business, we'll just take our beloved daughter." What did you think?'

Asha's eyes smarted with tears but she held them from falling.

'At least I can go home,' Asha mumbled. She drew the Chinese bag up to her chest and walked over to Purna's bedside. The Nepali girl shuddered and hugged herself tighter.

'Goodbye, sister,' Asha whispered. Purna turned away, her face was wet.

Leela snorted. She dug under her pillow for the make up she kept hidden there. 'Don't bother saying goodbye to me, I'm not going to miss you,' she growled over the top of her mirror. It wasn't even five o'clock yet. Her face was taut, the lipstick went on thick. The taxi outside sounded its horn again.

Meena watched Asha turn around slowly, her wide eyes memorising all that was in the room. Then she walked out the door.

'Little whore,' Leela spat. Asha's flip-flops clapped down the hall and away. 'Stupid little whore.' She glared at Meena, daring her to say something.

'You think they'll take her back? With her tight jeans and wasted thighs? With the sweet curve of her lips, they'll take one look and chuck her back where she came from. That's what they'll do. That's what they all do.'

Meena stared at her. There was something very sad under the smeared lipstick and caked foundation. 'Is that what happened to you?' Meena asked.

Leela tipped her head back, her mouth open. A harsh, horrible laugh escaped her. Lipstick globs dropping from her mouth in red sweating lumps. Her laughter stopped as suddenly as it had started, then she leaned across and spat blood-stained saliva onto Meena's lap.

'You're disgusting!' Meena said as she stood up.

'Am I? Well, you know what? I should have left you on the floor, on the stupid stinking floor like trash,' Leela shouted, her voice too loud for the room. 'That's what you are, all of you.'

Purna began whimpering.

Leela slumped over her now foggy mirror. Her lips sickly red, her eyes smudged. Her cheeks too coloured even for a joke. Meena's hand rolled into a fist but didn't move. She strode to the end of the room and climbed up onto the windowsill as she had seen Nahita do.

'You don't have to stay in here with her if you don't want to,' she called to Purna. Then she dropped to the ground, grazing her elbow on the wall. She heard the sound of glass smashing against concrete, then the panicked scurry of Purna's flip-flops escaping the other direction. Leela screamed, 'Whores! You're all whores, filthy, pus-weeping, disgusting whores ...'

Meena slipped from the shadows to the cool wall of the water tank. She could see the other girls now gathered around Asha. Some joked, others forced conversation. Sharmila stood at the back of them, an automatic smile plastered across her face. There was a small movement at the top of the dorm stairs and Meena could see Purna whimpering, tense and clinging to Didi at the top of the stairs as if afraid someone would push her into the taxi also.

'Come and say your goodbyes,' Maa called out as she joined the group. She carried a stuffed red-and-black backpack, plus a shopping bag full of fruit. Didi crossed the lawn to wrap Asha in a hug, the embrace triggering big wet tears on Asha's face. It was like they were sending her off to get married. Meena fingered the tasselled threads of Sarita's scarf. Had Sarita ever planned to take her leaving scarf home?

Maa shuffled to the taxi and tugged the back door open. Asha hesitated. She let her eyes move from girl to girl. Sharmila offered several bland well-wishing statements. Asha glanced in Meena's direction. At least Asha knew she didn't have HIV— what would it be like to go home positive? To face people's hatred, their fear and suspicions? Meena looked away.

She heard the taxi door shut. Heard the girls call out their farewells and good wishes for Asha's future. Only when the scrape of metal on bricks told her the guard was closing the gates, did she look up again. Didi and a small group of girls lingered by the gate, some were smiling, some crying. Didi was handing out little packets of tissues. Meena bent and twisted the water tap on. Water spurted out in a crooked stream, spraying the knees of her trousers. Slowly, Meena unwound the scarf from her neck. The silver threads she had admired so many times now clung together under the purple cottons, as if they were afraid of what the sun would do to them. Meena lowered the scarf under the water. The stream from the tap dragged the scarf from her fingers and crumpled purple to the ground. Meena squatted by the concrete tank and watched as the force of water dug and darkened the delicate fabric. The silver threads broke free from the dust and light streaked in sharp reflections into Meena's eyes. A heavy certainty set in her chest. She could never go home. No matter how strong the mountains called her, how much she longed for familiar tastes and smells, there was no home anymore. Not without Putali.

Mohan must have messaged the hotel manager because when they arrive, she is already waiting, leaning somewhat comfortably against a ground floor doorframe.

'Beautiful!' She gushes in an accented Hindi as Mohan introduces them. And she leans forward and grabs Putali's cheek. 'Very, very beautiful!'

Putali shrinks back and the manager just smiles at Mohan like he is her favourite son, even though Meena is sure they are about the same age. 'Very nice. Do come in.'

The hotel manager leads them through the doorway, the only one, Meena notices, that does not have a cage grill across it. Mohan prompts the girls forward but Meena hesitates. She glances quickly up the front of the hotel, looking for clues. Something, anything that might explain what is really going on. But the windows above the row of caged doorways are like all the others in this suburb—flapping with gaudy laundry. Tired, bored-looking girls lean elbows over balconies in slow conversation, ignoring Meena's gaze and unspoken questions. One of them has a scar across the side of her face.

A man squeezes past Mohan into the hotel, his eyes greedy on Putali in a way Meena recognises. She's seen that look before on one of her father's drinking friends. She takes a step backwards. The hotel manager notices and, dropping her wide smile, slaps the man roughly on the back, hurrying him inside and out of sight. Then she turns a silent, measured gaze in Meena's direction.

'We get all types here.'

Meena thinks she understands what the manager is saying, but she isn't sure. Her Hindi is learned only off the settlement TV. The hotel manager holds out a *mehndi*-covered hand to Putali. 'Enough waiting around,' she speaks quickly, making it even harder to understand. 'Come in. Come in. You must be hungry now. And thirsty too? Mumbai's hot these days, don't you think?'

Putali nods shyly at what she thinks she understands and Mohan gently prods her forwards. Up the steps, between the cages, and into the dark coolness of the hall inside. Meena hesitates only a second longer, then hurries after Putali, Mohan taking up the rear as if to make sure no one will follow them.

The hallway is long, dully lit, with doors off both sides and various sitting rooms decorated with lights and posters of scantily-clad Bollywood film stars. There are women everywhere, their conversations drawing to a hush as Putali and Meena walk past. One woman says something very inappropriate to Mohan and Meena flinches, expecting him to tell her off. But he doesn't. He just retorts something of his own, something in Hindi that feels to Meena equally rude, and hurries Meena forwards.

They come to a stop at a wide sitting room, partitioned from the rest of the floor by a heavy and ornate curtain. Inside is a navy upholstered lounge suite, a glass-topped coffee table, a flat-screen TV, and a variety of ornaments and vases poised full of bright fake flowers. Wealth is obvious and smells sweet, too sweet almost. Meena and Putali sit together on a small lounge. Mohan takes up another chair and the hotel manager the final one.

'Ganga!' the manager yells to someone beyond the curtain. 'Drinks!'

A Nepali girl, with a crooked hand and too much make up, enters with a tray of drinks. Sweet, warm tea. But the girl leaves again without lifting her eyes or speaking. Meena holds the tea between her hands but doesn't drink. It isn't even hot. Putali inches closer to her until their hips are together. This doesn't feel like a hotel. It doesn't even feel like a tea-shop. There are no waitresses. There isn't the comforting smell of frying onions or marinating chicken ...

'Is this really a hotel?' Meena blurts the words in Nepali before she can stop them.

The manager woman glares. Mohan stumbles over his words, a mixture of Hindi and Nepali. Putali puts her tea down and looks up at Meena, confused. 'It's okay,' Meena mumbles, patting Putali's knee, but she is watching the adults. It doesn't feel okay. It feels wrong. And too far from anything that is home.

'Of course, it's a hotel,' the manager woman speaks slowly. Each word articulated as if they are deaf. 'And I praise my cousin for bringing you here to work for me.'

Mohan stands as if on cue. The manager woman stands also, positioning herself between Mohan and the girls on the couch. She hands Mohan an envelope. 'I'll take them both,' Meena thinks she says, followed by the cryptic, 'Ask Ganga to take you to Princess before you leave.'

Meena watches Mohan blush.

'Mohanji?' Meena begins, gripping Putali's hand now. But Mohan just tucks the envelope deep into his pocket and disappears behind the curtain as if the girls had never been his concern.

Twenty-two

'I think it's clean now,' Didi said gently.

Meena blinked against the sunlight. Her eyes hurt, her back was stiff. Didi stood above her, on the grass beside the water tank, a dripping purple scarf in her fingers.

Meena stretched. How long had she been squatting here, staring at the water, at the sunlight, at nothing? Her head felt hot, her legs stiff and tingly.

Didi turned the tap off. She offered Meena a hand.

'Was it a gift?' Didi asked. She pulled Meena upright and kept a hold of her hand until Meena stopped wobbling. 'Was it a gift from a client?'

Meena shook her head. She took the scarf from Didi and stared at the silver threads—they weren't afraid of the sun anymore. Meena carefully wrung the scarf out.

'I need to hang it up,' she mumbled.

Didi walked with her to the clothesline. Meena straightened the scarf first, so it hung straight and flat. Drips of water ran down to the tasselled edges.

'It was Sarita's.'

Didi leaned forwards. 'Whose?'

'The girl I shared a room with. It was her leaving scarf. Like a promise to herself that one day she'd be free.'

'And she gave it to you?'

Meena nodded, unable to articulate what had happened that last day at Madam's. Unable to understand the implications of what Sarita had done, or even if Sarita had known what they would be.

Meena turned and stared at the gate. 'Asha's really gone, isn't she?'

'Yes. Maa will bring news in a few days.' Didi put her arm around Meena's shoulders. 'Her family love her, we have high hopes they will be willing to take her back.'

Meena nodded. 'I saw photos the other day. On Maa's desk. Nahita said Asha's parents had been looking for her.'

'Yes, that's true. It doesn't always work. But for Asha, it did. And it helped her have the confidence to try again. Would you like to see Maa's photos?'

'Now?' Meena asked, surprised. 'I'm allowed?'

'Of course, they aren't secret, just sad.' Didi took Meena by the hand and led her across the paving to the office. She pulled a key from around her neck and unlocked Maa's office, she flicked on the light-switch and walked to the back of the desk.

'Here, you can look at these.' Didi pulled a stack of photos from Maa's top drawer and handed them to Meena. Faces and faces of young girls, and the occasional boy, stared up at her. There were close-up shots of unsmiling girls in school uniforms, a few creased photos of red-and-gold saris and the tiny frightened face of a bride peeping out. She could tell their race by the shape of their nose, or the colour of their skin, or the style of clothing. Girls from Bangladesh, Pakistan, fair-skinned Indians from the north and dark-skinned ones from the south, girls from the Himalayan regions of Afghanistan, Nepali girls— lots of Nepali girls from almost every district. Meena's fingers began to shake.

'Are they are all locked up in brothels?'

'We don't know. Possibly. Sometimes young people just run away, they get lost, they get sick, they die. Sometimes they're able to find good jobs but don't know how to write, so they can't send a message home to reassure their parents. Unfortunately, in our experience, a lot of young women and girls do end up in brothels, even if they have not deliberately been trafficked to them.'

Meena stared at the faces. 'But some of these pictures are just little girls. Little girls grow up, they change, they wear make up and fancy clothes and look so different you can't tell who they are anymore.' Meena remembered Putali, plump, dressed and twirling like a beautiful tiny bride.

'It is difficult. The photos you saw the other day were probably about to be scanned. Sharmila takes copies of the photos we receive to local police stations. We also have some men who work for us in the red-light districts.'

Meena frowned. 'What do you mean?'

'We hire them to pose as clients. They go into brothels, pay for time with a girl and use that time to find information on people being held against their will. We then use this information to make a raid. But sometimes, even the police are corrupt. If everyone worked together, trafficking could be eliminated ...'

Meena stopped listening. She laid the photos, one after another, onto the table, searching for a face she knew—a small, kind face with soft cheeks and a serious smile. She'd recognise the face immediately if it was there. And it would be proof someone was looking. Looking for Putali. That her mother hadn't died, and maybe, maybe ... But the last photo landed on the desk. A stranger. 'Are there anymore?' Meena asked, her voice barely a whisper.

'More photos?' Didi rummaged in the drawer. 'I can't see any. I think that's all Maa has at the moment. She doesn't keep them for long; they get passed on to other rescue organisations in the city. Trying to rescue victims of slavery is an ongoing battle, Meena, the photos are just one step.'

'But the little girls are always locked away, only seen by the highest paying customers, and then only the ones Madam trusts. So a man pretending to be a client would never see them. And even if he spoke to the older girls, the ones downstairs or the ones that call men from the street, there is no guarantee they even know who is locked upstairs. Madam only lets her trusted girls travel the floors and hand out food, girls like ...' She was about to say 'Sarita' but stopped herself. Meena felt suddenly angry. She knew she was getting worked up but she couldn't help it. In her mind, she could see Devi's mouth moving behind the partition, prattling on about police raids and lipstick colours. Lalita's cheeks were wet behind the secret wall. Sarita was arguing with Madam behind the curtain and Putali ...Where was Putali? 'You haven't got a photo of everyone!' she burst.

Didi smiled kindly. 'Then we can only pray that we find them.'

Meena shoved at the photos on the desk, spilling them onto the floor. Didi shook her head. 'Do not scoff at prayer, little sister. You got out, didn't you? And you didn't have a photo.'

Meena stepped backwards, knocking the chair. 'But why?' Her voice was too loud. Warped by angry sobs. 'Why did I get out? It was Sarita's scarf! And what about the little girls upstairs? What about girls no one knows are there? Girls rich men with bulky jewellery bargain over, like they're goats in the market? What about Putali?!' Meena was shouting now, tears hot and wet down her cheeks. She spun from the office, shoving Sharmila on the way past, and ran across the yard to the dorm. She only slowed to snatch Sarita's scarf, still dripping, from the line and wrap it about her neck.

***

The following day the nurse called Meena into her office.

'Your blood tests came back,' the nurse said without smiling. 'You have mild anaemia, so I've ordered you some vitamins. And so far you are negative for HIV. So that's encouraging, but we'll need to do another test in a few months to double check.'

Meena glared out the window at the empty driveway. What good was a negative test result if it meant she had to be tested again? It meant nothing. Nothing at all. Meena strode back across the paving in agitation, annoyed and irritated by everyone and everything. Maa hadn't returned from taking Asha home. Sharmila continued her hawk-eye surveillance of Meena and the dorm felt empty without Asha's stubborn positivity to balance Leela's unpredictable moods.

Meena had tried to keep busy as Didi had suggested. She attended the lectures given by Sharmila, she listened as she explained the benefits of learning to read and even completed the chores allocated to her. One afternoon she attended a counselling session Maa had booked before she'd left, with a social worker who asked questions Meena didn't want to answer. In her free time, she worked the wool Didi had given her, slowly but steadily until the last skein ran out. Then there was nothing to do but climb the stairs, walk past the painted mountains in the hallway and face Didi again.

Didi was sitting on her couch with another girl when Meena arrived. This was a girl from one of the other dorm rooms. She had a crooked top lip that puckered in concentration as Didi taught her to weave the wool around her needles. Meena waited with her plastic bag by the door until Didi looked up.

'Come in, Meena. Sit down.'

Meena moved herself to the empty chair and tucked her legs tight under her knees. She gripped the bag on her lap, conscious of the missing needle lost somewhere between Little Sister and the bazaar. The other girl looked up briefly, but didn't smile. Meena stared back. The girl knew how to knit. She moved her painted fingers confidently, following the strange instructions that Didi was giving: knit one, decrease two, knit three. Meena fingered Sarita's scarf. She wouldn't be able to learn this. It was too hard. She stood up.

'Don't worry, Meena, Jaya is almost finished. She was just wondering how to shape the sleeve of her cardigan.' Didi never lifted her eyes from the other girl's work as she spoke. 'Sit back down.'

Meena sat. She waited. Eventually Jaya leaned back and began to knit without Didi's help. Didi grinned, she stood, stretched, then dragged the chair from under her desk to beside Meena's elbow.

'Okay, let's see how those balls of wool turned out.'

Meena lifted the balls, one by one, from the bag. Didi hummed with satisfaction as she inspected each one. 'See, I told you you could knit.'

'But I can't do that.' Meena pointed her needle at Jaya's speeding fingers.

'Well, Jaya has been learning for a while. This is her fourth project. And'—Didi took the lone needle from Meena's fingers with raised eyebrows—'she does have two needles.'

'I ...' Meena began but Didi just grinned.

'It's fine, I've got lots. Just try not to lose this set, okay?' Didi pulled a new pair of needles from her drawer and began teaching Meena to 'cast on'. The needles felt clumsy in Meena's hands, pokey and in the way. But eventually Meena could wind the thread, slip the needle underneath and pull new stitches out. One after the other after the other, until she had completed a row.

Didi squeezed Meena's shoulder. 'Look at that!' Didi praised. 'You're knitting!'

Meena just stared at the stitches tight and black against the needle. Stitches made by her fingers. Stitches she had made. She felt a tiny smile rise onto her cheeks.

'Do you think you could keep going like that?' Didi asked. 'Once you're confident, I'll teach you a different stitch and then we'll begin making a simple cardigan.'

Meena nodded. She watched Jaya pack up her work and walk outside. Meena did the same. But she hesitated in the hallway to stare at the painting again. The imperfect view clashing with her memories. Pickles. Stories. Home.

'Do you miss Nepal?' Didi came up behind her to ask.

'No,' Meena lied, but she didn't shift her gaze.

'Is it really as beautiful as this painting?'

Meena felt her heart swell with unexpected pride. 'More,' she whispered. Her heart ached for it. The longing rising stubbornly from wherever she'd locked it. 'But I can't go back.'

Twenty-three

Meena dropped her bag of wool and needles and newly-made stitches on the end of her bed, then she climbed out the dorm window and slipped through the side gate. She knew the way back to the bazaar now: up the alley, past the pile of rotting rubbish, the stream of passengers climbing in and out of buses.

There were only a few customers in Nahita's restaurant. One of them, a long thin Indian man, lounged against the side wall, his face lazy and happy. His long legs poked out the end of too-short trousers and ended in tough plastic sandals. His hair was oily, parted down the middle, trying to be trendy.

Meena slipped past him to where Nahita's dish-washing bowl was. Nahita was nowhere to be seen.

'She's out back,' the young Indian said. Meena ducked her head to avoid eye contact, and passed through the tables to the courtyard. The wire clothesline that spanned the open space was full of dripping washing. Meena could see Nahita's legs moving under a stained bed sheet. She was dancing, the off-tune lyrics from a dance song wove themselves round the open space.

'Just chill, chill, just chill ...' Nahita danced, her limping leg keeping speed with her other. Meena poked her head between the sheets. Nahita stopped dancing, slight concern crossing her face.

'Hi,' Meena said in English.

Nahita frowned and ignored the greeting. 'You didn't tell me you were coming today.' She glanced over Meena's shoulder to the restaurant.

'I didn't think I had to ... I came to buy henna.'

'I said I'd buy it,' Nahita snapped.

Meena was confused. Usually Nahita was pleased to see her, to share the dish-washing or bench wiping with someone. But today, the Bengali was agitated. 'What's wrong?'

'Nothing!' Nahita flustered.

Meena lifted the sheet and followed Nahita's gaze to the restaurant. The Indian man was sitting now, leaning forward, staring into the courtyard, staring at her. Meena tensed.

'Nahita, what's going on?'

Nahita pulled Meena back, out of view from the restaurant and glared at her. 'Don't tell Maa, just promise me you won't tell Maa.'

Meena shook herself free. 'Tell Maa what? They already warned me about you ...'

'Warned you?'

A dark hand shoved the sheets aside. 'Is she hassling you?'

It was the young Indian, his face tight, almost mad, his eyes on Nahita. They knew each other. They knew each other well.

'No. She just ...' Nahita reached out almost touching his hand before she pulled back, remembering Meena was with them. 'What are they saying about me?'

Meena frowned. 'Sharmila says you don't follow the rules. She says you're a rebel.'

'And what did you say?'

'Doesn't matter now, does it?'

Nahita glanced up at the Indian. He flicked his fingers upwards in question. Nahita answered, 'This is Meena, she's a friend.'

'And him?' Meena was cautious.

'He's my "breaking the rules".' Nahita waved the man off. He nodded at her, then disappeared through the restaurant onto the street. 'His name is Ramesh.'

'A boyfriend?!'

Nahita limped back to the shop and squatted by the bowl of dishes, her head down.

'You have a boyfriend?' Meena whispered again. 'But he's Indian!'

'So? I'm Bengali. He comes from a village north of Mumbai. He came in here to find work. We met. We like each other.'

'But you are HIV ...'

'So?' Nahita glared at her. 'Just because I have to watch my CD4 cell count, does that mean I can't live my life and be happy when I can? Is that what they've been telling you?'

'No, I mean ...'

'You don't know your result yet, you don't know what it's like to have to live life like this.'

'But,' Meena stammered, 'that's not what I meant. I was just wondering, does he know?'

Nahita took a deep breath and lowered her voice again, 'He knows, but she doesn't, so watch your words.' She pointed with her lips to the restaurant owner stretched out on an empty bench, her head on a folded newspaper, her eyes closed.

'But if he knows ...?'

'He's the same.'

Meena didn't understand.

'He's positive. Drug user, not now, used to be.'

'How do you know he isn't now?' Meena asked, remembering the relaxed, lazy expression that had been on Ramesh's face when she'd walked in from the street.

'You've been with drug users. You can tell those who are,

those who were. You can tell. He said he quit. I believe him. He's kind. He buys me presents—'

'That doesn't mean anything,' Meena hissed. 'Even Leela probably had clients that bought her presents and said they loved her.'

Nahita let her hair flop forward; it was just long enough to hide her eyes. 'He's not a client, and he won't sell me.'

'How do you know?'

'I just know.' Nahita ended the conversation. She turned her attention back to the dishes, scrubbing furiously.

'Can I stay?' Meena asked after a few minutes.

Nahita paused. She studied Meena. 'Will you tell Maa? Sharmila?'

'About Ramesh?' Meena shook her head. 'Why would I?'

Nahita relaxed and passed Meena a wet clean plate. 'You can stay. But be useful. We'll buy your henna after.'

***

That evening, after dinner and a special seminar on personal hygiene, Nahita called Meena into the dorm bathroom. The pink-tiled room was small, damp and windowless. The shower head was dripping and the area around the raised toilet platform newly cleaned. Nahita grinned as Meena came inside. She swirled a plastic bowl under Meena's nose. It contained dark, wet henna, mixed with water to form a sludgy green paste.

'Don't you love the smell?' Nahita inhaled deeply.

Meena scrunched her nose. Wet henna smelt like old grass. She held out her hand. Nahita released six tiny drops in the pattern of a flower onto the side of Meena's thumb. 'Is it ready?'

Meena checked the consistency. 'I think so.'

Nahita dragged an upside-down laundry bucket from under the sink. 'Sit,' she instructed.

Meena sat. The dampness from the base of the bucket immediately seeped into the rear of her trousers.

Nahita scooped the henna paste onto Meena's hair and began massaging it in, from scalp to ends.

'Little Sister Beauty Parlour.' She laughed when she finally rinsed her hands and tore open a plastic shopping bag to wind over Meena's head, sealing the henna underneath.

Meena stood up and eyed the reflection in the stained bathroom mirror. She hadn't really looked at herself since the time with Leela's mirror. She looked different now, and not just because of the plastic bag wrapped around her head. Her face was more rounded, evidence of the good health she'd gained since her arrival. And there was something else, something she'd never seen in Sarita's mirror: the echo of her mother. A silent tear slid down Meena's cheek.

Nahita didn't comment. She just dried her hands on a towel behind the door.

'When do I take the bag off?' Meena asked.

'If you keep the henna in overnight you'll get a better colour.'

'Won't the plastic come off? I'll stain the pillowcase.'

'If it was Purna, I'd worry, but not you. You sleep like a cut tree.'

'What?'

'You don't move. You close your eyes and snore away, completely still, like you used to get in trouble for wriggling or something!'

Meena turned the tap on and rinsed the six little drops of henna away. They left the stain of a tiny flower against her thumb. Nahita held her hands up, they were pale orange all over.

'I remember when I married the butcher, my aunt drew the henna in whirly patterns all over my feet and hands, almost up to my elbows. I think she drew them so slowly and so beautifully to help me forget about being afraid. It worked for a little while;

'I stared at my hands for the whole ceremony, they were so beautiful. I traced the vine lines and found tiny birds and hidden forests. I pretended I was a princess in a palace, with exquisite clothes and fancy food to eat every day. Some palace I ended up in ... I don't think I'll paint my hands when I marry Ramesh.'

'Marry Ramesh?' Meena stepped backwards and knocked the bucket over. 'What do you mean?'

Nahita brushed the hair away from her face in defence. She lowered her voice, 'We're going to go back to his village. He's going to work his father's land and I'm going to have his baby.'

'Are you ...?' Meena glanced down at Nahita's stomach.

'Not yet. But once we're in the village and settled. I'll get pregnant and no one will take my baby from me. I'll keep her and teach her to be strong and safe and independent ...'

'But can HIV positive girls have babies? What about AIDS?'

'I haven't got AIDS yet. Neither does Ramesh.' Nahita glared at her. 'I've been listening in on Sharmila's lectures, even if she thinks I haven't. And I've spoken with the nurse. As long as I'm careful, I can have a healthy baby just like everyone else. I'll go to a good hospital and get special medicine. There is a risk, but many HIV positive women have HIV negative babies. I'm not going to let my past, or HIV, take away my dreams.'

'But can Ramesh afford to send you to a good hospital? Would he let you go anyway? Women die because their men refuse to take them to hospital.' Her mother stared at her from the reflection.

Nahita shrugged. 'We've already talked about it. Ramesh understands. He says I can have a baby if I want. He wants a son but I told him I want a daughter. He said "Okay".

'He said okay? To a daughter?' Meena didn't believe it. Men wanted sons, not daughters.

But Nahita just restyled her hair, covering the scar on her cheek carefully. 'I'm going to marry Ramesh, and I'll have a daughter. You can come to her naming ceremony if you like.' Nahita smiled.

'Will you invite Maa and Sharmila?'

'Those old ladies? No way. They'd come and lecture me about STDs and contraception and the proper way to address the prime minister.'

Meena laughed. 'Sharmila isn't old.'

'No. But Maa is, and Maa thinks all love marriages result in trafficking.'

'But, isn't it true? Isn't that what happened to Sharmila?'

Nahita sighed, annoyed. 'Yes, but she was stupid. And Leela's boyfriend dumped her, pregnant, with a Nepali broker—he didn't even marry her. But just because it sometimes happens, doesn't mean it always will. Maa's too controlling. She doesn't even let us find our own friends or arrange our own weddings. You haven't been here when Maa arranges a wedding. She does it as often as she can. The last wedding was for Urmila. They couldn't find her family, so Maa found her a husband, some man whose wife had died and left him with a baby he couldn't look after. They held the ceremony here, I think it was to make sure Urmila went through with it. Maa provided the sari, the gifts, the feast. I don't even think his family came. Then Urmila was gone, faster than Asha. If I keep avoiding their attempts to return me to Bangladesh, they'll arrange a marriage. But I've told them I'm not going to marry anyone they choose.'

'And that's why Sharmila doesn't trust you?'

'Yeah, and because I think she's jealous. She's in the same situation as me—her family don't want her. She's afraid of what will happen if Maa decides she no longer needs her to work at Little Sister. So, every time I argue with Maa in lectures, or climb out windows—'

'I did that the other day.'

Nahita laughed. 'Oh dear! No wonder they're worried about you. I might be leading you astray!'

They are upstairs now, that much Meena knows. The mind-numbing effects of whatever it is Ganga adds to their meals is becoming more and more familiar. It makes them dozy. Makes them lean up against each other, gripping hands until their hold weakens and fears melt to fatigue. She can't count the days since Mohan left them at the hotel. Putali can't either. They just know that every day they wake heavy-headed to plates of lukewarm food, flavoured with unfamiliar spices and accompanied by sour tea. And if they don't eat they are beaten. A young man with a small goatee and accurate fists hits them. It took only a few days to realise it is safer to eat, even if they feel sick doing so, than to face the young man's fists. Their faces are healing now, the bruises softening. But there are other changes too. For one, Meena can feel the sleeves and waist of her *kurta-suruwal* growing tighter as days pass. And she has had her first menstruation—an event that was all but ignored except for the inconvenience of her requiring new clothes.

Sometimes, in odd waking times when food isn't before them, they talk. Putali worries about her mother and Meena tries to reassure her, making up stories of how neighbours will come to help her or how Putali's little brother has grown up so much and will be able to take on the family responsibility. Putali rests her head on Meena's shoulder as she listens and Meena can feel the silent trembling of tears. They aren't waitresses. They aren't doing work of any kind. They are waiting for something. Being fed, left alone mostly, sleeping, dozing, but always waiting.

It is, Meena thinks one day as she watches Putali eat more than she needs, as if they are skinny goats being fattened for a festival they know nothing about.

Twenty-four

Meena sat knitting on a plastic mat under the courtyard tree. Slowly, carefully, she lifted and wound the soft black wool around the knitting needles as Didi had taught her. Knit, knit, knit. The lines of wool, rows of stitches, wobbled under the needles. Didi had said she'd be able to knit a sweater, that she had the skill and the patience, and just needed a bit more practise.

Meena paused. It was three days since Maa had returned from taking Asha home. Returned alone. From what she could gather from the bits and pieces of information that floated around Little Sister, Asha's parents had been cautious but welcoming. Asha had chosen to return with them to the village, promising Maa she'd stay in touch and give them regular updates on how she was settling in. Since then, Maa had been too busy to speak with Meena individually. And today, she appeared preoccupied also. From where Meena sat she watched Maa and Didi come down the office steps to talk to Sharmila in the sunshine. Sharmila spoke with her hands, flicking her hair over her shoulder. Didi and Maa responded without the extra motion. Every now and then they looked towards the gate, and then over to Meena. She guessed they were waiting for someone and talking about her. Meena resumed her knitting and began another row. Didi and Maa returned inside and Sharmila crossed the paving to Meena. She slipped her heels off at the edge of the mat and sat cross-legged beside Meena.

'Your hair looks good. How long did you leave the henna in?' Sharmila asked.

'Overnight,' Meena answered.

'I can never do that; wriggle too much.' Sharmila laughed. She smoothed the hem of her *kurta* top, her fingernails perfect, her hair sprayed softly into place, her make up gentle, highlighting her natural features. Her appearance was perfect, right to the decorative *bindi* worn low on her forehead, matching the colours of her outfit.

'Why are you so pretty today?' Meena asked.

Sharmila blushed, 'Pretty? No reason.'

Meena didn't believe her. Sharmila was obviously dressed up for a reason.

'Didi says you're much improved since you arrived,' Sharmila said, changing the subject. 'She said you've been seeing the counsellor regularly too. That's really great. Maa's impressed with your commitment to rehabilitation.'

Meena hesitated over a stitch. She'd skipped several counselling sessions in the last week and gone to see Nahita instead. Obviously Sharmila hadn't received this report.

'Rehabilitation is something they don't count on, those traffickers. They think if they break us, we are broken forever. They forget we can heal. They don't realise that a girl who has once been trafficked can, in fact, become their strongest enemy. I know a lot of girls who have left Little Sister to become advocates, or community educators, for anti-trafficking organisations. Maybe that's something you'd like to do one day? After you return to Nepal?'

'I haven't thought about it,' Meena admitted. The future was blank and unfriendly before her.

'But hasn't Maa told you the good news?'

Meena looked up from her knitting. Sharmila tossed her hair over her shoulder, unusually oblivious to Meena's reaction.

'What news?' Meena asked.

'The man from Stop Trafficking Nepal is coming to see Maa today.'

'Stop Trafficking Nepal?'

'It's an organisation like us, sort of like Little Sister's big sister.' Sharmila laughed at her own joke. 'They have three rehab homes in Mumbai, plus four drop-in centres, one in each of the large red-light districts. Their main focus is rescuing Nepali girls, though they'll help anyone they can. One of their senior staff is coming here today. He's really nice.'

'Is he Nepali?'

'Oh no!' Sharmila made a face. 'He's one of the managers. He organises travel for groups of Nepali girls who have been rescued from brothels. They transport the victims back to Nepal, locate their families and reintegrate them into their communities. Maa's going to talk to Tarak to see if he can take you and Purna back.'

Sharmila continued to talk but Meena was no longer listening. Take her and Purna back? Back to Nepal? But they weren't ready. She wasn't ready. Meena struggled to focus. She dropped a stitch, tried to pick it up and lost another one. Sharmila kept talking. Her words were long and foreign sounding: reintegration, assimilation, reeducation, stereotypes, poverty. They circled in Meena's mind with a little voice from the past. A voice uncertain, trying to be braver than eleven-year-olds need to be: 'I didn't realise we'd be going so far ...' Meena dropped her knitting.

'Are you even listening to me?' Sharmila asked. But the sound of a motorbike at the front gate interrupted her. The motorbike honked its horn and the guard hurried from his hut to unlatch the gate and swung it open. Sharmila sat up straight, she pumped her lips and tossed her hair, so it hung soft around her shoulders.

'He's here,' Sharmila said, trying to keep her voice calm.

'Who?' Meena studied the man astride the motorbike, the focus of Sharmila's attention.

'The man I told you about, the man working for Stop Trafficking Nepal. His name is Tarak,' Sharmila spoke his name as if it were sacred.

Meena couldn't help but grin. 'You like him.'

'No, I don't.' Sharmila stood quickly and tugged the creases from her jeans. 'I just work with him when he comes here. We're professionals. Would you like to meet him?'

'No. I'm not going back to Nepal.'

Sharmila gave her a strange look, 'Perhaps you have been spending too much time around Nahita—'

'No. I'm just not ready to go back, not yet.'

'That's what Nahita says. Every time Maa tries to arrange a reintegration for her, she has a new excuse. She says she wants to learn to read first, but then she never makes the time to attend literacy classes. Some of the girls think Nahita has a boyfriend, and that's why she's always out there. Maa's worried about her.'

'Nahita isn't stupid.'

'No, but even smart people do stupid things,' Sharmila said. She slid her feet into her shoes with another glance at the Stop Trafficking Nepal man. He formed a greeting with his hands for her. Her face flushed as she returned it.

'See you later,' Sharmila said.

Meena didn't say anything. She watched Sharmila cross the lawn to the motorbike and swing her hair again. She could hear Sharmila chatting to the Stop Trafficking man. She was using her super sweet voice, trying to make a good impression.

Sharmila was smart, but she was stupid eyeing off a guy like that. From the way he walked, the tie around his neck, the wafts of after-shave that blew even far enough to reach her, Meena could tell he was rich. Well educated and far above girls like them—unless it meant easy sex. But when choosing a wife, which was what Sharmila would be dreaming of, a man like him wouldn't think twice about a girl who had been a sex worker. He wouldn't even learn her name. Sharmila was stupid.

Meena pushed her knitting onto the mat and stood up. Little flecks of wool stuck to her knees.

'That's Meena,' she heard Sharmila saying, pointing in her direction.

Meena ducked her head, avoiding eye contact with Tarak. If she left now and stayed in the bazaar for two hours, Sharmila's Stop Trafficking man would be gone. She dug her feet into the plastic flip-flops Little Sister had provided her and slipped out the back gate.

Twenty-five

She didn't stop until she reached the bazaar intersection. Two young women, made up and fancy, caught her attention. They were scanning the shelves of a beauty shop, fingering bangles and tubes of henna paste. They looked so much like Sarita. Not in physical appearance—they were nowhere near as pretty as Sarita—but from the way they cocked their heads and scanned the bazaar. They were out shopping on their time off, always keeping an eye open for a client. She watched them pump their lips at a tall Indian with greasy hair. One of them gestured towards him, beckoning him into a deal, but the Indian turned away, disinterested until he was facing Meena. Then his face flashed reluctant recognition. It was Nahita's Ramesh. 'Where's Nahita?' his voice was tense, his fingers gripping tightly on the bag of fruit at his side.

'Isn't she working?' Meena asked, pointing her lips to the restaurant.

Ramesh strode across the intersection. Meena waited. She saw Nahita emerge from the shadows. Ramesh gestured to her and tilted his head in Meena's direction, then Nahita pulled him inside the shop. Meena waited for two buses to pass, one of them carrying a bleached-haired Nepali fare-collector, then she crossed the road and walked under the shade to find Nahita.

'What do you want?' The restaurant owner was heaving

herself off the bench she had been resting on.

'Nahita.'

'She was doing the dishes, the lazy girl!'

Meena waited for her eyes to adjust to the restaurant's dimness. Nahita's spot by the bowl of dishes was empty. She walked between the tables and benches to the back courtyard. Washing hung on the line but Nahita was nowhere. Meena forced herself to think slowly: Ramesh had come in, with Nahita ... Meena walked back to the restaurant and scanned the benches again. She couldn't see either of them. Surely the restaurant owner wouldn't let her dish girl have a room during working hours? Meena turned back to the courtyard. The door at the end was slightly ajar. Meena pushed it. Past a grotty kitchen, she could see another alleyway. She hurried through and came out in the sunlight on the other side just in time to see Nahita and Ramesh turn the corner at the end of the alley.

'Nahita?' Meena jumped the drain and ran after them. At the corner, she could see Nahita and Ramesh slow down to check the road ahead. Ramesh was pulling his wallet from his pocket. They were getting ready to wait for a bus. Meena sped up, 'Nahita!' She pulled the Bengali girl round to face her. Nahita's cheeks were flushed dark with excitement.

'Where ... are you going?' Meena struggled to catch her breath. 'Are you going to leave? Just like that?'

'Ramesh got paid.'

'So?'

'She's mine now.' Ramesh frowned at her under his greasy hair. 'We're catching the next bus.'

'But your things? At Little Sister. You can't run away to get married without your things.' Meena looked to Ramesh for understanding. 'If she leaves with nothing, you'll have to spend all your money buying her new clothes,' Meena pressed. She knew what men were like. If Nahita cost him too much money, Ramesh would start regretting his choice; he'd be able to justify treating her like filth.

'She can't go back.' He tugged at Nahita's arm. She blushed like a virgin and turned to Meena.

'Ramesh got paid today,' she explained. 'If we don't leave today, his friends will come asking for loans to play cards or buy cheap drink and he can't say no. You know how it is, his money will be gone. We can't wait 'til next time.' She followed Ramesh further along the bus line.

'But ...' Meena's mind raced. 'Clothes cost money, so do blankets, and you have nothing but his bag of bruised bananas.'

'I know,' Nahita lowered her voice. 'But Maa knows I work from morning to evening. If I go back and pack my stuff, they'll get suspicious, they won't let me leave. We have to go now. We've got no choice.' Nahita ran her finger up the scar line on her face. Ramesh jittered on the spot. Two women carrying over-dressed babies stared openly at their discussion.

'Listen.' Meena pulled Nahita from the bus line. Ramesh frowned but didn't move. 'I haven't got regular habits like you, I can go back and get your things. I'll bring them to you, I'll meet you at the end of the alleyway in a few minutes.'

'Don't believe her. She'll run back and tell them everything.' Ramesh's voice was strained now. Nahita glared at Meena. 'We're leaving now. We're going!'

'I'll get your stuff.' Meena stepped backwards. 'If I don't come back, you can leave.'

'What about Sharmila and Maa?'

'I'll come back!'

Meena darted between the buses making them belch their horns in her direction, then she ran down the alley back to Little Sister. Inside the gate the garden was quiet. She slowed to a casual pace. The guard didn't even look up from admiring the Stop Trafficking Nepal man's motorbike as she passed him. She ran up the stairs to the dorm. Everyone else was out, in lessons or the recreation room. Meena hurried over to Nahita's bed. She found the cupboard key inside the pillowcase and opened Nahita's cupboard. It was stacked full of food and clothing. There were packets of biscuits, two-minute noodles and two boxed fruit drinks. Several new pairs of sandals, a pile of messy T-shirts and a cheap box of sanitary pads. Nahita was obviously a hoarder. There was more here than Meena could carry.

Quickly Meena reached for the Little Sister blanket that lay on Nahita's bed, then thought again and ran quickly to her own bed, pulling her blanket, the one she and Sarita had bought, free from the mattress. She lay the blanket on the floor and emptied the cupboard contents onto its centre. She added the pillow from Nahita's bed then tied up the blanket ends. She hefted the bundle up to the windowsill then, after checking the guard was still occupied, dropped it and herself to the ground below. Balancing Nahita's belongings on her hip, Meena took the long way to the side gate. Only Purna saw her from where she was hunched under a tree, but she made no move. Once in the narrow alley, she ran.

By the time she reached the end of the alley, her breathing was ragged. She clasped Nahita's bundle tight and scanned the intersection. Where was Nahita? The line by the bus stop was already eight people long. But Nahita and Ramesh were not among them. Meena staggered forward. Had they left already?

'Are you alone?' Ramesh appeared from behind a nearby street stall. Suspicion and distrust clear across his face.

'Where's Nahita?' Meena asked. Ramesh pointed with his lips towards the rubbish cart. The Bengali girl had been waiting, ready to run if Meena had turned up with anyone else. She came forwards now, eyeing the blanket bundle sceptically. 'That's your blanket.'

'So they don't notice you are gone so quickly.'

Nahita pursed her lips together. Ramesh unfolded his arms. 'Let's go then.'

'Okay.' Nahita took the bundle from Meena without looking at her face. 'Did you empty my cupboard?'

'As much as I could carry.'

Nahita let a tiny smile flick onto her face. Then she hefted the bundle onto her hip. 'We're really going,' she said, part dare.

Meena couldn't reply. Exhaustion from her task caught up with her. Her throat felt tight and dry. All she could do was stare. At the Bengali girl with the scar down her cheek. What would her daughter look like? Would she be safe and strong like Nahita's dreams? Ramesh began crossing the road to the bus stop. Nahita tilted her head in acknowledgment to Meena before limping after him.

Meena watched them go. Doubt crowded her mind. Questions squeezed into the cracks but she pushed them away. The Indian snack vendor saw her and began hurling insults in her direction. The foul odour from the rubbish cart beside her rose under the hot sun. Still, she didn't move away.

Nahita waited beside Ramesh. He held the bag of fruit, probably their first meal as a couple. They stood below a sign post that displayed a loop of red ribbon. The words beneath the symbol meant nothing to Meena. She couldn't read. Neither could Nahita. Meena doubted Ramesh could either. A bus pulled up between them, Meena on one side of the road, Nahita and Ramesh on the other. She lost sight of them for a few minutes, then their heads—Nahita, obvious with her hairstyle and Ramesh with his height—appeared again. They sat near the front. Nahita crowded almost onto Ramesh's knee, her face dark with anticipation.

'Go well,' Meena whispered.

The bus ground gears and pulled to the middle of the road. The owner of Nahita's restaurant glared from the front of her shop, her face red in rage at the disappearance of her dish girl. She spotted Meena and shouted something across the intersection. Meena turned away. Although the sun was bright, heaviness settled itself over her shoulders. Nahita was gone.

Part Four

Twenty-six

'What do you mean, "I haven't seen her"?' The dorm room light snapped on and Sharmila's voice split the evening silence. 'You eat beside her every night. You visit her in that grotty restaurant every day. You went to visit her today. I know you did, because you didn't want to meet Tarak!'

Meena pulled her thin sheet over her shoulders and rolled away from Sharmila. The other girls either groaned, complained or sat up to watch.

'Turn around and look at me! We're in this together, all of us. We're all exactly the same!' Sharmila kicked the leg of Meena's bed, then swore, obviously angrier at losing her temper than anything else. 'If you live at Little Sister, you have to obey the rules. And one of them is not covering for someone when they do something wrong.'

Leela snorted from where she lay. 'Well, Nahita obviously forgot to replace her pillow when she made her bed this morning. That's pretty bad!'

'Shut up, Leela, you know exactly what I'm talking about,' Sharmila snapped. 'You know exactly what's at stake!'

Leela didn't' say anything else. She just rolled over so her made-up face was directly opposite Meena's. Her expression tight, hidden and clouded, daring Meena to defend herself.

But Meena felt sick. Nahita was gone, somewhere in the

swirls of the city Mumbai. Gone with Ramesh, the ex-druggy, who claimed he wanted to marry her. Some part of her heart couldn't believe it would work out, and that part was now writhing under Leela's unwavering eyes.

'And where's your blanket?!' Sharmila asked and then swore again. 'Oh goodness, Meena, what have you done?'

Purna whimpered and began rocking, her bed creaking softly.

'Get up! Maa wants to see you in her office,' Sharmila ordered.

'She means you,' Leela said coolly to Meena, never shifting her measured gaze.

Meena dropped her feet over the edge of the bed and stood up. She followed Sharmila back through the dorm door and across the garden. The courtyard was still. The few outside lights lit circles of brightness: one over the water tap, one over the front gate now locked. Another light shone over the main building's doorway, and in the light stood Maa.

Gone was her typical *sari*. Instead, the narrow-faced woman wore trousers, wide-legged trousers and an oversized T-shirt— probably her sleeping clothes. When Meena reached the steps Maa turned and walked into her office. Meena followed, pushed ahead by Sharmila.

'Take a look at this,' Maa said as she held out a single photo.

Meena held the picture up, her anguish barely in check. A thin, bruised and sickly girl stared from the creased photo. She was dark-skinned, with untidy hair and cracked lips, her age indistinguishable, dressed in a too big T-shirt and tracksuit pants. Meena almost didn't recognise her, but for the scar down her cheek.

'This is what Nahita looked like when she arrived,' Maa said. 'Take it. Look at it.'

Meena didn't move.

'Where is she?'

'She didn't want to go home,' Meena croaked.

'That's not for you to say.' Maa sank back into a chair beside the desk.

'She was my friend, I knew her.'

'You did not know her for very long.'

'I knew her long enough to know she didn't want to go home.'

'And that gives you the right to participate in her trafficking?'

Meena felt her breath suck inwards so suddenly she couldn't speak. Maa continued, 'We have given you time to adjust to our routines. We understand that you have been abused and that kindness can be hard to believe, BUT we expect respect. We expect you to follow the rules of this centre while you are staying here. No matter how much you have suffered, there can be NO justification for assisting in the trafficking of someone you call a friend.'

Meena staggered backwards. 'I didn't sell her. I would never sell anyone.' Meena stared at Maa.

'Then what did you do? Why is she gone?'

'I ... she ...' Meena's mind raced through memories. Promises. Dreams. Lies. They knitted together, dropping stitches, threatening. Putali and Nahita together. Questioning. Accusing. 'I didn't—'

'Where's your blanket, Meena?' Sharmila leaned forward. 'Where's your blanket? Where's Nahita?'

'Nahita?'

'Nahita!' Maa's tongue sliced the word. 'What have you done to Nahita?'

Meena focused on them. She pulled a reign on her panic. Nahita. Nahita, not Putali. 'She's gone.'

'We know that. Where is she? Who took her?'

'I don't know. She didn't ... No one sold her. She's just gone.'

'I wished I could disappear into thin air every time Mr Scrawny came to my hotel room, but that sort of thing never happens, no matter how hard you wish it,' Sharmila said bitterly.

Maa scowled at the reference to the brothel.

'She didn't want to go home. She was HIV, they'd hate her.'

'They could be educated.'

'You can't educate some people,' Meena insisted.

Sharmila didn't disagree.

'Tell us what happened then.' Maa sat back, her arms crossed.

'She ran away. She met a man, an Indian. She was going to get married. They left today.'

'I knew it!' Sharmila cried. 'Didn't I tell you, didn't I say she had a boyfriend in the bazaar—'

Maa cut her off. 'But your blanket? Her things?'

Meena looked upwards. The single bulb refused to light the corners of the room.

'Where are her things?!' Sharmila demanded.

'I took it to her ...' Meena admitted.

'In your blanket so no one would suspect anything?' Sharmila's voice was incredulous.

Maa let out a loud, long sigh. 'You can go to bed now,' she said. She rolled her chair away from the desk and turned her back to the room.

Meena returned to the dorm without Sharmila's escort. She stood in the shadows by the window, ignoring Leela's unspoken questions, and watched the office until the light switched off and Maa, looking slumped like an old woman, trod across the garden to her flat. Then Meena lay down and went to sleep.

The next day Meena was called, almost immediately after the morning meal, to Maa's office again. Maa sat at her desk, dark circles under her eyes, several photos of Nahita spilling from an open file in front of her.

Meena sat in her normal chair and waited. Maa seemed to be waiting also. Meena heard the toilet under the stairs flush and then a pair of stiff boots marched towards the office. Meena looked up to see a police officer stride in and take a seat in the remaining empty chair. Meena tensed at the sight of his uniform. Was he here to take her back? Back to Madam? Had Maa decided she was too difficult?

'Officer,' Maa spoke with authority. The officer seemed to sit straighter. Meena waited for the instruction to arrest her, to transport her to Madam's hotel. But Maa was talking about Nahita. The officer tried to look interested.

'Yesterday one of our long-term residents disappeared. This girl'—she indicated with some distaste to Meena—'was the last one seen with her. I thought you might appreciate the opportunity to question her. So, you can begin your search.'

'Question me?' Meena stared at Maa, but the woman seemed determined to avoid eye contact.

The policeman pulled a dirty notebook from his pocket and held a pen lazily over it. 'Where did she say she was going?' he asked.

Meena kept her eyes fixed on Maa.

Maa answered for her: 'She said Nahita, who is a long-term Bengali resident in our program, travelled away with an Indian man.'

'She wanted to go with him.' Meena ignored the officer. 'They knew what they were doing.'

Maa finally looked at Meena, 'No, little sister, they did not. Nahita was HIV positive.'

'So was he.'

The police officer wiggled further back and tucked his boots under his chair.

Maa threw him a fierce look, then glared at Meena. 'Now tell the officer where you saw them leave, how they left and where they were going.'

'Why? So you can bring her back here against her will? Just like she was married to the old butcher against her will? And held in the brothel against her will? And lost her baby girl against her will?'

'We just want to make sure she isn't trafficked again.'

The police officer was sitting back now, watching.

'I don't think she'll be trafficked.'

'But if she is? How will we know? Do we just hang her photo out with all the rest and hope no more harm comes to her?'

Maa flung a set of photos across the desk to Meena. New photos, ones she must have received from Sharmila's Stop Trafficking Nepal guy. The police officer snorted at Maa's display of emotion.

'Do you know how hard it is to get girls out of brothels once we learn they are there? How hard it is to convince the corrupt police to make a raid and carry it out without accepting bribes from the madams?'

The officer coughed at the implication, but Maa kept going.

'If she has gone back, if this Indian who says he is HIV positive to secure her trust, has sold her, we will most likely never see her again. And you have been part of this, Meena. You.'

'Not me.' Meena stood up. The photos slid from her lap onto the floor. One almost slipped under the policeman's chair but he trapped it with his foot. The edge of his boot caught over the girl's plaits. Meena had seen enough.

She reached for it, but the police officer was faster.

'Here,' he said. Meena reached out her hand for the photo, but he placed it in Maa's hand instead. Meena watched the photo drop roughly into the top drawer of the desk. Then the desk slammed shut.

Maa looked up at her. 'You won't help us find her, then?'

Meena stared at the desk. She knew the girl in that photo. She knew the dark oiled braids. The soft, shy smile. The full cheeks.

'Whatever you know about where she is, you must tell us.' Maa leaned forwards.

'I don't know where she is,' Meena croaked. 'I don't know where she is.'

'You silly girl!' Maa huffed down in her chair. 'Go back to your room. You are now under strict curfew. You may not leave the compound unless you are accompanied by either Sharmila, Didi or myself. Do you understand?'

Meena didn't answer. She stood, stumbled, and somehow, she made it from the office to the stairs and down to the paving. The sun shone bright in her eyes, like when Sarita had carried her onto the street and placed her in the back of the jeep. Putali's photo was in the top drawer of Maa's desk!

Meena tried to sort her thoughts. Accusations. Suggestions. Didi's voice: 'Do you miss Nepal?' Sharmila's: 'Hasn't Maa told you the good news?' Home. Putali. The thought hit her with the force of Vishnu trying to keep her quiet: someone was looking for Putali. Someone had passed her photo on, recently. Asking for information, seeking their daughter. That meant Putali's father had returned ... or her *aama* was still alive ...

Meena sunk to the concrete at the base of the dorm stairs, the longing of home wrestling in her heart so hard she felt she could barely breathe. But how could she face Putali's mother now? After all this time? How could she explain? How could she return alone?

Meena's mind feels clear. Clearer than it has for a long time. Putali lies beside her, still asleep. Her hair messy and damp with sweat across her cheeks. Meena brushes the hair aside. How long have they been indoors now, without seeing the sun? How pale they must be—like plump, rich women who carry umbrellas everywhere!

Meena notices other details in her clarity too. She sees boards blocking the windows, the layer of dust on the unnecessary curtains. There are gecko droppings on the floor, and rat droppings by the cupboard where they keep their spare clothes. The bucket they use as their toilet has been emptied while she's been asleep. There is a new bucket next to it, a clean one with clear water, a dipping jug and a towel and soap beside it. There is a chair she hasn't noticed before too, to the left side of the locked blue door. On the chair lies some fabric, pink and green, sparkling under the perpetual light. Meena climbs down from the bed, hearing Putali stir behind her and holds up the fabric. It is an outfit, no, two outfits. Full flowing skirts with matching sequined tops. The pink one is too small for her, but perhaps it might fit Putali? The green one seems a good fit for herself.

There is a scraping sound; the latch shifting on the other side of the door. Meena drops the clothes. She hurries back to hold Putali's hand as the door swings open. But this time it isn't another plate of food and sour tea. Meena feels Putali's body tense as Zeshaan, the young man with the goatee, holds the door open for the hotel manager.

The woman eyes them both with something of satisfaction. 'Good, you are both awake.'

Meena grips Putali's hand and holds it steady. The younger girl is still woozy. The drugs affect her more than they do Meena.

'Get her cleaned up and put that outfit on her,' the manager says to Meena. 'She needs to be ready in ten minutes. You too.' The instructions are accompanied by a dare for defiance.

Meena drops her eyes.

'Do you understand, little girl?!' The hotel madam snaps.

Meena nods.

The door is shut again, the latch scrapes back in place. Putali lifts her confused face to Meena's. 'Get ready for what?'

'I don't know,' Meena answers. 'But we'd better do it.' She pulls Putali to the edge of the mattress and hurries her across the floor to where the towel and soap wait. Working faster as Putali wakes more, they strip off the tight, torn and stained *kurta-suruwal* and give Putali a gentle wash. Meena tries to make jokes as she helps, but Putali's fingers still shake. Then they slip the pink outfit over her pale skin. It fits perfectly, as if someone has taken her measurements while they have been sleeping. Have they? Meena feels suddenly sick.

'How do I look?' Putali asks as Meena reaches for the second outfit and begins changing.

Meena swallows and forces a smile. The outfit is perfect. Putali tries to spin, dizzily bumping the edge of the bed in her attempt. The latch scrapes yet again, and the hotel madam returns just as Meena manages the final button on her new green bodice.

'Good,' the manager notes. 'Now, make up. Ganga!'

The Nepali girl with the twisted hand enters the room with a tray of cosmetics. Without speaking, she settles Putali on the edge of the bed and begins applying base powder, *kohl* eyeliner, eye shadow, blusher and lipstick. Then comes jewellery—bracelets sparkling with jewels and gold that Meena can't decide if they are real or not. There is an anklet too, with bells, and a hairpiece that swings down to dangle on Putali's forehead. Her little friend has been transformed.

'You look like you're getting married!' Meena breathes. A disturbing thought battles the new clarity of her mind. It has been inching forward ever since Mohan left them with the instruction to visit 'Princess'. But Putali just smiles shyly, as if the thoughts Meena has couldn't possibly exist. She obeys Ganga's instructions to stand against the wall, to pose and twirl while the older girl takes several photos on her phone. Then Ganga returns to the bed and motions for Meena to take Putali's place. She repeats the routine with Meena, including twirling photos against the wall while Putali claps. Then she is finished, and the hotel madam nods and checks the photos on the phone. 'Exquisite,' she says with some satisfaction. 'Now, bring them to the Sitting Room,' she instructs. 'One at a time, the little one first.'

It is then that Putali turns to Meena, fear bigger than she's ever seen before, wide and panicked in her eyes. But before Meena can say anything, Zeshaan has separated them. The door is shut and Ganga is left to ignore Meena's questioning until finally Zeshaan returns, alone, to take Meena to the Sitting Room.

Twenty-seven

Meena stood at the top of the steps leading into the dorm. She pushed the uncomfortable memories away. The sunlight warmed her hair. The leaves on the trees rustled briefly. She hadn't left the compound for four whole days. Sharmila watched her like a hovering hawk, snapping and finding fault in her work. Maa expected regular recounts of educational seminars and chores completed. Meena's back ached now, from rehanging curtains in the recreation room with Renu. Her mind skittered about, sorting memories from fiction, dream from reality. Didi approached from her room beside the dorm. She must have just finished lunch.

'How about you fetch your knitting and come up to my office?' she suggested. 'You must be ready for the next set of instructions by now.'

Meena nodded.

'I'll wait for you,' Didi offered.

Meena collected her bag of wool from the dorm and followed Didi up the stairs. Even before they reached the painting, she felt the mountains mock her. Accusing her. Questioning her. Did you sell her?! Did she know?

No! Of course not. Surely Putali knew? Didn't she? That Meena had been as unaware as her? That they had both been tricked?

The mountains didn't answer. They hid themselves behind the cheap acrylic paints, denying any claim she had on them.

Meena turned quickly from the hall into Didi's office, blocking their accusations. She sat on Didi's couch and pulled her knitting from her bag with trembling fingers.

'Show me where you're up to,' Didi said.

Meena lifted her work, a short length of simple knitting hung from one of the needles. Didi murmured approval and began explaining how to proceed. But none of the instructions Didi gave sank in. Although her eyes followed the black wool—loop and pull over the needles—her mind wandered through tightly packed streets with caged balconies, *sari* fabric flapping between the bars. Cages? It was the word the hospital staff had used. How had she not noticed them for what they were? How had she been so stupid to believe Mohan's stories of waitressing jobs? Why had she tried so hard to convince Putali it had all been true? But what if she could remember more? If she could describe in detail to Maa, or Shushila's Tarak, how to get to the hotel Mohan had taken them to?

She cursed Madam for not letting her out. Sarita would know the area like the empty promises of her most regular clients. She had been allowed out to shop and visit friends and go to the temple. But Meena had been locked away. Madam had called her an asset: valuable due to her age and the colour of her skin. And her memories of the streets of Kamathipura were foggy, too foggy to be of any assistance in a search for one missing Nepali girl. But if she could go back, if she could retrace the steps ...' Do girls ever go back?' Meena interrupted Didi's explaining.

The woman lowered Meena's knitting and tilted her head to listen.

'Go back, to the brothels?' Meena continued.

'Did you leave a child behind, like Manju?'

Meena shook her head. She didn't know about Manju's child.

'What do you mean then?' Didi asked. 'Do you want to return to prostitution?'

'No!' The thought of it spun Meena's gut. 'I had ... my friend ...' Meena could barely say the words. 'She's still there.'

Didi nodded slowly. 'And you would like to find her?'

Meena barely nodded.

'As you know, sometimes Maa works with partner organisations to conduct raids. Particularly if there is reliable information about the location of trafficked women and girls. Do you know which red-light district you came from?'

'Kamathipura.'

Didi looked disappointed. 'That's one of the largest red-light districts in Mumbai. Do you know the name of the brothel you were in? Or where it was? Kamathipura is an enormous place, a whole suburb really. Without reliable details about the brothel, it'd be impossible for us to organise a raid. And far too dangerous for you to return on your own. Girls aged thirteen to sixteen are in the highest demand, and you still fall into that category. What other details do you have?'

'Her name, I know her name,'

'Well, that's a start. Maa could contact other organisations and see if they've found a girl by that name. Stop Trafficking Nepal might know—'

'No, they gave her photo to Maa. I saw it.'

Didi pursed her lips. 'In that case her name won't be very useful. Names change frequently in the red-light district, you probably know that more than I. Sex workers often change their names. I know Purna did and we don't even know what her real name is now.'

'But I know where she was sold. I can't remember properly, but if I go back, I might be able to find her. I might be able to—'

'No, Meena.' Didi held up an empty knitting needle. She shook her head. 'Kamathipura changes every day. Hotels are painted, rebranded. Pimps walk the streets on the look-out for vulnerable girls to sell and resell. And you were most likely drugged when you arrived there. Your memories are probably nothing more than a slide show of an area you never suspected was a red-light district. Unless you have clear and specific details about where your friend is, it would be foolish to even consider returning.'

Meena shook her head. She knew what Didi said was true and yet ...

She stared out the window. A bird with grey wings darted from a tree and out of sight.

'I don't want to discourage you, Meena. But thousands of girls are trafficked each year, and many of them are from Nepal like you and your friend. Of those that find themselves in brothels, it's only a very few that ever get freed. The fact that you are here is a miracle, and you're already asking for another one?'

Meena swallowed. She groped her mind for memories, details that might prove she knew enough to find the hotel. To find Putali. 'The hotel had grilled cages over the lower doors, and bars across the balconies ...' Meena stammered.

Didi shook her head again. 'Like I said, Kamathipura is enormous. You could be describing any number of streets.'

Didi handed Meena her knitting and guided her fingers for two rows without speaking. The phone rang. Didi answered it. She spoke using Hindi mixed with thick English. Meena stared at the stitches on her needle. Hopelessness crowded the room. Meena crushed her knitting into the plastic bag and stood up to leave.

Memories chased Meena back to the dorm. Hopscotch, Fanta, hot tea and stale rice donuts ... Mohan's smoky breath. She paced into the dorm and threw her knitting onto the bed. The bag slid onto the floor, the needles clacking against the concrete. Purna hovered at the doorway.

'What would you do?' Meena asked. As expected, Purna didn't answer, but neither did she leave. She just watched as Meena gathered the knitting from the floor, tugging the needles from where they had pierced the plastic.

Didi said keeping busy would help calm her mind, but right now her mind felt as skittish as a new kid. Meena perched on the edge of her bed and took a deep breath to slow her fingers. She looped the wool and began to knit a new row. She counted the growing stitches in Hindi. Then she tried counting in English, which some of the girls used when they were trying to show off, 'Wun, tooo, treee, pour, pive.' Her mind raced over the stitches, dropping them, picking them up again, counting, and counting again. Where was Putali, the girl who used to count with her when they played hopscotch drawn with stones on the road? Meena opened her mouth. Gingerly, for the first time in years, she tasted the subtle differences in sound of Nepali on her tongue and counted the next five stitches in her native tongue. No one came to beat her. No one bellowed for her to shut up. No one warned her from the other room. But behind her, someone was moving. It was Purna, her eyes, from across the room, were on Meena's needles. As Meena worked, Purna's mouth stumbled with her over the Nepali words.

'*Ek ... dui ... teen ...*' Purna walked closer. She sniffed and dragged her wrist across her nose. '*Chaar ... panch ...*' She came so close Meena could smell her body odour. So close the breath from her counting touched Meena's forehead.

Meena's fingers stopped moving.

Purna frowned, her eyes on the work, '*Ek ... dui ...*' She tried again.

Meena made a stitch.

'*Teen ...*'

Meena looped another.

'*Chaar ... panch ... ek ...*'

Meena looked up, Purna had returned to one again. One, two, three, four, five, one?

Tears started falling from Purna's eyes. She let them roll unchecked. The girl's tears dropped from her chin to Meena's knee, but she didn't make to move away. Meena continued knitting.

'*Ek, dui, teen, chaar, panch ...*' Purna whispered through her tears, 'After *panch*? What comes after *panch*?'

'*Chha*,' Meena said. She kept looping stitches.

'*Chha*?' Purna looked at her. '*Chha*? No, I have nothing.'

Meena stared up, Purna was speaking Nepali. The word for the number six is the same as the word for 'I have'. She had stopped counting at six because she thought she was saying she had something.

'*Chhaina*,' Purna continued, 'I have not. *Aama chhaina, baa chhaina,* sister *chhaina,* brother *chhaina,* grandmother *chhaina*—' Her voice caught. She climbed onto the bed beside Meena and curled into a heap, her eyes ever on the moving needles. '*Meri saathi pani chhaina,*' she cried softly. 'I don't even have a friend. But you ... you have.'

Meena can't see Putali anywhere. The Sitting Room is full of men. Shiny men with bulky jewellery and polished shoes. Men from different countries, some white—like Americans—and some dark—like Africans—and all the skin tones in between. These men sit silently, some smoking, others sipping alcohol from small glasses. They wear shirts and haircuts and belts that whisper of money. And they are all looking at her. A contained interest lurks on each man's face.

Zeshaan prods her forwards. She trips on the long skirt they've made her wear. One of the men chuckles softly. Another frowns. Meena feels herself watching them from behind the mask of make up. Does she look as beautiful as Putali had? Is that why they are staring at her?

Zeshaan speaks to the men. He speaks firmly as if explaining the rules of a detailed game the men already know how to play.

'Turn around,' he instructs Meena, and then softly, in Nepali, so the men can't hear, 'the way I told you to'.

Meena raises her arms and twirls her wrists. He has told her to dance, but there is no music. He told her to sway her hips, but the skirt feels too long for that. Her feet catch again and she stumbles clumsily. Zeshaan scowls. The chuckling man laughs aloud. The frowning one looks away. Then Zeshaan says something in Hindi, a term she doesn't understand and the men begin listing numbers. Large numbers. The white-skinned man, using a disinterested tone, offers 'yu ess dollars', which make two of the other men grizzle and increase the amount they've originally quoted.

Eventually the bargaining, for that is what it feels like, peters off. Zeshaan motions for her to leave the room and Ganga leads her along a hall and into a very glamorously decorated room.

'You do what he tells you,' is all Ganga says before she locks Meena inside.

Time drags on, like mud heavy off a plough. Finally the lock on the door makes a gentle click. Zeshaan and a man walk in. One of the men she had danced and stumbled before. The frowning one. Zeshaan holds out a syringe, but the man waves it away. So Zeshaan leaves, locking the door behind him.

The man eyes her, a small, soft, sickly smile reaching only as far as his lips. His eyes burn like a starved dog's, focusing on her neck, her shoulders, her waist, the new bumps on her chest. Meena feels her stomach knot. Back home, when she'd seen that expression on a drunk man, she'd known how to fight him off. But this man isn't drunk. He is entirely sober and it frightens her. He removes his jacket, lying it carefully over the back of a chair, then motions for her to sit with him on the edge of the bed.

Meena takes a step backward.

The man's smile dissolves. He steps towards her. In a swift, practised movement he snatches her hand and yanks her forwards, off balance and into his arms.

She wrestles free. Stumbling backwards, she trips on her skirt again and sprawls onto the floor, trapped in the skirt's silken, slippery lining. The man walks towards her, confidently, as if he's done this many times before, and steps on the skirt pinning her down. Then he reaches his long, thin arm down and unzips it.

Meena skitters suddenly backwards, free from the skirt. She clambers to the door. Pounding, clawing, willing the lock to give way. But the man just steps after her, without rush. A pair of footsteps approach outside.

'*Guhar*, help! Let me out!'

The footsteps pause. Surely they had heard her? But they don't stop. Meena spins to face the man. His eyes are hot now. His words ugly in a language she doesn't understand. But she knows enough to realise what this man is wanting. That he thinks he can have it because he's paid for it. That she has been fattened up, made beautiful, bargained for and sold. She feels him reach for her, the touch of his hand on her shoulder. She cries out once more. And this time the man hits her. He drags her towards the bed. Images flash through her mind—blurring, choking together. Her surroundings fade, and the face of the frowning man goes fuzzy.

Instead she sees Mohan tucking an envelope into his pocket.

Her uncle, ordering food at the border town restaurant.

Her aunt tossing soap sachets into the bathroom.

Rajit and Santosh leaning over their bikes.

And Putali, little Putali, hesitating by the river …

Meena's body is stinging. Burning. Blood, not her own, is foul in her mouth. Hair, his, in her fists. She retches, crouches, cries. The image of Putali beside the river, her eyes full of dreams, slams against her heart.

She curls herself as close to the wall as she can, away from the bed, away from the man. He slings on his jacket, sloshes water on his face from the little basin against the wall, and smooths his hair. Without another glance in her direction, he unlocks the door and strides out, leaving the door wide open. Zeshaan looks in and takes in Meena's battered nakedness, the mess around the bed and the expression on the frowning man's face. He waits only until the man has disappeared down the hall before coming in and kicking Meena so hard she sinks into darkness.

Twenty-eight

Meena tried to concentrate. Sharmila's voice droned on, lecturing about rights and freedom and strength from weakness, but Meena wanted to curl up and ignore it all. She felt the space beside her ache with emptiness.

Suddenly Sharmila paused. Her eyes widened in surprise as someone entered the meeting room late. Meena turned to look, half expecting Nahita to slide down the wall to her spot beside Meena. But it wasn't Nahita. It was Purna. She walked with her arms wrapped about her loose T-shirt, as if they were a sweater against the cold. Her dark eyes were wide, cautious and uncertain.

'Come in, Purna. Come and listen.' Sharmila switched to her sweet, coaxing voice. Purna barely responded. Her eyes roved the room in darts, stilling only when they found Meena. Then she shuffled over and knelt down.

'You have,' Purna whispered.

Sharmila opened her mouth, closed it, and opened it again. Her eyebrows raised towards Meena in a question. Meena shrugged. She hadn't done anything. Sharmila resumed the lecture. Her bossy tone softer now, wavering nervously, as if she expected Purna to panic. But she didn't. She just sat, and rocked, and occasionally bumped into Meena. It must have been the first educational seminar Purna had ever attended.

Sharmila flicked a new image onto the screen. It was a copy

of a newspaper clipping showing two policemen holding onto a man with a short beard.

'This man'—Sharmila pointed—'was a trafficker.'

There was a general murmur of approval from the girls. A trafficker in the hands of the police was certainly more interesting than blabber about human rights.

'Most girls who escape from the brothel, either by running away or by the freedom offered by their madam, don't ever think they could help to put traffickers in prison. But it can be done. This man'—Sharmila motioned to the screen—'sold his two nieces to a brothel in Pune. One of them escaped. She attended a rehabilitation home, received health care and participated in vocational training. She returned to her village. One day she saw her uncle walking through the bazaar. He had a fancy motorbike helmet under his arm and very expensive shoes. His niece was very angry that he should benefit from her experience, so she left the village and returned to the rehabilitation home. There, she contacted lawyers and filed a case against her uncle. It took four years, but finally he is being punished for his crime.'

The girls murmured again.

'Unfortunately, this is a rare story. Most traffickers get away with it. They continue to lure the vulnerable and sell them without being held accountable. But, as ex-trafficked women, we can help. By telling our story, we raise awareness. By taking those who sold us to court, we show the community that human trafficking is not acceptable.'

Renu spoke up, 'I know the woman who trafficked me. She told my mother I was going to school in America. She deserves to go to prison, but I wouldn't want to go to court. They'd take my photo and put it in the newspaper. Then everyone would know I'd been a whore in Mumbai. So much for starting again!'

Sharmila agreed, 'It can be very frightening, but Little

Sister and her partner organisations have lawyers who know the system. They work to bring these criminals to justice and protect your dignity at the same time. That's what they do.'

'And what do they want in return?' Leela called out.

The girls around Meena murmured. Sharmila shook her head. 'Many donate their services. It may surprise you, Leela, but there are people with integrity in this world.'

'There might be two,' Leela muttered.

Kani laughed.

Someone else called out a question: 'So, these lawyer men—'

'And women,' put in Sharmila proudly.

'Will they help anyone?'

'If you have evidence against the trafficker, then the case can be pursued. Sometimes criminals get away, there is a lot of corruption, but our lawyers don't give up easily. Until the community knows human trafficking is a punishable crime it will continue.'

Sharmila switched the projector off. 'Let's do a role play,' she suggested. 'We'll need a trafficker, a victim, her family, a lawyer, some policemen, a judge, and some onlookers.'

'I might as well be the trafficker, no one likes me anyway,' Leela called out, though not with her usual bitterness. 'Renu, I'll sell you.'

Renu scowled, but agreed. Manju opted for the role of Renu's mother.

'Meena?' Sharmila looked at her, some of her animosity gone now that Purna was present, 'What would you like to do?'

Meena hesitated. 'I'll be the lawyer.'

Sharmila left the girls discussing their roles for a few minutes then returned with a Lay's chips box, which she dumped in the centre of the room. Renu laughed and tipped the box up. 'Oohhh look at this!' She held up a sparkled *sari* skirt and matching blouse as Maa entered the room. 'I guess this is my whore suit?'

'We don't talk like that here, Renu,' Maa said, disapprovingly.

Sharmila began handing out the other pieces of clothing. There were several large scarfs, a Nepali *topi* cap, a T-shirt with Britney Spears on the front. There was even an old police officer's shirt that Rupa and Kani fought over. Meena found a creased men's jacket. She slung it over her shirt and then knotted Sarita's scarf as a tie around her neck.

'Okay,' called Sharmila from the front. 'Are you ready?'

The girls laughed their way through the drama. Renu played her role with such realism that the room fell silent and Purna began to cry. Maa came over and sat with her, stroking her hair as Leela took the stage. Leela's role suited her vocabulary, especially when Sharmila, who they had roped in to play the madam, wouldn't give her as much money as she was wanting for selling Renu.

But when Renu escaped the imaginary brothel and crept up to the door of Meena's lawyer office, her sparkled skirt rumpled and the lower buttons of her blouse popped, Meena could barely get the words out. All she saw was Putali. Putali, standing small before Uncle's appraising eyes. Putali, pulled along by Mohan. Putali, curled under a mound of sparkling fabric. And then there was Uncle again. Claiming he had nothing to do with Putali being in Mumbai, that there was another girl, an older girl they should arrest because she was the one who had left her friend to die...

'She is the victim!' Meena shouted suddenly. Renu stepped back in surprise and then giggled. 'You're good at this.'

'She was lured by lies and false pretences,' Meena continued. 'She is the victim of torture, abuse, cruelty and rape. And this man!' Meena pointed her finger across the room at Uncle, the cigarette balancing in his thin lips. 'This man benefited from her pain. This man!'

Leela's mouth was open.

'This man, broke not just the laws of the nation, but the law of being human! He's deserving of this punishment, and it will be served to him!'

Meena stepped back. She watched Kani and Rupa grab Leela by the elbows. They dragged her to an imaginary police cell and locked her up. Leela cursed in as many different languages as she could, then burst out laughing, big gawffing laughs that made Maa frown, but didn't hide the sudden wetness in her eyes. The coat on Meena's shoulders suddenly felt like lead. She shook it off. Purna crept forward to stand beside her. Maa started clapping. She spouted compliments like they were marigolds at a wedding. Sharmila clapped too, then Leela and Rupa joined in. Beside Meena, Purna put her hands together, her damp eyes on Meena, her palms together, raised to her forehead in a sign of respect.

They ate snacks together in the dorm kitchen. Leela and Renu joked about the role play, Manju ate in silence with Purna, but Meena barely tasted the curried beans. She bit the end off the chilli and pushed another strip of *puri* into her mouth. Uncle would never face the courts. There wasn't enough evidence. They'd twist it round onto her; blame her for the flow of events. They would say she wanted to come, say she was greedy, say she cared more about money than she did for her friend. And could she prove otherwise? Even her memories accused her. And now Putali was lost ...

Meena no longer felt hungry. She pushed her plate back.

'You've got to wash it,' Kani remarked.

Meena swore. She dumped the plate in the sink, scrubbed it quickly, then left the room. Regardless of what Didi said, Meena was sure if she went back to Kamathipura, during the day when hardly anyone worked, she'd be able to find the hotel Mohan had taken them to. And if she could find it, she could learn its name, and ask questions to find out if Putali was still there. Maybe?

She wrapped Sarita's scarf around her shoulders and headed for the front gate. Didi, who was talking to the guard, caught her by the shoulder.

'You can't go out, Meena.' Didi's voice was almost apologetic, but still very firm in the reminder of the curfew.

'I'm just going to the bazaar.' Meena shook Didi's hand away. 'The food here's horrible.'

'You can't go alone, you know that.'

Meena felt the anger grow within her. 'I thought it was the traffickers who deserved prison!' She spat the words. 'I thought we were supposed to be free, allowed out, to go for walks and shopping and ...'

'That was before you helped Nahita leave. You're on curfew now.'

The guard stepped into his hut but kept listening.

Meena fumed. 'She wanted to go. I told Maa, I told Sharmila, I told you: SHE WANTED TO LEAVE!'

'Helping her leave in secret like that'—Didi crossed her arms—'you put her life at risk.'

'But she wasn't being trafficked.'

'How do you know? It happens all the time. Girls from brothels are repeatedly trafficked, they search out hope and find hell.'

'But it's not always like that. It can't always be like that! I didn't do anything wrong, now let me go.' Meena glared at Didi.

'No, Meena.' The older woman placed a firm grip on Meena's arm.

'You can't stop me!' Meena almost screamed, pulling away but not escaping Didi's grip.

'Go back to the dorm. Find your knitting, do your laundry. If you are hungry, I have some fruit in my office.'

Meena glared at the open gate. Even if she sprinted, Didi would catch her. Didi's grip tightened, as if she read Meena's thoughts.

'Get your hands off me!' Meena twisted free. Didi stood solid, unmoving, between Meena and the gate. Meena sucked in the suddenly suffocating air. She could see Renu and Rupa now squatting by the water tap. They were watching her, whispering, their hands still over their laundry. The line was almost full; *kurta-suruwals*, jeans, shirts all flapped carelessly. The sun watched and stared and waited.

'Aaa*aau*uughhhh!!!' Meena cried. She ran under the clothesline. She yanked wet fabric and flung it to the ground.

'I hate you!' she yelled to Didi, who stood with arms crossed again near the gate.

'I hate you!' she yelled to Maa, to Sharmila, to the girls now quiet by the tap.

'I hate you!' That one was for Madam. 'I hate you.' For Rajit and her uncle and Mohan. 'And you.' Sarita. 'You.' Nahita, Ramesh, Leela, the man in the tie from Stop Trafficking Nepal.

'And you, I hate you, I hate you, I hate you!' she yelled at herself.

Meena raced her anger up the steps to the dorm room. Purna turned from where she had been staring at the window.

'*Chha*,' she said to Meena. '*Tapaai-ko chha*.' You have.

'*Mero ke chha?*' Meena shouted at the stupid girl. She, who couldn't even count to six, telling her she had something. 'What do I have?'

Purna quaked at the yelling. Her legs wobbled as if she didn't want to lie down for fear of what would happen.

'I'm not going to hurt you, you idiot! Why would I hurt

you?' Meena glared at her. Purna crashed onto Nahita's empty bed, missing the edge and falling to the floor. She yelped as her shoulder hit the ground, then tucked herself up into a ball, half under the bed. Like Durga's baby, back at the brothel, shoved out of the way when the clients came, dazed and shivering, but never daring to cry.

Meena opened her mouth to curse the world, but there was no sound left. She flung around and onto her own bed. She hated the world, she hated herself ...

But, you have.

Meena threw her pillow and leaned against the hardness of the wall. Her breath was ragged, like an old man trying too hard. The image set her retching.

You have. Have what?

She'd never had a safe place to live. She'd never had enough food. She'd never had clothes that kept her warm in winter or dry in the monsoon. But she'd had a friend once, a friend that laughed at her stupid jokes and shared old mandarins and let her come stay the night when things got too messy with Meena's father. She'd had a home and a friend and freedom.

The aching gulps of sadness rose from her chest.

Putali. Small Putali, who liked chicken meat and chillies. Who preferred Coke to Fanta. Who wished she could be a movie star, but knew she never would. She had known, Putali had always known, the trip wasn't going to work out well. And now?

Didi strode into the room. Meena tensed, but Didi didn't speak. She surveyed the scene, then knelt by Purna, coaxing her curled form from under the bed. Didi wordlessly scooped the fully-grown Nepali onto her lap and cradled her until the tight ball of fear relaxed. Then she lay Purna on her bed and pulled up the sheets.

'Rules are hard. I know,' Didi said when she finally

approached Meena's bedside and Purna's breathing had slowed. 'But it's our rules that make us a place of freedom.'

Meena didn't speak. The only sound in the room was what came from Purna, and the laughter of the girls outside.

Meena wakes to a soft moaning sound. Her whole body aches. The area between her legs stings. It aches. She opens her eyes, the room skews, her left eye is bruised shut. Her vision spins as she draws herself upright, memories of what has happened slamming into her.

'Putali?'

At the sound of her voice, the moaning pauses briefly, only to resume immediately after. Meena forces herself upright. Her bare legs stiff from the cold concrete. Her pink, ripped, sparkled top hangs open from her shoulders. She is practically naked. A *kurta-suruwal* has been tossed beside her. The fluorescent light above pains her eyes. What time is it? How long has she been unaware? Who had carried her—or dragged her—back to this place, the room she'd shared with Putali? The moaning continues.

Meena drags herself to the side of the bed. Her little friend lies curled under a pile of sparkling pink fabric, her arms hugging her chest, her heavily made up eyes squeezed shut. Meena pulls herself up and takes it all in. There are no bruises on Putali's face, so she has not been beaten, but her mouth hangs open at a strange angle and a thin line of wetness hangs from it.

'Putali.' Meena reaches out to touch Putali's shoulder. The little girl flinches, her eyes snapping open in dazed terror and then closing again in pain. Meena feels her chest pound. She's never seen Putali like this. Ever. Dread clambers over her. Her head spins, her body cringes in pain. She lies weakly beside her little friend and reaches for the blanket. To cover them both and still her trembling.

It is only after she wakes the second time that she notices the pool of blood seeping out from under Putali's skirt.

Twenty-nine

Three days later, Meena was still on curfew. She sat hunched by the turned dirt of Didi's tiny kitchen garden. The warm breeze that drifted about the compound blew lightly on her bare shins. She tugged her trouser legs down, brushing the dirt from her ankles. All morning she had worked like Didi had told her, digging up the stiff, stubborn soil. The dirt was dull, lifeless. Even Meena knew it needed more than turning over, but Didi was a city woman and Meena wasn't going to say anything.

She looked up to see the gate dragged open. Tarak from Stop Trafficking Nepal rode in on his motorbike. What was he doing here? Would Maa tell him about Nahita? Meena pulled the hoe closer and leaned on its handle. Tarak climbed off his bike and pulled his helmet off like he was in the Honda Heroes advertisement. Sharmila skipped down the office steps and blushed bright crimson at the sight of him. Tarak lifted his hands to greet her in the polite traditional manner. Meena spat the dust from her mouth and stood up. She mightn't know how to read books, but she knew enough to read Sharmila's face and to know she wanted more than politeness from Tarak-Sir. What were they talking about? Her? She watched them walk into Maa's office.

Meena carried the hoe around to the front of the dorm. She saw Purna, squatting by the water tap and holding out a worn pair of trousers under the unopened tap. She'd never actually seen Purna do laundry before, and here she was moving the dry trousers as if she was rinsing the soap out.

'Are you trying to wash them?' Meena asked. Purna looked up, half afraid. She drew the trousers into her chest.

'I'm not going to hurt you. I won't shout,' Meena said. She turned the tap on and watched Purna jump back with surprise as the water splashed onto the concrete. Purna made a narrow, squashed noise, it sounded something like disused laughter.

'Turn the water off when you're done.'

Purna nodded. She beat the trousers fiercely under the running water, blurring the soft sounds of Tarak, Maa and Sharmila's conversation.

Meena picked up the hoe again and went to return it to the garden shed. Thin lines of smoke were weaving their way up from a pile of burning rubbish behind the chicken hut. Meena strode towards it. She heard a sound of shuffling behind her. It was Purna, following slowly, wet trousers in her hand, the tap still running in the distance.

'Go turn the water off.' Meena pointed.

Purna ran clumsily back to the tap and Meena took the opportunity to duck unseen behind the chicken hut. Leela and Kani were smoking and tending the fire from a distance. Leela squatted with her trouser legs pulled up above the knees, showing off her skinny legs. They were crossed with scars from her ankles to her knees. The kind of scars made from knives or broken glass. Meena fingered the scarf at her neck. She had seen scars like that on Sarita.

'What'd you bring her for?' Leela muttered as Purna scurried around the side of the shed after Meena. Purna shrunk under Leela's glare.

'I didn't mean to,' Meena answered, then quickly changed

the subject as Purna squatted to stare absently into the fire beside her. 'The guy from Stop Trafficking Nepal turned up.'

Kani giggled. 'Oh yeah, doesn't Sharmila have her eyes on him?'

'As if he'd take her,' Leela spat, but Meena saw a flicker of thoughtfulness before the sarcasm.

They were silent for a while, each bar Purna, occupied with their own thoughts. Meena watched the grass around the fire curl and die.

'Would you ever go back?' She let the question go before she was ready.

'Go back? Where?' Kani asked.

'To the hotel, to the brothel?'

The girls just stared at her.

'I'd rather hang myself,' Kani finally muttered. 'The only people who go back are Madams.'

Leela pulled her trouser legs down and leaned in to poke the fire. 'There was a day when I had twenty-six clients,' she said. 'I remember 'cause I'd counted twenty-six lipstick dots on the wall.'

Meena didn't want to listen but she couldn't move.

'I told my madam twenty-six was too many. And Madam explained, as she was watching me get beaten, that she had been sold when she was nine, that she had been raped, that she had been starved, that men had poked pieces of glass inside her until she agreed to work and that, if she had been treated in that way, then she could do it to me. She said it was my fault I was in the brothel, that I asked for it, that it was what I deserved because I was nobody.'

Kani drew deep on her cigarette before handing it to Leela. Purna whimpered and disappeared.

'The next day she only sent five customers. But they were

monsters each time.' She glared at Meena. 'I will never go back. Even if I have to live here until I'm as old and boring as Maa. Never!'

Meena ducked her head. She could see the grass beside the rubbish heap, it had curled over and was dying. She took a breath of the foul air. 'But what if you had a friend? What if she was still inside?'

'We've all got friends inside,' Kani said softly. 'Was she in your brothel? Maybe she'll get out the same way you did.'

Meena shook her head. 'I haven't seen her since ... for three years.'

Leela snorted. 'Was she little? She's probably dead, or crazy, like Purna.' She dropped the cigarette to the ground. The red end glowed and the heat of it curled the leaves of grass until it went out and the leaves were left scarred. A breeze shifted the smoke into their faces. Meena coughed and stood up. She felt sick, dizzy, out of breath. 'I can't breathe.'

'You don't have to stay, you're not on rubbish duty,' Kani grumbled.

Meena covered her mouth and ran out of the smoke. She followed Purna back to the dorm. Leela's story sat sick in her mind. Was Putali's madam like that? Her photo was still in Maa's desk. How would they find her if Meena didn't say anything? If Meena didn't go back? Maybe Maa would agree to help. Or Tarak—he wanted to rescue Nepali girls, didn't he? Meena settled herself on the dorm steps with her knitting and waited for Tarak to leave. She'd go and talk to Maa about it this afternoon.

***

Eventually Tarak and Sharmila stepped from the office doors. They lingered by his motorbike, chatting for what seemed to Meena far too long to be 'professional', Tarak laughing at something Sharmila had said, and then Sharmila lowering her eyes and blushing shyly as Tarak replied. Finally he drove away, turning on his way out the gate for a final wave before he disappeared from view. Sharmila spun round dreamily, snapping her professional face into place at the sight of Meena.

'Quick, hurry inside.' She beckoned Meena over. 'Maa's got good news for you.'

Meena felt her stomach curdle with hope. Had Didi told Maa about Meena's friend in Kamathipura? Had Tarak been invited to make a plan? The smoke from the rubbish stuck at the back of her throat, but she managed to cross the paving to Maa's office.

The narrow-faced woman looked up from a pile of papers and smiled like a grandmother about to hand out expensive gifts.

'I was c... coming to talk to you ...' Meena started, but Maa had already begun talking.

'Meena, I have some good news. Please sit.'

Meena remained standing, but fumbled for the arm of the chair.

'You know the painting we have upstairs? Well, it looks like you'll be seeing the real view sooner than we both thought. Our colleague Tarak has arranged for you to travel with their next Stop Trafficking Nepal repatriation group. They have seven girls at their transit home, who will be moved to their main centre in Kathmandu, and a generous donor has made it possible for two of our Nepali girls to join them,' Maa announced triumphantly.

'Who's going?' Meena felt her legs go weak. She sank into the chair.

'Well, you and Purna of course,' Maa said.

Meena's eyes darted around the office for distraction.

Something to focus on, to still her mind, like Sarita had taught her. But the cobwebs near the airconditioner had been swept away. There was no evidence they had ever built their homes. No evidence at all ... But perhaps there was still time. Meena forced her voice to be calm. 'When?' she asked.

'Tomorrow! The Stop Trafficking Nepal mini bus will come in the morning to collect you, so you can both catch the noon train to Gorakhpur Junction.'

Meena shook her head. 'But I can't go. Not yet, not without ...' She still couldn't say it. Putali slipped further away.

Maa leaned forward. 'I know it feels very rushed. But both Didi and the nurse believe you will heal much better in your own country. Stop Trafficking Nepal have a very good reputation for rehabilitation and many more options for vocational training than we have here. Little Sister is only a small set-up,' Maa said, apologetically.

'That's not what I meant. I have a friend. You have her photo in your drawer. Her name is ...' Meena's voice began to waver.

'No, I haven't forgotten about Nahita. And that is one of the reasons we feel you would be safer in your own country. You're very lucky Stop Trafficking Nepal are willing to add you to their group, sometimes they have so many girls there isn't enough space for the Nepalis from Little Sister. You must be so excited? Yes?'

Meena couldn't respond. Her mind felt frozen thick like blocks of *kulfi* on wooden sticks. Eventually she would thaw and her words would slip messily all over the place, but for now, she was stuck, silent, dumb and stupid.

Maa nodded like she understood. 'You can go now. I'm sure you'll have lovely dreams tonight!'

Meena pounds on the door again. Screaming—though her voice sounds like someone else's. 'She's bleeding! Hurry up!'

Eventually the lock turns. Meena trips backwards as the door swings open. Zeshaan enters and whacks her hard across the face, bruising again her sore eye and knocking Meena off balance.

'Not me—her!' Meena feels anger rising. 'They've hurt her, she's bleeding—'

Ganga enters the room then, she scowls at Meena as if she is a stupid child. 'Of course she is; all little girls bleed after their first time.'

Meena feels herself gag with disgust. Zeshaan stands guard over Meena while Ganga approaches the bed. She lifts the skirt, muttering something about a doctor under her breath and returns to the hallway.

'Take her out,' she instructs as she passes Meena.

Zeshaan bends to grab Meena but she scuttles backwards. 'I won't go, I won't leave her.'

He grunts and grabs her arm—the sore one—and squeezes.

'*Hoina*, no!' Meena screams, half in pain, half in terror. 'I won't leave her!'

The moaning from Putali increases.

'You can't make me go. She needs me, she's bleeding, she's only little ...' Meena struggles, wriggling with a strength summoned from somewhere under Zeshaan's grasp.

The hotel manager enters the room with a well-dressed man carrying a black case. Zeshaan looks to the manager for instructions. Without making eye contact, she draws close enough to speak without Putali hearing. 'You've already caused us more trouble than you're worth. Do as you're told or you'll never see her again.'

And Meena feels herself rage forwards at the woman with such ferocity it takes two attempts from Zeshaan to regain his grip, but only one to toss her from the room. The last thing she hears is Putali's voice calling, confused, weak and full of terror. 'Meena? Don't leave me ...'

Thirty

Meena laid awake in the humidity and stared at the smudgy grey section of roof near the toilet door. The roller bird was grey like that. Grey until its wings spread and it flew away. She remembered the day she and Putali had chased it; over the paddy creek, past the ploughing oxen, up the dirt track to the settlement. She remembered the bitter radish Putali's mother served beside their rice that day. She couldn't sleep. She couldn't stay. She couldn't climb into the mini bus and wave to Maa and Sharmila and Leela like Asha had done. No, she had to go back. Back for Putali.

Meena waited until the only sounds that stirred the room were those of unsettled sleep. She slid her legs out from under the sheet and reached under her pillow for the key to her cupboard. The lock clicked like Sarita's tongue and the door swung open. With as little noise as possible, Meena changed from her bed clothes into a dark *kurta-suruwal* and tied the ends of another *kurta* top to make a bag. Into this she placed as much as she could carry from the collection of belongings she'd acquired since coming to Little Sister: the brown glass bottle of vitamins, a bar of soap, a comb and box of sanitary pads, as well as the few changes of clothes. But she hesitated at the bag of knitting. The soft wool, pitch black in the darkness, felt familiar, calming. There was no point taking it, without Didi's instructions she'd never know how to turn her rows of stitches into a cardigan. Meena pushed the knitting bag further back in the cupboard, then shut the door, closing but not locking her *kurta* bag of belongings inside. She was almost ready.

Climbing silently onto the sill of the ever open window, she jumped out, landing softly in the garden bed below. Ducking from shadow to shadow, she crept across the compound yard to the office building. Her heartbeat felt louder than her footsteps. From the shadows beside the doorway, she could hear two voices echo from upstairs—Maa and one of the office men. Their conversation seemed long and engaged, so Meena tiptoed up the steps to the foyer and pushed gently on Maa's office door. It swung open with a dull groan. Meena held her breath and listened, but the murmur of conversation continued.

It was dark and empty in Maa's office. Meena let her eyes adjust until she could see the cleared space that was Maa's desk and the vase without any flowers. She hurried behind the desk and pulled open the top drawer, the one she'd seen Maa drop Putali's photo in. She pulled the stack of pictures out, but the light was too dim. She couldn't pick features among the shadows. Someone moved upstairs. She heard a door pulled closed and steps, unhurried, moved towards the stairs. Meena reached into the drawer again. Pens and hair clips rattled against the cheap timber but there were no more photos. Putali's picture was either in the bundle she now held, or returned to the Stop Trafficking Nepal office. And there wasn't enough time to check. She'd have to take them all with her.

Meena slid the drawer closed. The footsteps upstairs slowed to a stop. The man had forgotten something in his office. Maa's voice echoed down the stairs. Meena hurried to the door, then hesitated. Maa's handbag sat—fat, squat and waiting—on the empty chair.

Money? Meena's memory jolted to the snack vendor outside Nahita's restaurant. She wouldn't get far without money. Quickly she reached into the handbag. Her fingers slipped on cool vinyl under a bottle of water. She pulled the purse out and clicked open the magnetic seal. From the slice of light coming from the hall she could see a photo of Maa and Didi taken at a conference somewhere. Meena squeezed the purse apart until the dirty grey rupees showed themselves. There weren't as many as Meena had expected, but it would be enough. The footsteps above returned to the stairs. They were coming down.

Meena steadied her hand. She pulled the money from its place, snapped the purse shut and shoved it back into the handbag. Maa's conversation wove its way down the stairs. Meena darted out the office and jumped down the steps and into the shadows of the garden.

'I'll finish the summaries tonight,' Meena heard the office man say.

'That would be good. The girls leave in the morning ...'

Meena heard Maa's voice fade off. 'I was sure I shut this door earlier.'

'Might have been the wind, it's that time of year,' the office man answered.

Meena hugged herself further back into the darkness.

'I suppose so. I haven't noticed the doors blowing open before though,' Maa said.

Meena gripped the photos and money to her chest. She watched Maa pull her office door shut, and then the large double doors at the front of the office building. She sighed when she turned, her expression hidden by a shadow, but Meena could tell Maa was looking around, scanning the courtyard for anything out of place. Meena held her breath. She concentrated on being still until she felt every pulse as a quake of thunder.

Maa mumbled a goodbye to the office man, who climbed onto his motorbike and disappeared out the gate. Meena didn't move.

She waited until the guard had locked the front gate and settled inside his little hut with his tin of food. She waited for Maa to slowly cross the paving. She waited for the light at the front room of Didi and Maa's residence to be switched off. Only then did she creep back across the yard and pull herself up through the dorm window. Sitting on the end of her bed, she held the stack of photos in the scrap of light that came from outside. Her fingers shook as one by one the little girls' faces shone up at her again. In the shadowy light, their blank expressions seemed to mock her. Their anonymity, their smileless faces; the very number of them taunted that what she was trying to do was futile. Didi would say she was being stupid, Leela would say worse, but the photo she had been searching for finally stared up at her. Two plaits on either side of her little girl face: Putali Maya. Butterfly Love. Meena could barely breathe, so strong were her memories. How had she forgotten? Her heart pounded in her chest. Hope curdling with desperation. Surely it wouldn't be too late?

Meena pushed the remaining photos under her pillow. Out of sight. She padded back to her cupboard and pushed Putali's photo, along with half of Maa's money, deep into the *kurta* bag. The rest of the money she tucked down her bra. Then she waited.

Sometime after midnight, Purna had a nightmare. She cried out so loud Meena was scared the other girls would wake. But although Manju stirred and Leela rolled over, no one woke. Purna continued to cry, softly now, the whimpers rattling in and out with her breath. Increasing in intensity. Meena slid from the covers and stood by the other Nepali girl's bedside. Purna writhed in her sleep like she was skirting beatings across the floor of a locked room.

'Shhhh,' Meena whispered urgently, willing Purna to stay asleep. If the girl woke in hysterics, they'd have to call Sharmila and then they'd notice Meena was dressed. Meena leaned closer. 'Shhhh.' The sound of it seemed to sooth Purna slightly, but still the nightmare raged. Meena sat gingerly on the edge of Purna's bed and placed her fingers on the crying girl's shoulder. 'Shhhh,' she whispered again. Slowly the tension eased from Purna's body and the whimpering lessened. Meena didn't move. She couldn't. Her hand was now tucked at Purna's neck as the girl rolled slightly and continued to sleep. Meena sat like that and waited.

Eventually she heard the first rumblings of pre-dawn traffic from the bazaar. Meena stared down at Purna. Her mouth was open and soft, little snoring noises came out. Meena eased her hand from Purna's neck and shoulder and rose. She lifted the *kurta* bag from her cupboard and laid the key on the shelf with the knitting. The cupboard clicked closed and someone rustled in bed behind her. Meena froze. She held the *kurta* bag close to her body, masking it in the shadows before she turned around, but the room was still. Even Leela continued to sleep, her face strangely make-up free. Meena tiptoed over to the window and lifted herself up one last time.

Part Five

Thirty-one

Meena gripped her bag to her chest and ran. The back gate was locked, as she'd expected, but she pulled herself up using the hinges for footholds and launched herself over to the other side. The metal spikes at the top of the gate scraped her shin on the way over and she landed too hard and fast on her left foot. She bit her lip to stop herself from crying out before hurrying on.

The pre-dawn bazaar was just waking. Shutters were being rolled open, snack vendors were unlocking their carts. The few tea shops that were open were crowded with early morning commuters, snatching bites to eat before the buses arrived. Meena hurried across the road, conscious that she wasn't dressed like them for work in an office, and joined a queue. She could feel them watching her, staring at her bag, wondering what her story was. But she kept her head down and refused eye contact.

The first bus arrived and filled up before Meena reached the front of the line. The ticket conductor flicked her away as the bus drove off. The next bus pulled up empty. Meena poked her head through one of the open doors. It smelt funny, like urine.

'Kamathipura? Do you go to Kamathipura?'

The ticket collector eyed her with mixed disgust and interest. 'No. Too far.'

Meena stepped back onto the street. She tried the next bus and received a similar answer. She asked the third the same question.

'Kamathipura? What do you want to go there for?' The fare collector spoke Nepali to her. She lowered her eyes. Sarita had been with Nepali men. Meena hadn't. She felt suddenly shy.

'*Hos*, okay. I said nothing.' The ticket collector turned back to the rearview vision mirror, adjusted his earring and rearranged his hair.

Passengers climbed in after her, trapping her by the open door but without a ticket anywhere. They all knew where they were going. Meena felt the enormity of what she was trying to do rise.

'If you want to go to Kamathipura, you have to get to Mumbai Central,' the Nepali conductor said. He turned from collecting passenger payments to look at Meena. 'We go to Mumbai Central. Are you getting on or off?'

Meena flustered at the bus door. A woman in a suit bustled past her impatiently, taking the last seat. The aisle began to fill. Meena stumbled. The bus engine started. The conductor held out his palm and quoted a fare. She clumsily pulled the money from her shirt to pay, then gripped a handle hanging from the roof. The bus smelt like exhaust and hair oil, men's perfume and freshly baked pastries. Meena's stomach growled. She regretted not eating last night's meal and clutched her bag tighter. The bus heaved away from the bazaar and the sky finally gave up its darkness for the day.

On and on the bus drove, stopping regularly to let passengers off and allow new ones on until the entire bus population had changed—except for Meena, the conductor and the weary-faced driver. She had a seat now, against the window, close to the door, but nothing she saw was familiar. The city sprawled, as it had the other times she'd journeyed through it, like a never ending maze. She was alone now, really alone, and there was no going back to Little Sister. She'd never find her way back, she didn't even know what the bazaar was called, or what suburb Little Sister was located in. She had never thought to ask.

Eventually the bus heaved to a stop.

'Mumbai Central, Mumbai Central, Mumbai Central!' the Nepali conductor called as the bus began emptying. Meena allowed herself to be pulled along by the crowds. The bus station was huge and bustling. The noise of horns bellowing, drivers cursing and fare collectors slapping the sides of the buses pounded Meena's mind. Signposts hung from almost every telegraph pole, but no one looked at them. Everyone around her seemed to know where they were going without consulting the signs. Meena felt the crowds writhe around her. There was something familiar about this place. But not quite enough.

'Tea? Donut?' A pre-teen boy lifted a cage of tea filled glasses before her.

Meena nodded. The scent of fresh donuts and burnt milk drifted from a nearby stall. Meena reached into her shirt for a few crumpled rupees.

'Where is Kamathipura?' she asked the boy as he delivered her food. She waited for him to juggle the glasses and plop some chilli chutney on the edge of her paper plate.

'Down that road,' he pointed.

'Is it too far to walk?'

The boy shrugged. He went to find another customer. Meena dunked her donut in the spicy sauce. The chilli stung her lips, but the donut was warm and fresh and good. She finished all but the sludgy tea leave dregs at the bottom of her glass before stepping back onto the busy street, heading in the direction the boy had pointed.

Meena gripped the *kurta* bag to her chest. Four, five and six-storey buildings leaned over the narrowing streets. In the distance, between the heads of pedestrians, Meena could see the clean buildings lessen. More tin roofs and older style hotels began to crowd closer together, but it wasn't until Meena had crossed four more intersections that Meena saw the prostitute.

She was leaning against the outer wall of a building, her hair untied and loose past her shoulders. Her sleeveless satin *sari* blouse was stained under the arms and the shoulder section slipped to reveal the wide strip of dark flesh that was her belly. The woman looked tired. A cigarette balanced between her swollen lips. She waited for her child, a boy, to finish urinating into a drain. The woman stared at the footpath, disinterested. Then she yanked the boy, bare-bottomed, onto her hip and began walking away. Meena followed at a distance. The child began to call out for sweets or bananas or twisted toffee candy or whatever other food vendor they passed. But his mother ignored him. She walked on towards the tin roofs and turned into a tired, crowded street Meena had almost missed.

Meena hesitated. The street was littered with potholes and rubbish and half-clad children. No cars drove up this road. The inhabitants made their home in the street. Cheap wooden beds were pulled out into the morning sunlight. The buildings were old, their timber doorframes chipped. Along the lowest balconies and from the occasional roof, Meena could see the flapping of gaudy clothing, trying to dry in the smog. This wasn't where Mohan had brought them—there were no grills over doors on this street, and the women were too dark. But it was close. Nowhere else did women lie exhausted on such open beds so early in the morning than in suburbs where their work wasn't mudding floors and cooking the morning meal. No, the women who lounged in these doorways were like the woman Meena had followed: prostitutes. And this was Kamathipura.

The light slaps Meena's face. Excruciating. Putali!

She struggles to stand, to clear the pain from her head. From her whole body.

Putali ...

'Get up!' the voice is foreign. Hindi, harsh and scratched.

Meena tries to sort the memories. Zeshaan's beating. Ganga calling for the doctor. The hotel manager. Putali's torn body ... and her voice. Calling. Calling her.

'Putali!' Meena calls out.

The only answer is a slap, red and raw across her left cheek. Then, 'Stand up!'

Meena tries to obey. Her legs are thick and clumsy. She's never been drugged like this before. She forces her eyes to stay open. The woman in front of her wears a red cotton *sari*. She studies Meena like a newly acquired purchase.

'Hmmm.' The woman frowns. 'They certainly gave you some bruises. Still, we can hide them with make up. How old are you?' She tilts Meena's face upwards. Roughly. Meena cranes to see behind the woman. The air feels different, it smells different. The ceilings are lower. Where is Putali?

Another slap. 'Age?'

'I'm ...' Meena wills herself to remember. 'Twelve.'

The woman crows in pleasure. 'It's not often Anchita sells her new little girls. You must have given them some trouble, ehh? But not anymore.'

Meena understands the Hindi threat more than the words themselves. She hears footsteps.

'Putali?'

The footsteps halt and a tall, attractive Indian woman with black strappy heels and tight blue jeans appears.

Meena falters. 'I can't stay here. I have to go back ...'

The fat woman ignores her. She turns to the girl in blue jeans. 'Give her a wash, then take her upstairs, to the empty room. She's obviously not a virgin, but she's fair and if you clean her up, we may get away with it for a couple of months before anyone notices.'

The girl on heels nods.

'But Putali ...' Meena tries to explain. Her head pounds, the image of her little friend writhing on the bed fills her mind. 'They've still got her. I need to go back. I need to get her. She's bleeding. We don't belong here—'

'Well, actually, you do.' The fat woman snaps. 'I bought you.'

'But I'm not for sale.' Meena struggles to remain upright. 'And Putali—'

'I don't know or care who she is.' The woman shuts Meena down. 'I paid for you. Good money. Lots of money. That sounds like a sale to me. But if you don't want to stay ...'

Meena sits up as straight as she can. 'I don't!'

'Fine.' The woman looks only marginally annoyed. She holds her hand out, palm up. 'But I'll be needing my money back. All forty-three thousand, five hundred rupees of it.'

'But I don't have any ...' Meena trips over the sickening realisation.

'No, I didn't think so,' the woman snaps. 'Get her ready to work.'

The floor rises to catch Meena as she falls. The girl with heels steps forward to catch her head.

'My friend, Putali ...' Meena tries again. But the girl pulls the door behind her closed and lowers her voice. 'Listen to me, listen carefully.'

Meena tries to focus.

'You have no friends. There is no one called Putali. You will not mention her name again. You will forget all about her.'

'But—'

'No!' The girl slaps her. Her eyes narrow and in them, Meena reads an urgency she doesn't want to believe. 'If you want to survive, you will do what I say. If I say forget, you forget. If I say lie still, you lie still. You weren't cheap, but you're fair and beautiful— yes, even with all that Anchita's men have done to you. You'll be able to make enough money to keep Madam happy. And if she's happy, you will survive. Do you understand? Madam is not kind.'

'But Putali—' The force of the girl's fist slams Meena's head against the wall. 'You can remember when you are free,' the girl retorts. 'But not here.'

Meena feels the tears before she hears them. Hot wetness running down and mingling with the bruises on her face. Defeat rises. And with it, anger. Meena screams. She lunges at the girl, but trips and lands crumpled against the floor. Something akin to compassion skitters briefly across the girl's face. But she pulls it in check as quickly as it had come.

'What's your name?' the girl asks.

Meena sobs her name into the concrete.

'Well, mine's Sarita,' the girl responds with a click of her tongue. 'And I promise, if I can, to keep you alive.'

Thirty-two

Meena's feet led her further into Kamathipura, her heart pounding so hard she felt short of breath. The air reeked of urine, frying fat and cheap perfume. Meena stumbled over a cracked piece of bitumen but no one gave her a second look, so she readjusted Sarita's scarf and kept walking. She could see the suburb's wealth now: expensive shoes on the occasional businessman, a private cafe with computer cubicles and a growing number of men gathered around tables in cafes playing cards and *carrom*.

Sarita had once talked of a hierarchy of hotels. Now Meena saw it. Dark-skinned girls and women—some so old or ugly they would only get a few rupees for the most unpleasant acts—lay resting outside. Their children played beside them with smooth pebbles or bottle tops. Other girls, with fairer skin and tidier outfits, rested behind barred doorways, curled asleep on hard beds. The air stirred of dirty incense and unshowered bodies. But every now and then a different kind of hotel broke the line and no women lingered outside. The paint work on these was fresh and new. Tubes of unlit neon lights waited patiently to call clients in from the night. From these hotels' upper floors airconditioners jutted out over the street, their balconies and windows barred to the world.

Meena reached into her *kurta* bag and pulled out Putali's

stained photo. How fair had she been? Why could she remember Putali's laughter, her hands working the wet washing, but not her face? She pushed the photo back into the bag and stared at the hotel in front of her, willing herself to remember: Mohan's hands gripping hers, Putali's worried comments. What was the hotel like, where they had been promised good jobs waitressing or in bustling kitchens?

A memory flitted through her mind of a hotel, tall and white with multiple caged doorways along the road side but only one door without a grill. The upper floors had flapped with laundry, just like so many in this suburb. Meena felt despair rise. The scarf around her neck too tight, too warm in the near midday sun.

Meena felt the panic climb, her mind fogging over, the details slipping from reach. She spun around, searching, comparing, willing the hotel Mohan had taken them to appear. But while some hotels had grilled doorways, their balconies were locked. Others had laundry flapping—but no cages. Meena stumbled forward. The smell of the street, the leery glances from men waiting at drinking rooms, the puffs of cheap cigarette smoke in her nose—it all made her retch. The donut in her stomach suddenly rejected.

What had she thought she'd be able to do? The streets were a maze, the buildings leaned too close, the air stagnant. Down every alley more women lay on beds, more clean-painted hotels shut their doors to the world, more large-busted madams sized her up as she floundered confused by their doorways. Meena began to run, her fingers slipping on the *kurta* bag in her hands. She could hear the men laughing at her clumsy gait, feel the poking of the polished fingers pointing from the open balconies above.

Why had she come?

She retched against an electricity pillar. The donut chunks joining the rubbish collected at its base. She leaned her face against the chipped concrete and gasped for breath. What was she doing? What had she expected? Didi was right, it was foolish, so foolish. There was nowhere to hide from the staring faces, the faces that watched her run as if she were entertainment. People stood around her at all angles. Hotels, restaurants, drinking stalls, carom bars, and *paan* corners everywhere, all asking for her money or her body or...

Meena choked. She pushed herself from the pillar and staggered into the street again. She had to get away, to get somewhere, anywhere.

But a pop song rang out from one of the tea shops, calling of love and devotion and forever together. Someone was singing along to the lyrics, slapping their thighs in time with the dance beat. Meena felt her shoulders tense. She knew that voice. It was the man Sarita had called 'her *babu*'. But a *babu* was a girl's favourite client, the man to whom she gave discounts or free sex because they promised presents and treats and true love. Meena had never wanted a *babu*. Instead she had given him the name Waman in conversations behind his back; Waman which meant short. The memories were so many and so thick she could almost smell him.

Meena forced her legs forward, away from the music, away from the voice. But something about the scene before her made her stop. Her will to hide fought the instinct to study the buildings. She scanned the cheap signboards, English words, Hindi words— they shouted accusation at her. A rickshaw almost ran her into a drain.

Why wouldn't her legs move? What was it about this place? Meena turned, the sense of dread at facing Waman only defeated by the nagging familiarity. Yes, she did remember it. It was the tea shop Mohan had taken them to. Where he'd ordered cold *samosa*s and Fanta. Meena groped her memory for more details but Waman spotted her. His thin frame emerged from the tea shop shadows.

'Puja, Puja, Puja,' the man sung her working name in his high nasal voice—the name Madam had allocated her once she'd given up the fight.

'I've missed my little Puja.' Waman leered over her. 'They told me you had gone home, back to your little village and your little mountain hut.'

Meena tried to ignore him.

'Are you pleased to see your *babu*? You were always my favourite, my special girl.'

Meena took a step backwards. She could smell the hair oil he used, the non-effective deodorant, the beetle-nut on his breath.

Waman cocked his head to one side, properly taking in her appearance. 'Why aren't you wearing make up? I almost didn't recognise you 'till I saw you walk. But then I thought, 'ooooh yeah', I know that back end. My favourite ass in the whole of Kamathipura it is, and I was right.'

Meena felt sick but didn't speak. She had never had conversation with Waman before. He never asked for it.

'Come, I'll buy you a drink.' Waman pulled her by the elbow back into the tea shop. Memories assaulted Meena. Waman didn't seem to notice, he just pushed her onto a bench with a laugh and went to order drinks. One tall bottle of beer and a cup. He poured the cup half full and slid it across the table to Meena. Then he sucked at the bottle as if he was parched, never taking his eyes off Meena. When he was finished, the bottle hit the table again with the noise like Devi's head against the partition wall. 'Drink!'

Meena lifted the metal cup to her lips. The scarf around her neck felt too tight. The beer bitter on her tongue. She drank it all under his glare, then placed the empty cup on the table. Waman nodded, satisfied.

'Where can we go? Where's your bed if you're not sharing the room with that sour bitch anymore?' He leaned forward, referring to Sarita. The woman behind the counter chuckled. Waman grinned like it was a compliment.

Meena let her eyes wander past him, out over his shoulder, the nagging connection of memories growing ever stronger. She dug into the *kurta* bag, feeling for Putali's photo, but the photo had slid further down in the bag and the movement of her elbow made the table shake, knocking the bottle over. Waman swore and lunged to catch it. 'What are you doing, you clumsy dog?! I only gave you one cup. I've seen you drink twice that much!'

Meena ignored him, she felt the alcohol hit her bloodstream, but she steadied herself. She was close now. She felt it. She strode back out to the street. The sunlight stubborn. The hotels lazy before the evening rush.

'Where are you going? I just bought you a drink!' Waman complained.

The hotel at the end of the road tugged her memories.

'You work there? Good Hotel's expensive. Let's go somewhere else, somewhere ... intimate.'

But Meena just stared at the hotel. She didn't recognise the muscled Indian guard, or the fresh coat of yellow paint. But there were three grilled doorways against the street, each with a space for displaying a girl. And above them, a balcony, with richly decorated *sari* skirts tugging gently in the breeze. A man dressed in an expensive suit coat and gold watch slipped out from the only ungrilled door and nodded acknowledgment to the guard. He crossed the street and brushed past on his way, smelling foul of sweat and perfume. Meena drew a wavering breath.

Waman gripped her shoulder. 'Let's go.'

'No,' Meena whispered, only barely aware of Waman now. The memories colliding with hope, then curling in fear. What had been her plan? What did she think she was going to do? The guard wouldn't just let her in ...

Waman leaned closer, clamping his hand around her wrist. 'Do you have a friend in Good Hotel?'

Meena tried not to nod, but her fingers were shaking now. Waman noticed and grinned.

'Is she locked up? Is she little, like you used to be?'

Meena nodded, hating herself for it. Hating the alcohol. Hating him.

'What does she look like? Is she fair? Like you?'

Meena clamped her lips together. She felt her eyes fill with tears, the tears Sarita had warned her about. Tears that made her seem weak. And she was weak. The *kurta* bag slipped. Soap, shirts and sanitary pads fell to the road. And then Putali's photo. Landing in the mud and *paan* for everyone to see. Waman's lips twisted into a putrid smile. Meena lunged, but Waman was faster. He snatched the photo from the mud and held it out of reach. Little Putali stared down at them with dark, shy, unsmiling eyes.

'Is this her?' He sounded hungry.

Meena wiped furiously at the wetness on her face. What had she done? Waman laughed—a cruel, sick laugh. Slowly and with deliberate care that she was watching, he slipped Putali's photo into his top shirt pocket.

'Mine now,' he snickered.

'No!'

'No? Then show me where we can go.'

She didn't understand.

'I bought you a drink. You owe me. And now'—he patted his pocket—'give me what I want and you can have it back.'

He wrapped an arm around her waist and pulled her closer. A dull automation fought in Meena's chest. She saw the lines of alcohol in the whites of his eyes. She saw the row of prickles the barber had missed when shaving. She saw the stinging red of the gums above his chipped tooth. She knew what he was like. She knew about the tiny sores he wore under his trousers. But he had her photo. The only link she had to the past. To Putali ...

'Where can we go?' Waman asked.

And Meena felt her soul cower in silent shame.

Thirty-three

Sarita had told her once about a place with small rooms in the bazaar. Space she used for private customers who gave generous tips away from Madam. She used to laugh about its location between a shrine and a beauty parlour.

'Take me to the shrine opposite the beauty parlour,' Meena instructed, her voice sounding distant, like it belonged to someone else.

Waman didn't seem to notice. He just led the way without further instruction. Up a laneway, past a water tap and around a bend.

'Here it is.' Waman pointed.

The shrine was just as Sarita had described; squat and dark, pasted with orange powder paste of multiple rituals and worship, a stone image of the god honoured to protect from disease and keep children safe or unborn. Meena couldn't look at it.

'Hurry up!' Waman's eagerness made her stomach cringe. 'Where's the room?'

Defeat clambered up Meena's spine. Putali's photo now poked from the top of Waman's shirt pocket. Meena swallowed the lump of yuck that rose in her throat and turned to the dark hotel with its street counter slouching low between the shrine and the parlour. The woman behind the counter motioned Meena closer.

'We have space, small, but enough for what you need.' The woman spoke to Meena, ignoring Waman.

Meena didn't move. The doorway behind the woman was crowded with dark women and men in stained *lungi*s, some moving in, others moving out. Waman pushed her forward but the woman at the counter thrust out an arm to block their entrance.

'Space isn't free,' she barked.

Meena glanced at Waman. He just grinned, 'I'll pay if you want, but that means I get to keep the photo of your little friend, which will make it easier for me to locate her when I save up enough to visit the Good—'

'No!' Meena pulled Maa's money from inside her shirt. Maa's money. She fingered the dusty notes just for a second before Waman snatched them away. He bargained with the woman at the counter, then pushed three notes into her hand, the rest into his pocket. The woman waved her arm, bangled with cheap and dented jewellery, down the hall to the curtained spaces behind. Already, before it was even midday, Meena could hear the groans, grunting and sharp intakes of breath indicating several spaces were in use.

Waman strode down the hall until he found an empty cubical. Meena knew what would be inside. Sarita had described it once: a bed, a thin mattress and curtains for walls all the way around.

'Come!' Waman ordered. He held a curtain up. All civility was gone. Meena's mind felt numb, and yet she could hear Sharmila lecturing her, bossing on about how she was worth much more than this, so much more. That she deserved to be loved. Not bought. Not sold. And that love didn't come with a price like this.

Not 35 rupees for the space Waman needed.

Not 43,500 rupees to repay a 'debt'.

But Waman was growing impatient. She saw the shadow of anger flick across his face. Behind another curtain, she heard a woman cry out in pain, just once before the sound was muffled. Fear rose from a hidden place in Meena's stomach and she stepped backwards. She couldn't do this, not again, not with Waman and his sores and his thin cold hands. Not in there, with the dirt and the grime and the wetness from someone else. Not now, not after Nahita and Maa and Didi.

Shaking, she turned from the counter. She shouldn't have finished the drink Waman had given her. Her mind felt thick and fuzzy, but she could feel the sunlight now, shoving its way through the smog to see her. She felt its pull. She tasted the thread of freedom on a putrid gust of wind.

'Where are you going?' Waman shouted from behind stained and flapping curtains.

Meena took another step. Away. She knew it now. She couldn't go with him. Not even for Putali. Her chest crushed itself with grief. A sob rose harsh and hard.

'Get back here! You can't steal from me, you dirty little whore!'

Meena glanced in time to see him storm from the curtained hallway. His belt was loose, his fly half-unzipped, the bulge in his trousers angry. Meena backed away.

'Come here!' He grabbed, the fabric of her shirt. She pulled from his grasp. Her feet slipping in the mud.

'What did you think?' Waman sneered, holding his balance. 'That you could back out, and I'd just let you. You think I was going to give this photo back?' He ripped Putali's photo from his shirt pocket and shoved it against his mouth. 'You don't think I'd have her too? Have her rough and—'

'Nooooo!' Meena ran at him. She beat him with all her strength, scraped her nails into his neck. Waman staggered backwards in surprise and anger. She had never fought him in the past, she'd always shut up and laid still, locking the memories away. But not anymore.

'I'm not your whore!' Meena screamed at him. The woman from the grotty hotel was now standing in the street. The girls from the beauty parlour gathered to giggle and watch. 'You don't own me! You have never been and will never be my *babu*!'

Something like a growl rose from Waman's throat. His face surged with anger and humiliation. Meena turned and ran. She ran past the parlour and around the bend, past a water tap and the women lined up waiting. She ran on until she came to the intersection where Good Hotel stood.

'Putali Maya!' Meena screamed. The name aloud now. Out for the first time in three years. 'Putali!'

She scanned the grilled windows, willing one to open, willing a girl with plaits to appear.

'Putali!' Pain welled in her chest, hope was slipping. She felt, rather than saw, the crowd gathering, people taunting, teasing her.

'Crazy bitch,' they called out.

'Drug whore!' someone else spat.

Windows began to open, girls appeared on balconies, men began to stare and watch. The guard at the front of Good Hotel was joined by a girl. A Nepali girl with a twisted hand and angry expression. Ganga. She muttered something to the guard who hurried inside.

Meena ran forwards. Ganga blocked the way. 'Shut up,' she hissed, gripping Meena by the shoulders.

'But Putali ...' Meena felt the words clog in her throat.

A flicker of recognition twitched across the other girl's face. 'You can't go in. They'll lock you up.'

'But she's in there—'

The girl gripped her shoulders even tighter, as if willing her to understand the most basic facts. 'No, she's not.'

'But I ... I ...' Meena couldn't say it. Over Ganga's shoulder she could see the guard returning with the hotel manager.

The girl shoved Meena hard and fierce. She pushed her face into Meena's. 'You were too much trouble, so Anchita sold you. I remember it well. But your little friend, she's not here either. She jumped, two years ago. Anchita was furious. You don't get much for a cripple, even if they are young and beautiful.'

'No ...' Meena felt her legs dissolve, her eyes lifting to the only open balcony three floors up.

'She's not here anymore.' The girl shoved Meena again. 'And I don't know where she is, so run now before Anchita locks you up instead.'

Meena staggered backwards. She felt the faces staring at her, hating her, wanting her, baiting her. Ganga disappeared. The hotel manager pointed. The guard stepped onto the street. Meena turned and began to run. The road cluttered up before her. Tripping her up. The guard came after her, but he was large and clumsy, and a group of older women blocked his way, buying Meena time. She raced on, down a narrow alley, one she could see the end of, one with no neon signs and no posh hotels. Her heart pounded, her tread uneven. On and on she ran. Without her *kurta* bag, without money or ideas of where to go or how. Only conscious of the instinct to be away.

'Putali ...' she sobbed. Weak, wrecked, hopeless. She was an idiot. Leela had been right, and Didi and Maa. Even Waman had known it with his lies and promises to find her friend. She staggered forwards, the world spun about her. Suddenly Kamathipura ended and Meena had reached a main road. She stumbled, staggering clumsy, out of the way of an angry bus, when she heard someone call: 'Meena!'

'Meena!' It came again. And then there was a stream of curses—harsh, beautiful swearing. Meena blinked against the sunlight of the street. Panic paused. Leela, red-faced and make-up free spun into vision. And behind her came Sharmila and a wordless embrace so tight Meena could barely breathe.

Thirty-four

'What are you doing back here? You idiot!' Leela barked when Sharmila finally released Meena and stood back to wipe something from her eye.

'You've been drinking, haven't you?'

Meena wobbled. She felt the ground spin, her head light. She was going to faint.

'Let's take her to Maa,' Leela barked. She grabbed Meena's elbow as Sharmila quickly typed a message into her phone. Then they turned her back to Kamathipura.

'No!' Meena struggled against them. Her legs weak and feet slipping on the bitumen.

'Don't worry,' Sharmila explained. 'We'll meet Maa at the Little Sister Drop-in Centre. It's just around the corner. It's safe.'

The drop-in centre? Where Sarita had visited. Where she got the card? And Maa? Meena pulled back.

'I took …' She choked, remembering the money, now tucked deep in Waman's pocket. Waman. She retched.

'Gross!' Leela let go but Sharmila frowned until she retook Meena's elbow.

They led her around the first corner and into an unassuming building with a small cafe at the front. From a side room, in a silent swish of yellow sari, Maa appeared.

Meena drew a hesitant breath. Maa should be angry, furious, and yet the hardness on her face wasn't fury. She looked much older than Meena had ever seen her, but not angry. It was as if Maa was relieved about something. Meena's legs gave way. Two strong arms caught her but Meena didn't look up. She could tell by the smell of yesterday's expensive aftershave, and the way Sharmila rushed to help, that it was Tarak who had caught her. Tarak was here too?

Meena struggled to find her balance.

'Let's sit down,' Maa suggested.

Meena nodded. Her throat felt like it would break from holding in the pain. She let Tarak hold her up and guide her to a sitting room where he deposited her into one of the upholstered chairs. Then he went to sit beside Sharmila. Two members of staff from the drop-in centre hovered in the doorway.

'Do you want to go home now?' Maa asked, and lowered herself into the chair opposite. Leela remained standing, as if on watch.

Meena didn't answer.

'We would like you to come back to Little Sister with us. But,' Maa spoke slowly, as if she knew Meena's mind was in turmoil, 'we will not force you. If this is where you want to stay—'

'She is a bitch if she wants to stay here!' Leela cut in.

Maa frowned.

'Please come back,' Sharmila said.

'If she wants to stay, that is her choice,' Maa said firmly.

'I ...' Meena ducked her head.

'You stole my money. I know. But that's not why we're here. We care about you, Meena. We want to help you.'

They were the same words Sharmila had said the first time they had met. Meena glanced at the once-prostitute now. Sharmila's shirt was bright orange, the same shirt she had worn to find Meena in the hospital. But today there were damp spots under the arms; she wouldn't smell so pretty now. And yet, somehow, although she was almost leaning on Tarak's shoulder, his nose didn't scrunch up in disgust.

'Will you come back with us?' Maa asked.

'I was looking for ...' Meena tried again. The words sounded cheap on her tongue.

Maa nodded. 'I know. Didi told me about your friend, and Purna found the photos under your pillow. I suppose that was what you were trying to tell me yesterday, only I wasn't really listening.'

Leela swore.

'Enough of that, Leela.' Maa raised her voice. She leaned forward. 'Do you know where your friend is? Were you able to locate her brothel?'

'Yes ...' Meena choked. 'No ... I found the brothel, Good Hotel.' Meena spat the name from her lips. 'But she's gone. The girl said she'd jumped, she said ... it's too far from the third floor!'

Leela kicked the wall, then glared at the drop-in staff member who frowned at her. Maa looked to Tarak, then back at Meena. 'Who told you she jumped?'

'No one. Just a girl ... she told me to run ... told me they'd catch me ... told me Putali had gone,' Meena stuttered. Her world was shutting down, her head pounded, darkness was creeping in.

Maa tapped the table in front of Meena. 'Listen. Do you still have her photo?'

Meena groaned, she held her head in her hands. The memory of Waman's face glared at her.

Maa sighed. 'Don't give up, Meena. She may still be there, or she may have survived. Desperation can sometimes be a girl's greatest strength.'

'And we'll organise a raid on the hotel, just to make sure,' Tarak put in. Meena watched Maa nod without much faith.

'I wish we could help your friend today, Meena. But we need to go now. Purna needs you.'

'Purna?' Meena croaked.

Maa nodded. 'It was Purna who discovered you had run away,' Maa explained.

Leela gave a dry laugh. 'Discovered she had run away? That's a nice way of putting it, more like she completely lost it and wouldn't stop punching me and shouting Nepali at me until I promised we'd come and find you ... Why do you think I'm here now? If it wasn't to get away from a Nepali beating?!'

Maa frowned and Leela looked away, seeming suddenly embarrassed.

'If you are not yet ready to return to Nepal, we can wait. There is no rush. Nepal will not lift her skirts and move. But we would like you back at Little Sister, if you are willing to return with us.' Maa looked so tired, more tired than she had looked after Nahita's disappearance.

Meena unwound Sarita's leaving scarf from around her neck, its threads slippery between her fingers.

'Please, Meena, won't you come home with us?' Sharmila begged.

Leela put out her hand. 'Are you coming?' she asked, her voice hard.

'You didn't put your lipstick on,' Meena choked.

Leela ran a finger over her naked lips, 'I guess I forgot, ehh? It's not a big deal.' She narrowed her eyes, but they held no unkindness.

Sharmila slipped out the doorway with Tarak. Maa stood and followed them to call for a taxi. Eventually it was only Leela and the two drop-in staff members left with Meena.

'It's time to leave,' Leela said.

Meena felt the tears pull at her cheeks. She looked up to the closest drop-in staff member, a pockscarred woman in her forties. 'Do you know Sarita?' Meena choked out the question.

The woman hesitated, paused and then nodded. 'I know two. Although one is no longer allowed to visit us. Something happened three months ago and her madam won't let her out anymore. Says she has to pay back a debt.'

The sob escaped before Meena could stop it. Leela hurried forward.

'Can ... can you give this to her?' Meena pushed the scarf further across the table. 'Tell her I don't need it anymore. Tell her that I'm ... that she kept her promise.'

The woman lifted the scarf from the table as if it was something precious. 'I will,' she said. Then Leela helped Meena out to where Didi and the taxi were waiting.

The taxi crawled through the crowded streets. Maa sat in the front. She called Didi on a silver mobile phone.

'Yes, we found her.' Her voice was weary, but relieved, under the noise of the taxi's engine. 'And she's coming home.'

Meena sat between Maa and Sharmila. They smelt of sweat, both of them. They didn't speak. Meena kept her eyes straight ahead. Her rib cage felt too small, too tight. She tried not to think.

Eventually Meena recognised the intersection where Nahita's restaurant stood. The taxi zigzagged through the midday bazaar and after several small bribes from Maa, continued down the unpaved road to the black gates of Little Sister Rescue Home. It pulled up beside Tarak's already parked motorbike. Tarak and Didi stood at the edge of the paving, Didi had her hands folded across her chest.

Maa paid the driver and climbed out. So did Sharmila and

Leela. Meena just sat. The vinyl of the seats was cracked red. Like the lips of a girl with too many sores.

'Come on.' Sharmila bent to look into the taxi. 'We're home now.'

Meena wouldn't meet her gaze. Her heart felt left somewhere, forgotten and trampled on in a shuffled alley.

Sharmila leaned further in, her fingernails shiny. 'Come on ...'

But Meena couldn't move. The driver fiddled with the gears, preparing to leave. At the rev of the engine a frantic cry sirened from the dorm entrance, '*Na-jaau! Bahini, na-jaau!*'

Purna hurtled down the dorm stairs, almost tripping over her bare feet as she charged across the yard. 'Na-j*aau*, don't go. Don't go with them!' Her voice was wrought with tension but the words she used were common-form Nepali, the kind used to speak to children or close friends. Purna shoved Sharmila aside and reached into the taxi to drag Meena out. Her mouth never stopped its movement; the words spilled forth. She practically dragged Meena from the taxi and back across the yard. Only when she had pulled Meena up the dorm stairs and into their room did Purna's voice soften, like a mother speaking to her frightened child. '*Aau*, come now, lie down. Rest ...'

Meena obeyed. The sob, deep and bitter wrenched in her chest.

'*Na-ru,*' Purna whispered. She climbed onto the bed with Meena and curled beside her. Meena felt the tears break loose and slide hot down her cheeks. She cried for the death of her mother. For the day her father forgot she was his daughter. She cried for the red ribbons she could never wear in her hair. She cried for Lalita and Devi and Sarita. The sobs rose wretched and poisonous.

'Putali ...' The name escaped her lips.

Putali Maya. Where was she now? Who was she now? Was she living, alive, free? Or not ...

But Purna tugged Meena closer. She stroked her dusty hair and began to rock. The embrace moved ever so softly to a rhythm from long ago. In her mind, Meena could hear Putali laughing at warm water from a tap, she could smell the pickles on Putali's fingers. There was nothing else she could do.

'*Gyani nani*,' Purna crooned, her hands as gentle as her words. 'Good little girl. Good, lovely, beautiful little girl.'

Epilogue

The train pulls into the station several minutes late. A goat, someone had said, ran onto the tracks just out of Gorakhpur and caused the delay. But Meena isn't listening to their complaints. She stares out the window. The platform is as crowded as the last time she had been here. A young boy is trying to sell cucumber slices to thirsty passengers. He looks like a hill tribe Nepali.

'*Aao*, Meena, Purna, come.' Maa pushes herself from the seat across the aisle. She acts as if her body is heavy after the long journey. She will go no further today. Meena rises. She clutches at the backpack, a gift from Little Sister, full of clean clothes, toiletries and the black cardigan Didi had helped her finish yesterday.

'Follow me,' Maa instructs.

They thread through the harried travellers to the end of the carriage and then onto the platform. The boy selling cucumbers switches easily to Nepali as he spots the girls. Meena looks past him. Maa has found the woman in the turquoise *kurta-suruwal* suit, the woman they are meeting from Stop Trafficking Nepal. She looks older than Meena, but still young—about Purna's age— and she greets Maa with efficient politeness.

'So these are your Nepali girls? Welcome to Gorakhpur. My name is Kausilla.'

Purna sidles up to Maa's side. She is hugging herself again, and beginning to rock. Maa frowns.

'Come, you must be exhausted, let's have tea.' Kausilla

smiles. She leads them out of the station, under the huge arch and onto the busy street in front. Along the footpath a row of small shops stand awaiting customers. Kausilla chooses the third shop. It smells of fried pastries, strong milky tea and cheap cigarettes. They enter, sit on hard plastic chairs and wait for their tea to arrive.

Maa pulls two cardboard folders from her bag and passes them across the table to Kausilla. Meena recognises the folders. They are the ones holding all Maa's information about them. Details on HIV status, ages, years in the brothel, sickness treated, psychological issues present. They will say that Meena is HIV negative, but Purna has started showing symptoms of AIDS. They will say that Meena has no family, that she was trafficked to India by people not related to her. They will say Purna once lived in a village with a smelly buffalo and that is all she can remember. Somewhere among the papers will be a comment, written in by Maa at Meena's instruction, that Meena had a friend once, a friend whose name meant 'butterfly' and 'love'.

But Kausilla doesn't open the folders. She tucks them into a pocket of her fake leather brief case. She smiles at Meena, and then at Purna. 'Are you ready to go back to Nepal?' she asks.

Purna looks at Meena for the correct answer. Meena doesn't reply. She knows what needs to be done, that she must face Putali's mother. Must tell her story and ask for hope. Their tea arrives to break the silence. Purna slurps it like a child. Maa and Kausilla chat about numbers of girls crossing the border and the weather and the new AIDS drug being trialled in Delhi. Over Kausilla's silhouetted shoulder, Meena can see a row of billboards. One is advertising a happy couple and a bottle of expensive whiskey. Another is advertising a fair skinned model and a yellow bar of soap. The last one is a picture of a girl and a man, the man is holding a false grin on his face and a stash of money behind his back. She knows, without sounding out the letters underneath, what the poster means now. It is a warning, a pleading.

'My train will leave soon,' Maa says as she stands up. A strange expression is on her face. Something Meena cannot read but Purna suddenly drops to the ground, her knees on the dusty shop floor. She joins her hands in the deepest sign of respect, to her forehead, to Maa's feet, to her forehead again. Over and over. Purna makes the motion of gratitude, a soft strangled sob noise coming from her lips. Maa lifts her eyes to Meena; there is wetness in the old woman's eyes. 'You'll take care of my little sister, won't you?' she asks.

Meena tilts her head to the side. She scoops Purna up from the floor. She uses the edge of her shirt to wipe the wetness from Purna's face. Maa strides past them, her yellow *sari* swinging in the dust. Out, past the line of shops, back to the train, back to Mumbai and Leela and Kani and Sharmila ...

'Let's go. We'll catch a bus to Sunauli. S.T.N. have a border home there where we can stay overnight. The staff are all returned sex workers like yourselves. They're very understanding. Tomorrow we'll catch the bus to Kathmandu.'

Kausilla takes Purna's hand. She guides the shaking girl away from the staring tea shop faces, towards the bus park. She keeps talking when she can, to keep Purna moving. She tells them of the centre in Kathmandu, and the legal services available to ex-trafficked girls, and the cooking classes some girls have been taking to work in the fanciest tourist hotels in Nepal. But suddenly, Meena isn't listening. Something has darted over the traffic and ducked into the branches of a single decorative tree. Meena squints around the heads of bustling pedestrians. The grey something stops and seems to tilt its head at Meena. Yes. It is a bird, a grey Indian roller bird. Meena stares, almost forgetting to walk. The bird is watching her, half afraid, half brave in the smoggy city. A taxi horn bellows, but the bird doesn't flinch. It studies Meena for one more second then jumps from an outer branch. Its wings spread. Bright and brilliant blue swoops low over Meena's head. She turns to follow its flight as it scoops and darts perfectly, ever north, towards the fields and open spaces.

Onwards to Nepal.

One day, she knows, she'll return to Mumbai. She'll learn to read and write. She'll paint the sign for Sharmila's wedding, and she'll go with Tarak and Maa and Leela into the brothels. She'll find the girls trapped in secret cupboards and hidden rooms, and she'll tell their story to the world until someone begins to take notice. Until Putali is free. Because people, like butterflies and roller birds, were never meant for cages.

Purna tugs her arm.

'*Jaum?*' The girl's expression is paused, unsure, with questions she is too afraid to ask. Meena slips her arm around Purna's thin shoulders. She is stronger already.

'*Jaum*,' she says. 'Let's go home.'

For more resources on child and teen trafficking:

www.destinyrescue.org.au
www.ijm.org
www.a21.org
www.stopthetraffik.com.au
www.oasisin.org
www.maitinepal.org

Glossary

Nepali Words

aama –	mother
aau –	come
baa –	father
bahini –	little sister
bajai-aama –	grandmother
bhaisi –	water buffalo
chaar –	the number four
chha –	the number six, also meaning 'to have'
chitto –	fast
chhya –	eew!
dal –	a lentil stew dish
dhaka –	a traditional Nepali woven fabric design
doko –	a large open–weave cane basket
dui –	the number two
ek-dum dublo –	very, very skinny
ek –	the number one
guhar! –	help!
gyani nani –	good little girl
hario –	green
himal –	snow capped mountain

hoina –	no
haus –	okay
jaum –	let's go
timi-lai kasto chha? –	how are you?
ke garne? –	what to do?
khana –	food
Machhapuchhre –	a famous 6,997 metre–high, fish–tail–shaped mountain, clearly visible from the Pokhara valley
masu –	meat
meri saathi pani chhaina –	I don't even have a friend
mero ke chha? –	what do I have?
mo mo –	a Tibetan/Nepali snack; steamed dumplings
na-jaau! –	don't go!
na-ru –	don't cry
Newari –	a people group of Nepal, predominantly found around the Kathmandu valley
panch –	the number five
pir na-garra –	don't be afraid
rani –	queen
roksi –	alcohol
tapaai-ko chha –	you have
Terai –	the plains of Nepal, closest to the Indian border
teen –	the number three
topi –	hat, usually a traditional Nepali hat for men

Hindi Words

aacha –	good
aao –	come
babu –	informal word implying 'sweetheart'
bahana –	little sister
bhojana –	food
bimara –	sick
bindi –	a decorative dot worn on the forehead. Traditionally a sign of Hindu worship, but also a fashion accessory
buddhoo –	person with intellectual disability
carrom –	a strike and pocket game, similar to billiards but without a cue
ghee –	clarified butter used in Indian cooking
ghinauna –	disgusting
kancho –	youngest brother
kohl –	a black eyeliner
kulfi –	Indian frozen dessert
kurta –	long shirt to be worn over trousers
kurta-suruwal –	an outfit consisting of a matching long shirt and trousers
lungi –	an article of clothing consisting of a length of fabric worn wrapped around the waist and legs
mehndi –	henna paste, usually painted into decorative designs on the hands and/or feet
nain –	no
Namaste –	traditional Hindu greeting
Namaskar –	a more respectful version of *Namaste*
paan –	betel nut, lime and spices chewed like tobacco

paisa –	the smallest form of Indian currency
puri –	a fried Indian bread often served with curry
samosa –	triangular pastries
sari –	an outfit worn by women consisting of a short, cropped blouse and several meters of fabric wrapped and pleated around the waist and over the shoulder
suno –	listen
thika –	okay

Acronyms

AIDS - Acquired Immune Deficiency Syndrome is a condition caused by HIV that results in the weakening of the body's system for fighting disease, resulting in death.

CD4 cells - Immune cells in the blood. A person living with HIV can monitor the amount of CD4 cells in their body to determine the health of their immune system.

HIV - Human Immunodeficiency Virus is the virus that causes AIDS. Over time HIV weakens the immune system until the symptoms of AIDS begin to show and a person becomes sick.

OPD - Out Patients Department in a hospital.

STD - Sexually transmitted disease.

Places

Bhairahawa –	A town close to the Indian border with Nepal. Very popular transit point for people moving in and out of Nepal.
Butwal –	A busy town halfway between Pokhara and the border to India.
Delhi –	India's capital city.
Dhaka –	The capital city of Bangladesh, east of India.
Gorakhpur –	The first large city on the Indian side from Bhairahawa. There is a large train station there with trains running to various parts of India.
Kamathipura –	Mumbai's largest red-light district
Kolkata –	Previously known as Calcutta. A major Indian City north of Bangladesh.
Mumbai –	Previously known as Bombay. A major city on the west coast of India, home to the Bollywood film industry.
Pokhara –	The largest city in Nepal's western district, seven hours bus ride from Kathmandu.
Sunauli –	A town that straddles the border to India.

Map

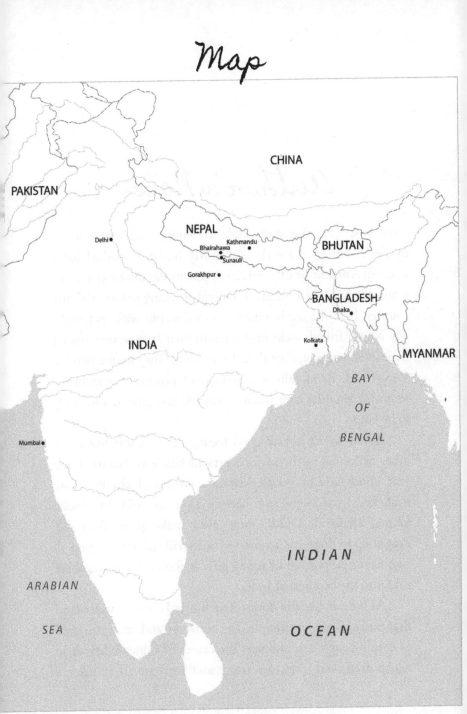

Author's Note

I began writing this story while my family and I were living in Nepal during the early 2000s. My husband worked for a non-government health and development organisation and we made our home in Pokhara. I remember falling in love with the country. Not just the beautiful mountains, but with its people. My Nepali friends welcomed me into their homes; they shared their lives with me; they shared their food. They let me bumble along beside them, calf-deep in the mud, planting rice and then returning months later when it was tall and golden and ready to be cut.

But it wasn't just all good feelings. Nepal, just like every other nation on earth, carries heartache beside its beauty. Each year, thousands of people—women, men and children—are trafficked from Nepal into slavery. They are sold into India, China, Thailand, Dubai, some even make it to Australia, caught up in domestic service—visa-less, illegal and trapped. A significant proportion of young girls trafficked from Nepal are sold into the brothels of India.

As I researched the stories of such girls, I came to understand that trafficking is not simple. The networks and strategies used to entrap people are complex. The causes of vulnerability, upon which traffickers prey, are many and intricate. If it takes a village to raise a child, it will take nations to eradicate slavery. And that begins with me. And with you. And with the very real organisations upon whom I've based the fictional Little Sister Rescue Foundation and Stop Trafficking Nepal. These organisations risk everything to fight for freedom: they educate communities about the risks of trafficking; they organise raids; they pursue justice for traffickers; they advocate change in government policy; they offer hope and healing to victims of unimaginable abuse. Very often these same organisations are staffed by survivors, like Sharmila and Leela and Meena. They work tirelessly, unnoticed and without glory, because they have chosen to hope despite it all.

I wrote *Out of the Cages* as something of a prayer, that one day we might live in a world that no longer accepts any form of slavery as common place. Until that day comes, though, we've got a fight on our hands. A fight that has already begun, but a fight worth joining.

Acknowledgements

There are so, so many people behind this book. In particular I need to thank the staff at Maiti Nepal (especially Dhruba Gurung who went out of her way to assist me), Indu Aryal and the staff at ABC Nepal, Shanta Sapkota and the young women I met at SPK Kathmandu and in other rehabilitation centres. Thank you too to Oasis India, Vasu Vital, Carolyn Kitto, Stop the Traffik and the WOS India Team of 2013.

A huge thank you to Jyoti Nepali, Abigail Sherpa, Asha Nepali, Binu Pradhan, Ambika Baniya and Daisy George for their help with language related questions.

Thank you to my early readers: Susan Bosquanet, Jacqui Conlon and Katie Robert. Your feedback made all the difference. Also to Naomi Reed, Heidi Cassise, Lois Dingley, Janine Clarke and Sierra Hadfield. Thank you to Rosanne Hawke, for your encouragement and support.

To my publisher, Rochelle Manners, thank you for believing in me and in this book. I am so thankful for your courage. And to the team at Rhiza Edge, especially Emily Lighezzolo, for seeing the vision for this book and working so hard to bring it to print, thank you.

Thank you to my family: my parents Rob and Rhonda Hadfield for their unfading support, my children Lillian,

Zachary and Patrick for not only putting up with having a writer for a mum, but sharing the ups and downs along the way. And my husband Richard, thank you for every time you told me this book would make it, and every little thing you did to help along the way.

I certainly didn't write this book alone!

About the Author

Penny Jaye writes books for children and older readers. Although she was born in Ballarat, Victoria, she has lived in many different places since then including Arnhem Land, Bangladesh, Papua New Guinea and Nepal. She is currently living in western Sydney, with her husband and three children, and is studying towards her Master of Arts (writing and literature at Deakin university).

Penny enjoys the challenges and opportunities of juggling family life with writing commitments and author visits, and can also be found writing as *Penny Reeve*.

Family movie nights, sharing lunch by the river and being tucked up in bed to read a new young adult novel are just a few of her favourite things.